THIS KISS

By Deanna Roy

USA Today bestselling author of

Forever Innocent ~ Forever Loved
Forever Sheltered ~ Forever Bound
Forever Family ~ Forever Christmas
Stella and Dane

Forbidden Dance ~ Wounded Dance
Wicked Dance ~ Tender Dance
Final Dance ~ Billionaire's Dance

Never miss a new release.
Sign up for emails or texts at www.deannaroy.com/news

Copyright © 2023 by Deanna Roy. All rights reserved.

No part of this book may be used or reproduced by any means, graphic, electronic, or mechanical, including photocopying, taping, and recording without written permission, except in the case of brief quotations embodied in critical articles and reviews.

This is a work of fiction. All the characters, organizations, and events portrayed in this novel are either products of the author's imagination or used fictitiously.

Ebook edition 1.1

Casey Shay Press
PO Box 160116
Austin, TX 78716
www.caseyshaypress.com

Paperback Edition ISBN: 9781938150999

*For Elizabeth
My epilepsy warrior
You have taught me about strength,
tenacity, and grace.*

Go forth and keep fighting.

*Purple day is March 26.
Wear purple and post instructions from epilepsy.com to raise awareness on how to help someone who might have a seizure in front of you.*

The heart remembers.

CHAPTER 1
Ava

The first time I lost all memory of Tucker, we had just met.

A nurse in pale pink scrubs led me to the disco room of the epilepsy ward of our children's hospital, assuring me that the lights and dancing would help induce a seizure. Once the doctors had the data they needed, I could go home.

Colored starbursts cut through the semi-darkness, music pulsing from a speaker in the corner. A tall man in scrubs stood by the door and nodded at me as I stepped inside.

The nurse had assured me the disco room would be swarming with other teen patients, but at first it appeared completely empty.

Then I saw him.

A boy leaned against the far wall, a mirrored ball spinning confetti bits of light across his face. White gauze fastened with blue tape covered the electrodes glued to his head.

The colors muted and changed, breaking my view of him into fragmented pieces like a puzzle not yet put together. Even so, I could tell he was close to seventeen, same as me.

I never got to meet boys my age. Or any boys. Mother made sure of that.

My fingers trailed along the textured wall, my head angled down to conceal my interest. Music blasted through the space, thrashing like a mechanical monster trying to escape. I didn't recognize the song, but that wasn't unusual. I wasn't allowed television, movies, or the internet. My mother controlled my home environment completely.

But not here.

I paused to adjust the cluster of wires snaking from my scalp to a backpack on my shoulder. There was no point in getting to know this boy, even if I dared to approach. Once the seizure struck, everything would be lost. My favorite food. The books I loved. My entire history. Even my name.

The person I knew as myself would be wiped, and I'd be transparent as newly Windexed glass. Vulnerable, too. My hard-won toughness would be replaced with confusion. The next iteration of Ava might be meek. She might even enjoy her mother's company, at least for a while.

I'd been through this before.

I stole another glance. The boy tapped a glowing white shoe. I couldn't tell if he was looking at me. We were supposed to dance, get overheated and tired. They needed data from our heads to flow down the wires to our backpacks. The disco room was the last resort for those of us whose brains weren't cooperating. This boy was probably in the same boat.

We stood on opposite polarities, on the brink of the next terrible thing. Would we collapse at the same time, or would one bear witness to the other?

I began walking again. The two nurses remained near the door, one occasionally checking the bright rectangle of a phone. But they weren't close to us, which meant I still had time.

Before today, I'd never known precisely when the erasure was coming. My seizures struck on their own schedule, often years apart. Scarcity was my condition's only good point because it took weeks, sometimes months, to read my journals and reorient myself to the girl I once had been.

But this hospital visit was a planned reset. I'd prepared as best I could, spreading notes to myself throughout my room. My mother was undoubtedly searching for them while I was away, ready to remove any evidence of my past that she disliked. She had her reasons.

I left easy ones to fool her, placed between clothes in my suitcase or sticking out of books. But the good stuff would be impossible for her to find, words in Sharpie written along the edge of the shower curtain in the hospital bathroom. Others were bits of paper hidden in plain sight, tucked among the safety notices tacked on the bulletin board.

The absolutely critical information was written on my body, low enough on my belly to prevent easy detection. I'd been writing on myself since I was old enough to understand that I should.

Trust only this handwriting.
Find your notes.
Remember your life.

I moved within a few feet of the boy, and he looked right at me. I froze, not sure what I was doing. If I had no record of him, no notes or references, he'd be lost to me completely as quickly as he'd arrived.

But maybe that was good. I could live in this moment, only this very one.

His brown hair spilled out beneath the strips of gauze and covered the tops of his ears. I spotted a name stitched on an oval patch over the pocket of his shirt. I couldn't read it from here, and I didn't want to stare.

The song ended, and in the moment of quiet, I could almost hear his breathing. My heart thumped so loud it could have been the opening beats to the next melody.

But then another edgy pulse of notes filled the room, making my body vibrate.

The male nurse approached the boy and nudged his shoulder. They both looked at me. I could only assume his nurse wanted him to introduce himself.

Did *I* want that?

Maybe.

I shifted in my sandals, tugging on the bottom of my shirt. Mother had forgotten I would need a button-down due to the wires. Ransacking my closet this morning before we left turned up only a girl-sized, pink-flowered number. It was snug.

The boy pushed away from the wall. His gaze remained on the floor until the very last moment, when he stopped in front of me and our eyes met.

His mouth made a sound, but the music drowned out his words. I shook my head, uncomprehending. He stepped closer. I caught the scent of laundry detergent and something chocolate. He must have eaten the cake that arrived on the dinner tray. I had, too.

"I'm Tucker!" He was so near, I could have turned my head for a kiss. Not that I would. I'd seen precious few kisses on screen and none in real life.

My head buzzed with anxiety as I said, "I'm Ava."

"I think we're already there!" he shouted.

"What?"

"We're already there!"

I had no idea what he meant. "Where?"

He pointed at the speaker. "Hell."

I didn't know why he was bringing this up, but I said, "Sure."

He tilted his head, then laughed so loudly that the sound cut through the music. A swoop fluttered through my belly like a butterfly leaving the safety of its perch to wing into the sky.

"What's so funny?"

He leaned in again, and this time I felt the heat of his nearness. "It's the song. It's called 'Highway to Hell.'"

"Oh!" He'd made a joke. "Yes, we're already there. In hell."

"Come here often?" His eyes penetrated mine, dark and filled with amusement. I couldn't tell their color in the crisscross of light, but they made me smile.

"Never. Do you?"

He laughed again. "God, I hope not."

He tapped his foot, his head nodding to the beat. His proximity made me feel off-center, as if the core of who I was no longer resided in my body but in the narrow slice of air between us. No book I'd read had ever described a feeling like this. Even with my faulty memory, surely I'd recognize it if I'd felt it before.

The music began to wind down, and our nurses approached. My elation washed over with fear. Was it time to go back to my room? Or to lose everything?

The light changed from its gentle confetti to a flashing strobe. My head spun like I'd been turning in circles. I felt sick and reached out for anything to steady me.

The regular lights popped on as the music died out. A warning tone sounded. The dizzying whirl sharpened to a buzz. I sizzled like a lightning rod, head to belly to hands and feet.

My legs crumpled, and the nurse grasped my body to help me slide safely to the ground. The last thing I saw was his face, watching me with concern.

Tucker.

CHAPTER 2
Tucker

"Ava!"

I dropped to my knees, but not from a seizure. Strobe lights don't trigger them for me.

Ava was down, her skin pale, her body twitching. My stomach tightened as I was forced to witness what others saw in me. I got it now. Their fear, why they kept their distance.

It was like watching someone die.

I'd never met anyone else with epilepsy. I knew kids my age had it because more than one school nurse had referred to them when I was stuck on a cot in a sick room. But I guess their seizures were under control, because I'd never seen anybody doing what I did.

DeShawn, my nurse, laid a hand on my shoulder. "Tucker, come back over here."

"I'm fine."

"I'm not worried about you," DeShawn said. "We need to give them some room."

The nurse on the floor pushed Ava's dark hair from her cheeks. "Ava, come on out of it. Time to start breathing."

I stood and backed away. Since I'd had about a bazillion and one seizures, I wasn't worried that Ava was having one now. But as the seconds ticked by, I sensed the tension in DeShawn and the other nurse.

"Time check?" the nurse asked.

"One minute thirty," DeShawn said. "What's her typical?"

"Mom says a couple of minutes."

More seconds passed. I squeezed my hands into fists, then loosened them again.

"You want me to order diazepam?" DeShawn asked.

"Let's give it thirty more seconds," Ava's nurse said.

We waited. I gripped my backpack strap so tightly my fingers howled.

DeShawn looked over at me. "You doing okay, Tucker?"

"Bang-up," I said. But I wasn't. My longest seizure had been eighty-five seconds. We were pushing two minutes on this one.

Another minute and nothing.

"Call for diazepam," the nurse said.

"I need to get him out of here," DeShawn said. He meant me.

"Grab Cindy. She's at the desk."

"Will do." DeShawn got on his phone and gave several terse instructions I couldn't follow.

I didn't want to go. Ava lay completely still, her color the grayish-blue of somebody who wasn't ever going to breathe again.

I knew that color. I'd seen it before.

My mom, my dad, my brother. All of them looked like that after the car accident. I'd been the only one to survive, with the parting gift of a brain injury that caused my seizures. But I'd been awake when they loaded me on the stretcher. When they covered everyone else in my family with plastic.

"Go grab your phone," DeShawn told me.

This seemed unreasonably practical, given there was a girl lying on the ground who hadn't breathed in over two minutes.

But I walked over to the speaker, unhooked my phone, and followed him out. Two more nurses with a cart between them hustled down the hall toward the room. Ava really was in danger.

A sick feeling welled in my gut. I got it after a night of bad dreams, nonstop sirens and the smell of leaking gas, asphalt too close to my face.

Like death was near.

DeShawn handed me off to a blonde lady sitting behind the desk.

"You know your room number?" she asked.

I waved vaguely in the direction of my hall. "210."

"All right. Let's go." She stood to escort me back.

The epilepsy section of the hospital was small. I'd find Ava. I'd pester everybody to find out how she was.

I had to know she was okay.

CHAPTER 3
Ava

I sank into softness, a bed that stayed still instead of rolled. People walked in and out, murmuring, shining light onto my face. My belly shook and my eyes got wet. I wiped and wiped until the words started returning. Tears. Cry. Hospital. Nurse. Pain.

My head hurt.

A woman sat in a chair by the bed. Some people called her Mrs. Roberts. Another called her Geneva. Then someone said she was my mom.

When I tried to sit up, she pressed me back down. "Rest, Ava." So I did.

I woke to a low, aching pressure in my belly. I shifted from side to side, but each movement made it worse. I sat up, a roar in my ears, my hands on my stomach.

Mom jumped from her chair and helped me stand up. "You probably have to use the bathroom."

She led me to another small room, arranging the wires that trailed behind me. They attached to my head. What were they for? Mom didn't have them. The nurses either.

"This is the bathroom," she said. "Normally I show

you what to do, but we're not home." She glanced back at the bigger room.

The air was colder in the small space. I stared at things until the words came. Toilet. Toilet paper. Sink.

She closed the door. "You sit there. The water will come out." She smiled. "Your body will know what to do." She reached out, but when she unzipped my clothes, I saw words on my skin and panicked. I pushed her out, hot and frightened. Something in me knew those words were only for me.

"Ava!" Mom called. "The wires!"

I slid the colored lines under the door. There was space. Then I pressed my back to the wall, trying to breathe. My chest felt tight. Why had the words scared me so much?

I bent over, touching each letter until I slowly made them out.

Trust only this handwriting.

Find your notes.

Notes?

I closed my eyes. I had so little to hold onto, scenes that began with the rolling bed, the blur of the halls. Then the room. I carefully pictured each one, weighing it against this terrible jittering in my body.

I walked to the toilet and spun the roll of soft paper. It piled on the floor.

It was for soaking up water that would come out if I sat down.

The phrase "sit on the toilet" felt natural when I said it inside my head.

I could do this.

My clothes were in the way, so I lowered them and sat. Water ran out, a release of the jittery feeling.

I stayed sitting on the toilet, not sure if the water would come again. I peered down at the words on my belly.

The next line read, *Remember your life*.

But I did remember. The rolling bed. Nurses. Mom. This bathroom.

There was one more line.

Read the shower curtain.

I glanced over at the sheet of plastic that separated the shower from the rest of the bathroom. It had no words on it, only a long fall of bright white.

What did the words mean?

I picked up some of the toilet paper and dried my body. It took a moment to work the zipper, but I discovered if I didn't look, my hands knew what to do.

I turned and pushed a lever on the toilet, then jumped back at the loud noise. The water and paper moved down. I had known to do that. Parts of me remembered. *Flush*.

I looked around to see what else I could learn. The room had a sink and a mirror.

I walked up to the shiny glass. I knew this was me. The body wore the clothes I could see when I looked down. It moved when I did.

But I had never seen my face before.

Long dark hair swirled on my shoulders, disappearing into the white wrapping on my head. My eyes were blue with little brown specks. I leaned in and stared until my breath changed part of the mirror into fog.

A noise on the door made me jump.

"Ava?" It was Mom.

"I'm here," I said, not sure what else to say.

"Are you okay?"

"Yes."

I approached the shower. I had to hurry, or she might

come in.

I ran my hand along the length of the curtain. The white was unbroken. There were no notes. No handwriting. I examined it closely and found a small tag. It read, "Do not remove."

Was that my message?

I walked inside and pulled the curtain closed. I liked the feeling. Safe. Alone. I leaned against the cold wall.

Was this what the note meant? Do not remove myself?

I slid to the floor. My feet were bare, and I wiggled my toes. I worked my way up, naming every part of my body. Ankle. Knees. Legs. The words piled up and comforted me, something for my thoughts to rest on.

Then I spotted it. A group of letters on the bottom corner of the shower curtain.

A word!

I snatched it close. More words ran up the side, written small.

Open the book History of the World. *Do not let Mother see the notes inside. If no book, find the paper flowers at home. Trust no one.*

I read it again and again and again. *History of the World*. Paper flowers.

Trust no one.

Mother meant Mom. *Mother* felt right when I whispered it, although it made my stomach turn over, hot and uneasy. I didn't know why, but I understood I could not let the woman in my room see inside the book.

I had to be brave enough to go out there and find it.

CHAPTER 4
Tucker

I paced my hospital room, sometimes stepping into the hall as far as the wires would go.

Gram sat on the sofa bed by the window, knitting a Pokémon hat. A Squirtle. She started making them when I was six and never stopped, even though I quit playing Pokémon years ago.

"You're going to wear a hole in the floor." She held up the pale-blue Squirtle. Its round head and big eyes looked amazingly like her, even without her mass of gray curls. "Am I getting it right?"

I coughed to cover my laugh. "It's great."

"Is all this wandering about that girl?"

I didn't have to answer. She could read my damn mind. Of course she could. It had been nothing but the two of us since I was twelve. Since my life caved in after the accident.

This hospital visit was supposed to change everything. I'd have a seizure while wired to the gizmos, and they'd figure out the problem and fix it. We'd hinged all our hopes on it.

I would graduate high school in June. How long could I live with my gram? I wanted a real life. To drive a car more than a few months here and there when my seizures were under control. To get a job. And college. I wanted to go. I had Mom and Dad's life insurance money set aside for it.

But how could I do any of that if I couldn't beat this thing? Sometimes I spent weeks lying in bed because sitting up for too long gave me muscle tremors. Then came the migraines.

It was no life at all.

This week was supposed to make things happen for me. Only we were on day four—and nothing.

At least right now I could walk around. For five hours a day I was stuck sitting in bed next to a dude holding a syringe. He had to be ready to pump his radioactive sauce into my veins the minute a seizure started. Surely he was tired of me. My failure. My nothing.

The only thing that had been worth it was that girl.

I plunked down on a chair.

"What was her name?" Gram asked.

"Ava."

"That's a nice name. I knew an Ava once. She married a young man named Horace."

I loved Gram, but I did not want to hear about Ava and Horace. I wanted to find *my* Ava. I had to know she was all right.

A nurse popped into the room. She was cute, but like most of the staff, she treated me like I was ten. "Quick vitals check!" She tugged a blood pressure cuff from the stand.

"Were you able to find out anything about Ava?" I'd asked all the night nurses since the disco room incident, but nobody would tell me anything. I was hoping the morning ones would tell me something. At least that she was alive.

"We've been talking about you two. Hold on." She held up a finger until the cuff deflated.

My heart sped up. Maybe I would get some answers. "How is she?"

She pulled the stethoscope from her ears. "I think it's cute you talked to her."

"Not cute enough to tell me if she's okay? She wasn't breathing."

The nurse glanced over at Gram and leaned in close to remove the cuff. "She's okay," she said softly. "She's in her room."

Relief flooded through me. "I don't guess you'd tell me which one."

She flashed me a look of pure *don't push your luck*. "You want to try the disco room again tonight?"

"Will she be there?"

"I doubt it." The nurse hesitated, as if she might say something more. But she only repeated, "I doubt it."

"Then, no."

"Okay, we'll do the strobes in here. They're going to order sleep deprivation for you tonight," she said. "And I'm thinking they'll make you ride a recumbent bike around two in the morning."

Gram stood up at that. "Ride a bike? In the middle of the night?"

The nurse nodded. "Exhaustion. Trying to induce that seizure."

"Great," I said.

"Sorry. Anything else?" She headed toward the door,

pausing a moment to see if I would answer. I shook my head and she disappeared.

Gram walked over and rubbed my shoulder. "Don't be blue. The seizure will happen."

"All this time we hoped it wouldn't, and now we're hoping it will." I flopped back on the bed.

"I tell you what," Gram said. "When the nuclear person arrives, I'll take a little walk. See if I can nose around for this Ava."

"You'd do that?"

"Of course. Anything you want me to tell her?"

I couldn't imagine what Gram might say. *Would you like some tea with my grandson?*

"No, Gram. Just tell me how she is. Remember, long brown hair. Shirt with pink flowers. Maybe. She might have changed."

"I'll find her," Gram assures me. "Old ladies can walk in anywhere and act all confused while they perform their covert ops."

I had to laugh. Gram loved spy movies.

The nuclear medicine tech, a lanky man with a bald head and lumberjack beard, arrived a while later. Gram told him she'd take a break in the cafeteria since he was there. Seizure patients weren't allowed to be alone.

An alarm sounded in the room next door. Lucky duck. All around me, other kids had their seizures, got their scans, and went home. I was stuck.

Although Ava had gone through a seizure and was still here.

"You have anybody else taking as long as me?" I asked the technician.

He checked my IV port, rearranging the line. "It happens. The worst is when you get to the end of the week with nothing, check out, and then have one in the parking lot."

Great. That better not happen to me.

"Have you been in a room with a girl named Ava? She's a friend of mine."

"Nope, just you this week, buddy."

"I'm your full-time job?"

"Right now you are. Other than writing reports and looking over records."

I stared up at the ceiling. The black bubble over the video camera displayed my warped reflection.

When Gram returned a half-hour later, I could tell instantly that she had news. Her face had bloomed pink.

"What did you find?" I asked.

"Two things that are going to make your day. One is a cupcake." She set a plastic container on my tray. It held a chocolate cupcake the size of my face.

I wasted no time opening it. "What's the other?"

"The girl is still on the ward. Room 205."

I wanted to kiss her.

"How do I see her?" I asked. "I'm all wired."

"You could go back to the disco room," she said.

"But she won't be there. The nurse said so."

Gram sat back down on the sofa. "Surely there is some other activity you can do. At least to allow you to walk by her room."

The tech gave me a knowing smile. "A girl, huh? There's a support group they let teens go to."

"Will she be there?"

He shrugged. "No way to know, but at least it would get you back in the mobile unit." He picked up the wires leading to the wall. "You'd have to be moved to a backpack and escorted, same as for the disco room. That has to be arranged in advance. But it's doable once I'm gone."

I turned to Gram. "Let's call the nurse. I'm ready for a second shot."

The hours with the nuclear medicine tech felt like a year. I watched TV and played Scrabble with Gram. I tried on her Squirtle hat over my gauze, much to the amusement of the tech guy. He ended up taking the hat home for one of his kids. This lit a fire under Gram, who decided she needed to make them for all the nurses.

Finally, the EEG tech arrived to rewire me from the wall to the backpack. I practiced all my opening lines.

So, you decided blue wasn't your color?

No, no, no. She might be self-conscious about going *un*conscious.

Not the first time I've made a lady swoon.

Okay, that was worse.

DeShawn popped in to say he was coming on shift in five minutes. He'd been the one pushing me to talk to Ava last night, so I waited for him to walk me down. When he finally came to fetch me, Gram looked up from her newest creation, a Charmander.

"I hope you find what you're looking for," Gram said with a wink.

The moment we were out in the hall, I scanned the nearby room numbers. The epilepsy ward was a long hall lined with circular wards. In each section, all the doors faced a nurses' desk in the center.

Ava's 205 opened directly across the circle from me. Technically, I could stand at my door and she could stand at hers and we could wave to each other without ever leaving our rooms.

Not that I intended to do that. Best-case scenario was that I'd be able to get her phone number and we could text each other. But an occasional visual from across a crowded nursing station worked, too.

DeShawn tried to take me the wrong way around the circle, the direction that wouldn't pass her room. But I didn't follow him.

My heart beat ninety-to-nothing as I approached 205. What was I going to say? Would it be any better than the last thing I'd said? I didn't have AC/DC to help me this time.

I spotted her right away through the half-open door. She was sitting on her bed, holding a giant textbook.

My shoulders relaxed. For the first time in my life, someone had recovered from the blue-gray skin of death.

DeShawn came up behind me. "Oh, I get it."

Ava still wore the button-down shirt with pink flowers. But she looked perfect. They must've adjusted her head gauze at some point because I distinctly remembered her tape last night being pink, and now it was yellow.

I wasn't sure if I should knock or clear my throat or hope the laser beams of my eyes would make her look up. I couldn't see much of the room, just the slice that had her in it.

But she was oblivious to me.

I waited another beat, then I couldn't stand it. "Ava. Hey."

Her head popped up, her gaze meeting mine.

"I'm so glad you're all right." Everything about her was exactly as I remembered. Those bright eyes. Long legs in denim shorts. Instead of shoes, she wore the hospital-issue nubby-footed socks.

As her head tilted, surveying me in her doorway, my knees went liquid. I wanted her to be happy to see me.

But her words dashed my hopes.

"Do I know you?"

Crap. She didn't remember me. That sometimes happened. I often lost the ten or fifteen minutes right before a seizure. We'd barely met before she went down.

A woman approached the head of the bed. Probably her mother. She had the same brown hair, only cut more severely near her chin. Her eyes bore into me like she was contemplating stabbing me with a cafeteria fork. "Ava can't have guests."

I didn't want to cause Ava any distress. But moms were moms and this one definitely seemed overprotective.

"I understand, ma'am," I said, but that didn't stop me from speaking to Ava anyway. "I wanted to see you again. There's a—"

The mother cut me off. "Please leave."

My gut clenched. I wasn't going to be deterred until I took my shot.

Ava gazed up at her mom, then back at me, like she was trying to work this out.

"Are you my boyfriend?" she asked.

Of all the things I thought she might say, this wasn't even on the list. She turned to her mother. "Did you mess with my journal?"

"Of course not," her mother said.

Now I was worried. The animosity coming off these two could have melted the ice caps.

"Are you okay?" I asked.

Ava swung her legs over the edge of the bed and

patted the spot next to her on the mattress. "You *are* my boyfriend. Come over here and let's make out."

"Ava!" her mother said. "I never should have let you watch TV!"

This conversation was a surprise a minute. I wasn't sure what else to do, so I walked in and sat down next to her. She lifted my hand and held it in hers, soft and warm.

"Ava, stop it," her mother said. "Stop this instant. You don't even know that boy." She snatched up the bed remote and pressed the red call button.

DeShawn took a step into the room. "Tucker, let's go."

Ava leaned in until our shoulders brushed. "No. I want him here." She tilted her face up to me, and I was knocked backward by the look of pure hope in her expression. "Are we madly in love?"

If Ava wanted to involve me in some scheme against her mother, I was all in.

"Absolutely," I told her.

"I thought so." Ava grabbed my face with both hands. Her lips met mine.

First kiss.

I was too flabbergasted to do anything but kiss her back. I'd never kissed anyone before. My tendency to fall on the floor in a blur of muscle spasms generally meant girls didn't deem me worthy of locking lips.

Ava smelled faintly floral. She deepened the kiss, tasting of chicken salad from the hospital lunch. My body tried to react too fast, and I had to will it down. We had all these spectators.

Still, I was high, practically floating. Her lips were warm, and her hands held onto me like I was the last anchor in a storm.

The mom's shrill voice could have shattered glass. "I will not stand for this!"

DeShawn's tone conveyed his concern. "Tucker, we have to go."

Lighter footsteps rushed into the room, but I refused to open my eyes. This was too perfect, too unexpected. I wasn't going to let go of this moment until they dragged me away in chains.

"Is everything okay in here?" A female voice, probably the nurse who got called.

"This boy came in here and started kissing my daughter."

"That's not exactly how it went down," DeShawn said. "But Tucker, we gotta go."

"Call security right now," the mother said.

"That isn't necessary," DeShawn shot back.

We reluctantly broke apart. Ava kept her hands on my face. Her eyes were the pale blue of a summer sky.

I refused to look at anyone else. "Are you going to the support group meeting?"

She touched her mouth, as if she was as surprised as I was at what she'd done. "What's a support group?"

"Where all the teens our age sit and talk."

Her eyes widened. "Yes, yes! Where do I go?"

"Next door to the disco room."

"What's the disco room?"

Whoa. "It's where we met. It has music. And lights."

"Ooooh. Let's go again!"

But my elation dropped. If she didn't know about the disco room, then she had lost more than my introduction. How much amnesia did she have?

DeShawn walked up, towering over us.

I had to work fast. "We were there last night. They turned on the strobes. You had a seizure."

"That's enough," the mother said. "Escort him out of here or I'm calling 911. Clearly there isn't any sort of security here."

DeShawn put his hand on my arm to pull me up. "Tucker, we have to go. Now."

Ava stood with me. "I'm going with him."

"You're not wired to walk around," her nurse said.

"You need to be in here on the video monitor," her mother said. "That's why we admitted you. It's for your safety."

Ava turned to the nurse. "I'd like to see a…" She looked frantically around the room. "Someone. I'm sad. I cry a lot. I need to go to a support group so I can talk. Get… support. I need a…" She frowned again.

"Social worker," I whispered.

"That's right. A social worker," she said. "I need a social worker to send me to the support group because I'm sad. Depressed! I should take an SSRI, which may cause dry mouth and have side effects I should tell my doctor about." She seemed elated to have thought of all this.

Her mother rounded the bed. "No more television."

Ava lunged toward the nurse and grabbed her arm. "Please call a social worker. I need to talk." She bit her lip. "I need help away from this mother."

Her mother went still. "Ava? What are you doing?"

Ava stood straighter. "You said I was here to get help. I'm getting it."

"You're here to get a doctor's opinion," her mother said.

Ava turned back to the nurse. "Please, a social worker. My mother… hurts me."

"Ava! Stop it!" Her mother's face contorted with fear.

The nurse paused, wide-eyed. "I'll get someone up here right away." She looked back and forth between the mother and Ava. "I think I'll wait here for her to arrive." She pulled her phone from her pocket and tapped a hurried message.

DeShawn tugged on my arm. "Come on, Tucker. *Now*."

This time I let him lead me away. When we were in the hall, I asked him, "Do you believe all that?"

He shook his head. "I believe you are about to get your butt thrown out of here."

"I think she's in some sort of trouble."

"Ava doesn't remember who you are. Let them sort this out."

"I lose some memory when I have seizures. I forget things for a while. It comes back."

"That's not going to happen to Ava," DeShawn said. "When she has a seizure, her memory loss is permanent."

"Permanent? Like gone, gone?"

DeShawn grimaced. "Gone for good. Now, come on."

I barely registered the walls as they blurred past, giant portraits of smiling kids in colorful frames. Ava lost everything with a seizure.

How could you live that way?

Would she have another one today? Would she lose the memory of kissing me?

I'd never forget it. Her blue eyes. Her joy. For the first time in my life, someone had pinned their hopes on me.

I decided right then and there, her seizures didn't matter. Because after losing my parents and brother, there was one thing I knew about memories. As long as you were alive, you could always make *more*.

CHAPTER 5
Ava

I was free.

With that boy's help, I'd stumbled upon magic words. *Social worker. Mother hurts me.* I would use those any time I had to. Because even if I didn't know exactly why, my notes in my history book told me not to trust that woman. That she would tell me I was someone I wasn't. She would write a diary and say the words were mine. She would destroy my own notes so I always forgot how I felt about her.

Trust only this handwriting.

When I got home to my paper flowers, hopefully I would learn why.

I'd been careful since the social worker took me to her office. I paid very close attention to how she leaned in, when her red lips pinched, and when she scribbled in her book.

I didn't tell her about the hidden notes or the words on my body. Whenever I opened my mouth to speak about them, my belly trembled. So I said I couldn't remember things, but my mother made me afraid.

That was the truth.

The social worker decided I needed to be around kids my age, so after closing her notebook, she walked me to the support group meeting.

"I hear you've been watching a lot of television today," she said. "Did you find something you liked?"

This was my new favorite subject. Mother didn't want to talk about it. She would have prevented me from watching anything after I kissed the boy, but while the tech person moved my wires to a backpack, I kept the nurse button in my hand. I had a weapon.

"Everything," I said. "*Grey's Anatomy* is amazing. They were having a marathon! I didn't even know about marathons, but I love them!"

The social worked laughed. "Much better to watch them than run in them."

I had no idea what she meant by that, but I said, "It's a lot easier than talking to real people. That makes my head hurt."

"That's expected," she said. "You have very little functional memory. If you feel uncomfortable in the group, let the counselor know."

I knew I wouldn't. The boy who kissed me would be there. "I'll be fine."

Her red lips smiled at that. "I like your spirit."

We paused outside a door, and she cracked it open. "We have one more!" she called.

"Come in!" said a voice inside.

Four people sat in chairs, but I ignored everyone else when I saw the boy I kissed. I rushed forward. "Boyfriend!"

He jumped up to move an empty chair next to him.

We sat down, although the social worker stayed by the

door. Her lips pinched as she watched us. That was bad, but I didn't care. I reached for the boy's hand and held it. His fingers squeezed mine, and my body warmed over.

I wished I could remember his name. Things had happened too fast for me to keep up.

But I remembered the kiss. It was better than TV. When he did it, I felt perfect inside, like I was sprouting happiness in my body. No trembling. No fear.

I wanted to do it again.

A gray-haired woman spoke. "Ava, I'm Morena, the counselor. Ria just told us that she's sixteen and plays the flute." She turned to a boy slouched down in his chair. "Jared, what about you?"

"I've had two surgeries already. I'm over it." He pointed a finger at his head and made a strange sound with his mouth, like *peckow*. "No help. Keto. VNS. Four failed meds."

Ria snorted. "Four failed meds? I've had four*teen*."

"This isn't a contest." Morena wrote something on her paper then smiled at my boyfriend. "Would you like to take a turn?"

"Sure. I like bowling." He pointed to his shirt. "And I pretty much live for video games where I get to kill off zombies."

Bowling. Zombies. I couldn't picture those things. They weren't words I knew.

"Very good," Morena said. "We are all so much more than our diagnosis."

"Diagnosis?" He grabbed his head with his free hand, startling me. "Is something wrong with me? Am I dying? Should I find Jesus?"

Ria let out a giggle.

Morena smiled. "You have a great sense of humor."

THIS KISS

I grinned. "He's my boyfriend."

Morena shuffled through her papers. "You two know each other?"

I lifted our joined hands to my cheek. "Of course. We've been making out like Meredith Grey and Dr. McDreamy in the residents' bunk room."

He laughed. "You like *Grey's Anatomy*?"

"*Love* it!" I said. "I watched a *marathon*. Didn't run in one, though."

Jared and Ria burst out laughing. I looked at them, then at Morena. "Is that funny?"

The social worker moved forward from where she'd been watching at the door and handed Morena another piece of paper. "Here's a little background on Ava."

Morena scanned it. "So you had a memory loss event last night, Ava?"

This got everybody quiet.

"I admit nothing," I said. People liked saying that on *Judge Judy*.

My boyfriend turned to me with a broad smile. *Yes*. I said the right thing.

Morena turned to the social worker. "She has amnesia?"

My body buzzed with energy. "I'm right here," I said. "I can tell you myself."

The social worker's lips pinched the tightest I'd seen, but it no longer made me anxious. I was a fighter. The notes I left in my history book said so. I had to fight.

She tapped the paper Morena held. "Memory loss, declarative. She was tested this morning. All procedural intact. She can walk, talk, seems normal. Only episodic memory is gone."

"Jabber jabber jabber," I said, each word like a shard of

glass aimed at the woman. Every scene from the TV shows I'd watched that day were like treasure troves, words and emotions I could fire like the guns the cops carried in *Law and Order*. "I'm fine. Look at me. My boyfriend is right here. I'm all good."

Jared perked up. "Dang." He and Ria were paying full attention.

Morena tucked the new paper into her clipboard. "Ava, do you remember anything before last night?"

"Of course I do." I flipped my hair with my hand like a shampoo commercial, forgetting the wires, and had to disentangle my fingers. "Nobody can tell what I know or don't know."

Morena's gaze clashed with the social worker. The social worker subtly shook her head *no*.

A fighter instinct rose in me, heat curling through my belly. No one was going to tell me I was weak. I wrote on my skin. I found the shower curtain. I read about who I was. I was smart and fierce, and none of these people would take me down.

"All right, Ava," Morena said. "What did you do yesterday?"

"The same crap we always do." I glanced at my boyfriend. "Right, honey?"

His grin made my stomach swoop just like the kiss. "Absolutely. You got here yesterday morning, checked in by the fish tank. Told me the blue one was your favorite."

I had no notes about him, but it didn't matter. Here he was. Perfection in jeans and an orange and brown shirt. His smile told me he would help.

"Nope, it was the red," I said. "Blue was *your* favorite."

"I stand corrected," he said, his grin even bigger. "And it took forever for them to wire you up. We tried to arrange being here at the same time, but I got here several days ago." He lifted my hand and kissed the back of it. My belly positively vibrated with joy. We were fierce *together*. "I've purposefully held off having a seizure so I could be here with you."

Morena pulled her pencil out. She was going to take notes, too. This was a *test*. "Ava, have you met me before?"

I looked her dead in the eye. "Nope. The only person I know is my boyfriend."

Morena lifted one of her eyebrows. "So, you really are her boyfriend?"

He sat up straight. "With all the rights and privileges thereof."

"Ava, it's okay to acknowledge your condition," Morena said. "Has this happened before?"

"It hasn't happened now." The more I spoke with confidence, the better I felt. This was the way to live. Not scared in a bathroom shower. Old Ava told me in the notes that I learned quickly. I would turn eighteen in a couple of months. Then I could leave home no matter what Mother said.

And now I had a boyfriend. Boyfriends were good, if they were like Dr. McDreamy for Meredith. Or bad, if they made you cry, like Alex. I wasn't sure how often either thing happened, but this felt like the right kind.

I held our joined hands to my chest. "Tad and I are about to celebrate four months of boyfriend and girlfriend bliss."

I immediately caught myself. Tad? Where had that come from?

Jared slid back down in his chair. Ria's mouth became a frown.

I'd messed up. I would not pass the test.

Morena lifted both eyebrows this time. "His name is Tucker."

I had to fix this. My gaze moved from the counselor to the other teens while I thought about it. Then I said, "I call him Tad."

Tucker put his arm around me. "She thinks Tucker is hokey."

My belly swooped again. I ran through the episodes of the shows I'd watched, thinking fast for a way to prove we had memories together. Then I had it. *The Simpsons*. "Tad swept me off my feet at a school dance," I said. "He tried to do some fancy dip, and I ended up on the ground."

"Super embarrassing," he added.

I squeezed his hand. "But in true Tad fashion, he picked me right up again, and we continued dancing." I grinned up at him and was rewarded with a glorious smile in return. "And since then, he's picked me up every time I've fallen."

His smile faltered.

Oh no. I'd said the wrong thing.

But his expression must have meant something good because he lifted my hand to his lips and kissed my knuckles. The feeling became more than a swoop. It was a glow. An assurance that everything was absolutely right. I sank into it like the blankets on the bed. It was the most secure, the most safe I'd felt since reading the shower curtain.

"That's what people do," he said. "When they're in love. They pick each other up."

I didn't know if love worked this way. I hadn't seen enough TV or lived enough life to know for sure.

But I believed him. Because when Tucker said he'd pick

me up when I fell, the gooey goodness inside told me it was absolutely true.

CHAPTER 6
Tucker

My life had taken an unexpected turn for the best. After group, my feet scarcely touched the ground as I walked Ava back to her room with the nurses, our hands joined. Everything was happening fast, but my friend Bill said it was the same with his girlfriend. One minute he was sure nobody would take a second look at him, and the next, he was buying flowers for Valentine's Day.

Sleep deprivation was ordered, but it didn't matter. I couldn't have come down from this high if I wanted to. I rode the stationary bike every few hours. Watched movies. Texted Bill my latest thoughts about Ava.

Gram stayed up with me through the power of coffee. Around six a.m., the nurse came in and said I was allowed to sleep a few hours, and we both finally crashed.

I woke to Gram shaking my shoulder. "Tucker, you need to get up."

It took me a moment to remember where I was, but the wires and gauze were quick to remind me.

I sat up. "Is the nuclear med guy here?"

"No, he's delayed his visit," she said. "Apparently, you got signed up for an art therapy class."

I dropped my head onto the pillow. "Really? Do I have to?"

"The counselor felt it would be good for you and *your girlfriend* to explore your feelings."

I sat up. "Ava's going to be there?"

"It seems so. She's your girlfriend already?"

"Maybe. How long do I have until this art therapy thing?"

Gram glanced at the clock. "Fifteen minutes. I let you sleep as long as possible since you were up all night."

"Oh man, oh man." I jumped up. "I can't shower. What do I do?"

"Get a washcloth and wipe yourself down," she said with a laugh. She pushed me toward the bathroom, holding out the backpack. The tech must have transferred my wires while I slept. "Go on."

After the best sort of wash-down I could manage, I changed into my father's other bowling shirt, a green and blue one.

It hadn't been worn in years. Most of my family's things were in storage. Gram had the idea that we'd go back and sort through them one day, but we never felt up to the task.

But I'd kept the bowling shirts with me, part of the stash I took from my old house before it was packed away.

They were part of my best history. Mom used to host these girls' nights where she would play some dice game with her friends. Dad would take me and my brother Stephen bowling to get us out of her hair.

Stephen was only nine and pretty terrible. But I had good aim for a kid. Dad admired my ability to outscore him. That final year, Mom got us all matching bowling shirts. After the accident, I wore mine every time it was clean until I finally grew enough that I couldn't button it anymore.

Only when we were packing to come to the hospital did I dig out the two that were Dad's. I never wore button-down shirts, but I needed some due to the wires.

They fit perfectly, and I was positive they would bring me luck in the hospital. I examined myself in the mirror. I looked like hell. Dark circles under my eyes. Random tufts of hair sticking out from beneath the gauze.

Ava would look at me today and wonder what she was thinking. I smashed my hair the best I could and headed back into the room.

Nurse DeShawn waited for me at the door.

"Are you always here?" I asked.

He clapped me on the back. "I'm going to pretend you're asking that because you're glad to see me every day."

"I thought nurses only worked two days a week or something."

"I'm four on and three off," DeShawn said. "So you've got me today and tomorrow."

"Cool."

He grinned. "Come on. Let's go see that so-called girlfriend of yours." He shook his head. "Can't believe that stunt you pulled actually worked."

"When it's meant to be, it's meant to be."

The art room was farther afield, in the main part of the hospital away from the epilepsy unit. Apparently, I would not be live monitored, but the cameras in the room would record my activity so it could be played back should something happen.

At this point, I didn't expect it. My seizures came in clusters, sometimes a few days apart, sometimes weeks or even months. Catching them while we were at the hospital was like throwing a dart at the moon.

Ava was already there when we walked in. She had changed into a soft green button-up sweater that looked far too large. Probably her mother's. Gram often wore something similar.

That didn't matter. Her expression lit up when she saw me, and that was the best thing.

I sat next to her. The table must have been intended for preschoolers because when I squatted on the little chair, my knees bumped the edge.

Ava laughed. "We are giants."

"From the land of the Lilliputians," I said.

She looked at me quizzically. "What does that mean?"

"From *Gulliver's Travels*. It's a book about a giant and a bunch of very tiny people."

"I've probably never read it. I'm homeschooled."

"You seem very well-adjusted for someone who lost her memory," I said.

"I'm good at faking it," she said. "My mother told me that this morning."

"You really don't remember anything from before the disco room?"

"No. Thank God I found my hidden notes."

"You write everything down?"

"Always. But Mother destroys anything she doesn't want me to remember. Pretty much the very first letter I discovered was a warning to myself about her. By the way, thank you for telling me about social workers. The old Ava didn't have a word for that."

"The old Ava?"

"Yeah, I start over every year or two. The only reason I know anything is my system of notes."

"You're organized."

"I don't have a choice."

A lady in a red smock passed out large sheets of heavy white paper and spread tubs of paint and small brushes out on the tables. "Just paint whatever comes from your heart," she said before moving on to the other tables.

Ava and I looked at each other and busted out laughing.

"I might have a black, black heart," Ava said.

"Then it will be a perfect match for mine."

Ava shook her head. "No way. I may only have two days of memories and fifty-three TV shows under my belt, but I can already tell you're the cowboy with the white hat on." She leaned closer to me, and my head spun for a moment with the memory of kissing her. "Speaking of that, where *are* all the cowboys? This is Texas, right? Shouldn't there be cowboys everywhere?"

I laughed so loud the other kids turned to stare. We were alone at our table, thankfully, since we were the oldest by a long shot.

When I finally reined it in, I told her, "You can't believe everything you see on television."

"Bummer," she said. "Cowboys are wild. They shoot first and ask questions later."

"That's one way to live," I said. "But most of us ask plenty of questions."

"Right. Like about this." She lifted the bottom of her sweater.

My face heated as I saw the skin of her belly. I didn't want to stare at it too hard, but there were lines of blurry ink. "What's that?"

"I wrote it with a marker. It says to trust only this handwriting. It's how I knew to read the shower curtain."

"Shower curtain?"

"I have to leave notes where my mother can't steal them."

"Why would she do that?"

Ava picked up a brush and started painting a tree. It exactly matched the sample set out on the table. "As far as I can tell, my mother has been controlling my life by what she allows me to relearn after each seizure."

"That's terrible."

She shrugged. "It's her messed up way of protecting me. I have to check the handwriting of my old notes because sometimes she adds her own words to them. *I love my mom* and stuff like that."

"But you do love her, right? Or is that hard with your memory?" That was probably too much to ask, but the whole situation seemed so screwed up. I'd seen Ava's mother overreact. And the way Ava instinctively knew to be afraid. Something wasn't right.

Ava concentrated a moment on a red tulip, its jagged top and round bottom copied from the example. I thought she wasn't going to answer, but finally she stopped painting and said, "I've seen the mothers on the shows. Some of them are obviously supposed to be bad, making fun of their kids or hitting them. Others, the good ones, I guess, hug them and pack their lunches. The worst thing they do is make them eat their vegetables." She dunked her brush in the water. "But mine is different."

"Different how?"

She dried the brush on a paper towel. "When she talks, the words don't match the look in her eyes. Her words are fine. But her eyes are not."

"And it scares you?"

Ava dipped a brush in the white paint and gave the red tulip big white eyes. Then she went back to the red and rubbed them out. "I feel scared about most things. So I don't know. But I don't trust her, and apparently I never have. The memory problem means I have to always warn myself."

"Do I scare you?"

"You're the only thing that doesn't." The way her gaze met mine as she said it made my heart thunder.

She trusted me. I would never, ever betray that trust.

The art teacher approached our table and tapped Ava's painting. "Nice work." She looked at my blank page meaningfully. I stuck a brush in a pot of green and made a random swirl on my page.

When she moved on, I asked Ava, "Do you know how many times you've lost your memory?"

"I'm not totally sure. I don't get to see my medical records. But the notes say I had two seizures between eight and twelve, and several since I've been a teen. I don't know why they got worse. And I don't know if I've found all the notes."

"Are they in your hospital room?"

"They're taped inside that giant history textbook I was holding when you came in yesterday."

"You're clever."

She shrugged and returned to her painting with its yellow sun, green grass, and bright flowers. She examined it for a moment, then stuck her brush in the black pot and began obliterating it.

A protective urge rose in me. "What are you going to do when you get out of the hospital?"

"According to my notes, I'm planning to blow out of

my mother's house the moment I turn eighteen. I think that's why she stuck me in here. They thought I was too dumb or confused to understand their conversation this morning. But I can figure out what 'medically incompetent' means. If she can prove I can't make my own medical decisions, I won't be considered an adult even after my birthday."

"That's bad," I said. "Can she do that?"

"She's already working on it." She lifted the brush from the page. It was completely blacked out.

"I want to help you."

Her gaze held mine. "I'm not sure anybody can."

"I'd like to try."

The art teacher wandered over, frowning at my plain green spiral and Ava's black page. "You ruined your perfect picture!" she said.

"I sure did." Ava tilted her head to the woman. "I think it would help me a lot if you brought me back here tomorrow to try again."

I had to bite back my smile. Nobody was going to put one over on her.

Ava was a fighter.

Things got pretty grim for me the next day. I hadn't had a seizure and I was due to be evicted from the hospital in less than twenty-four hours. We'd tried everything. They gave me antihistamines. Kept me up all night. Bike rides. Strobes. I breathed heavy for huff tests until I thought my head would pop off.

But nothing.

The hospital protocol didn't force me to go hungry, but

Gram and I agreed that I would stop eating on top of everything else. Insurance refused to pay for any more hours with the pricey nuclear medicine guy, so my day was even emptier than before.

Despite all that, I was on a natural high. No sleep? No problem. No food? I could live on air as long as Ava was close by.

She didn't have a cell phone. Given her mother, that didn't surprise me. As we left art therapy yesterday, we agreed that at the top of every hour, we would walk to our doors and wave. Since the wires to the wall let us go as far as our bathrooms, the door was easy.

She didn't always make it, and unlike me, she didn't have sleep deprivation orders keeping her up around the clock. But we'd managed six waves since we parted.

We attended another art class. Ava asked me to paint her a flower, and I drew yellow daffodils because they were my mother's favorite.

She peered at them. "They seem familiar. What are they?"

"Daffodils. My mom liked how they had fluffy snouts."

She leaned over the image. "They're so happy."

"Yellow is a happy color."

"Are they listening?"

"The flowers?"

"Yes. They look like they are listening, you know, the way they lean over."

I laughed. "They do. I suppose we can tell the daffodils our secrets." I leaned down to the page. "I like her."

She laughed too and bent close to the page. "I like him, too."

She chucked her page and started over, making her own secret-loving daffodils. We wrote the wrong name and room number on the backs so they would be delivered to each other after they dried.

The nurses seemed to be conspiring to help us, possibly for Ava's sake as much as mine. I kept my door propped open so I could see Ava's room, and I'd spotted the social worker go in and out twice.

I had no idea how she was coping. She didn't know any music, any current events, not even the President. I had to keep myself in check when we were in art class, or else I felt the need to explain everything from radio to virtual reality.

But I did show her things that mattered. When she said she'd never heard music, I pulled out my phone and split my earbuds between us while we painted. I played AC/DC and told her the crashing melodies helped when I felt life weighing on me. She agreed that it canceled out all the noise in her head.

Lots of teen girls liked Taylor Swift, so I played some. At first she didn't like it, then she heard a love song and insisted I play it over and over again. The longing spoke to her, and she kept her head on my shoulder. I'd listen to Taylor all day if this was the result.

But when I played Lizzo, Ava went wild. She stood up and danced in front of the whole art class. She figured out the repeating chorus, but didn't realize some of the words were completely inappropriate around kids. The teacher shut her down in a hurry. Still, she insisted I let her hear it again later as we walked back to our rooms. DeShawn even took us the long way through the labyrinth of halls to stretch out our time together.

When I sat back down on my bed after art, Gram said, "Well, isn't this a lovely romance?" She'd stopped knitting

Pokémon hats and was working on a pillow shaped like a heart.

"Feeling inspired?" I asked.

"I may be old," she said. "But I'm nothing if not sneaky."

She turned the pillow to the side and showed off a secret pocket that could be accessed between the seams.

"I thought you could use a way of sending her a message that her mother wouldn't suspect."

"Gram! You're like a love spy!"

"I have my ways."

"I don't think her mother will let her keep anything from me," I said. "I'm not exactly on her good side."

"I'm aware. I'll be posing as a hospital volunteer. I'll make sure the young lady knows this heart is from you."

I gave her a big, squeezy hug. "You're the best."

"I know."

As the day wore on, Gram and I ran out of ideas on how to make me have a seizure. So did the nurses.

I was due to be ejected from the hospital by the afternoon, so they decided to use the final hours to test a different medicine to see if it would alter my EEG as it entered my bloodstream. Gram consulted with the neurologist. I half listened, only commenting when they talked about side effects, like my liver dying or my hair falling out.

They settled on one, and I took the first dose while I was still wired up. Ava and I kept up our hourly waves at the door. Since I had nothing left to lose at this point, I asked DeShawn to pass her a note. To my surprise, he did, slipping it into her hand while she was at the door.

An hour before I was due to leave, I got a note back.

I had asked Ava how I could get in touch with her after

we left. I already knew she didn't have an email address or phone number.

She copied the home address from her medical form onto the piece of paper, saying she hoped it was her current one. That was my only way to find her.

"What do I do, Gram? I can't just show up at her house. Her mom would never let me in."

Gram was putting the finishing touches on her heart pillow. "You could send her letters."

Typical Gram. So old-fashioned.

"I'm sure her mother checks the mail and would toss them."

"Ava is smart. If she knows things are coming from you, she'll find a way to get the mail herself."

I couldn't count on it. As the minutes ticked down to when I would no longer get to wave at Ava from across the hall, I made a decision. Gram wouldn't like it. But she was my gram, and she would forgive me.

I asked her for the heart pillow she was planning to take Ava as we left.

I scribbled a note, explaining how to turn on my cell phone and what the cord was for. I took nothing for granted.

While Gram packed the room, I shoved my cell phone and power cord into the hidden compartment of the pillow and buttoned it. I had to admire Gram's work. She'd knitted loops and buttons all around the edge of the pillow, but only one of them released the secret compartment. I could only hope Ava would figure out how to open it. Otherwise, I had sent my phone to a dark and lonely death.

I missed my last hourly wave to Ava because the tech arrived to pull my electrodes. I hoped to jump into the shower immediately and get rid of the glue and grease from having spent so many days in the hospital without a proper shower. I wanted Ava to see me looking normal at least once.

But the nurses were already gathering my towels and sheets and clearing the room.

Gram warned me not to pass Ava's door. "If that mother of hers sees us together, the jig is up."

So we avoided that side of the unit until we turned the corner.

"I'm going back to do the old lady act and leave the pillow," she said. "You wait here."

I hated not saying goodbye to Ava, but Gram was right. I had to sacrifice this last meeting for the hope she'd get my pillow and my phone, and we'd talk outside the hospital.

I stood around the corner with my duffel, waiting to hear if the pillow plan had worked, when pretty much the luckiest thing of my life happened. On the other side of the courtyard, I spotted Ava. She was no longer wired and walked down the opposite hall with the counselor who had led the support group.

This was my chance. I raced to her.

"Tucker!" Morena said. "You're not wired. Are you leaving?"

"Yes, right now," I said. "I need to borrow Ava for five seconds."

"I can't let you do that."

I didn't listen as I pulled Ava out of earshot. "My grandmother made you a secret pillow. It's shaped like a heart. Hopefully, it's on your bed or somewhere in your room. I hid my cell phone inside it, and a note about how to use it. I'll have another phone by tomorrow, and I'll text you. It won't make any noise at all. Just check it every once in a while and plug it into the wall if it goes dead."

Ava's face lit with happiness. "You thought of everything."

"I'm never going to give you up." I pressed a quick kiss to her lips.

Morena stood only a few feet away, arms crossed. "Come along, Ava."

I let her go, elated. I had done exactly the right thing.

CHAPTER 7
Ava

The day we checked out of the hospital, I had one last meeting with the social worker, this time with Mother present. We would be given the decision on my medical competency.

I caught myself squirming in my seat like the little kids in art therapy. Were they as nervous as I was now? I'd been fine alone with the social worker, but this felt too important.

The woman was far more formal than when we talked alone. She folded her hands together on a stack of papers, her red mouth serious. "Geneva, Ava, I'm here to discuss the findings of the ethics committee on whether Ava is sufficiently capable of living independently as an adult when she turns eighteen later this year."

Mother shifted in her chair. So she was nervous, too.

The counselor smiled at me. "Ava is incredibly resilient after her memory loss. She passed her cognitive tests within twenty-four hours of the event, and we can all see how well she was able to cope here in the hospital. She created original art, as well as read books and remembered what they contained. She even made new friends."

Mother's eyes got narrow. "You mean that boy."

The counselor skipped over that comment. "The new medication is working. The neurologist's report shows that Ava's EEG is perfectly normal while on it."

"Of course it is," Mother snapped. "She only has these things on rare occasions. Do you know how many EEGs we've done? How normal they all looked until they weren't?"

The counselor's smile tightened in the corners. "I understand your fear, Geneva. I'm going to include the card for a therapist who might be able to help you. I've also provided a list of books to give you some insight on managing an empty nest after raising a child with a disability."

When Mother inhaled sharply, the woman added, "Of course, we expect Ava will live with you for a while. But if she does choose to leave at her legal majority, you will have no recourse to force her back."

I refused to look directly at Mother, but I could sense how she sank in her chair. "Of course, she'll live with me," Mother said. Her voice had a tremble I'd never heard before. "She has no means to support herself. If she lost her memory, who would help her?"

"We understand how hard it is to raise a child with a rare condition like Ava's. Finding ways to reorient herself to the world in the event of a breakthrough seizure will be part of the action plan we send home with you both." The woman turned to me. "Ava, it's very critical that you keep scrapbooks and journals to help you re-enter your own life after these events. Medication has failed you in the past, so you should prepare for the possibility of it happening again."

I figured that out when I was eight. "I have journals," I said. And now I had a phone, but of course I wouldn't mention that. I couldn't wait to get home to a room away from Mother. I would learn how to use it. Listen to music. Talk to Tucker!

Mother's voice wasn't any more stable when she spoke again. "So Ava is going to be left to fend for herself? Despite everything? Even if she's angry at me only because she doesn't know her whole story?"

I wanted to shout, *And why don't I know it?* But I wouldn't. I had the phone. I was medically competent. I could wait until my birthday. The medicine would keep me safe. I would write on my belly to take it. To never, ever forget.

The social worker gathered her papers into a folder. "I hope the two of you will come to an amicable place and create a lifestyle that works for you both. These activities and books can help."

Mother stood. "Right. A book. As if I haven't read everything I could get my hands on already. If that is all, I'd like to get our things packed."

The social worker slid the folder across the desk. "The teen years are always hard, Geneva. Ava, do your best to find common ground with your mother. She is your best advocate as you move into adulthood."

Ha. I doubted that. When Mother didn't reach for the paperwork, I took it myself. I wasn't any more interested in the activities than Mother was. But I wanted any documentation I could get my hands on. It was important to hide it away for the next time I needed to figure out what the hell was happening to me.

We drove home in a banged-up car that stuttered and wheezed at every intersection. I gripped the door handle, sure the whole thing was going to blow up any minute like the cars in the cop shows.

When we arrived at a funny house with two front doors, I couldn't get out of the car fast enough, dragging my suitcase along the ground with both hands.

Two sets of stairs led to the doors. One side was spilling over with flowers, the other bare with peeling white paint. I started up the colorful side.

"Ava!" Mother called from the car, where she was struggling to pull out her bags. "Not that one. An old lady lives in the other half of the duplex. She isn't kind, and you don't want to bother her."

I hesitated, sure I was welcome among those flowers. But I backed down the stairs and headed up the other side.

As I waited for Mother to unlock the door, I compared our barren porch to the other. My mind stumbled over the names of the blooms.

Then I spotted a pot of yellow flowers shaped like stars with long fluffy snouts.

Daffodils!

My heart turned over. This was a sign, like when Phoebe on *Friends* saw the franks and burger and knew she had to see her dad!

I reached over the rail between our porches to touch one of the blooms. Everything about the smells and color and feathery softness made my body wash over with contentment and peace, completely the opposite of what Mother told me about the woman who lived there.

My distrust of her inched up another notch.

But now we were alone. I had no nurses, no social worker, and no Tucker to help me.

I gripped the red pillow with its secret inside. I hadn't dared to take the phone out while at the hospital. Carrying the pillow into the bathroom would have seemed strange, and Mother watched my every move. I would have to wait until late at night, when Mother slept. It would take time to figure out how to use it.

The door opened to a room not much larger than the one at the hospital. It was furnished like the places I saw on television. A sofa with a low table in front. A set of shelves with books and folders stacked inside.

A small television sat on a stand on the back wall. I headed straight for it. It was the one familiar thing.

Mother shut the door. "Don't assume you'll be able to watch those horrible shows here. No cable. No antenna. We have a few movies, though. You've always liked them."

Movies? I wanted to ask her what they were, but I was too eager to see the rest of my house. I set down the suitcase and walked through another open doorway.

Here was a kitchen with a small table and chairs, cabinets, a sink, stove, and refrigerator. I recognized the function of most everything, other than a few strange metal objects on the counter. I lifted one, pushing down on a lever. The metal grew hot and I dropped it back to the counter with a clang.

"You forgot the toaster this time?" Mother asked, lifting the lever so that it popped back into place.

Right. Toaster.

"Do I usually remember it?"

"I bought this one recently."

I wanted to ask her more, but I didn't trust the answers.

A friendly man had come to my hospital room,

showing me pictures of everyday objects and asking me to recite sentences and strings of numbers. He'd explained about the different types of memory and how they were stored in the brain. But I couldn't keep up with all the thoughts and ideas.

I wished I could talk to him again. Now that I was someplace I ought to know, I had so many questions. Why did I recognize the refrigerator but not the toaster? Why did I know what some things were for, like spoons, but not others, like shoelaces? I'd had no idea how to tie them when we left.

"Your bedroom is down the hall," Mother said. "The one with the pink bedspread. Take your suitcase. I'll make some tea."

She opened a cabinet and removed a small box that read, *Black tea*.

Good. She'd be busy, and I could look around on my own.

I returned to the first room and picked up my suitcase. Another opening sent me into a short hall. There were three doors.

The first room had a green bedspread, a dresser, and a table in the corner. I could tell it was Mother's by the muted tones. The air smelled like her.

The second room was a bathroom, much smaller than the one in the hospital.

The third room held a narrow bed covered in a pink blanket. A small white dresser sat on the side wall, next to the closet door.

I breathed in. I couldn't describe the scent of it, but it felt right. I set down the suitcase and turned to the wall behind me.

Flowers. So many flowers. They covered every inch,

floor to ceiling. Pink ones. Red ones. White ones. Orange. Purple. Blue. All had green stems and leaves.

I touched one.

Paper.

The paper flowers.

I placed the heart pillow on my bed and carefully examined the flowers. They held all my secrets. Multiple notes said so. But where? How?

I stepped back. Did they make a pattern? Point to something?

The mattress dipped as I sat down. I couldn't find any significance in the colors or rows. I knew the different styles probably had names, but I only knew two of them. *Rose* because all the women on the show with the bachelor had wanted one. And *daffodil*, thanks to Tucker.

I stared at them until my eyes blurred, then I realized some of the leaves had fine details, tiny markings that were barely perceptible.

I walked close to them. Not every flower had these markings. I pulled a pink one from the wall and brought it over to the small window for more light.

I turned it over and immediately registered the markings.

Words.

I had written words on the back of the flower, and the bleed-through made it appear as though they were little lines to give the leaves texture.

I greedily read the message.

Journal taped under middle dresser drawer.

Really?

I hurried to the dresser, setting down the flower and pulling out the drawer. I felt around, and sure enough, a sheaf of papers was fastened to the bottom.

I pulled it down.

The front cover had words similar to the ones on my belly.

Trust only this handwriting.
This is the book.
Remember your life.

The handwriting was a match. I'd carefully kept it on my skin with a marker from the art room. The teacher had let me take it.

I shoved the papers beneath some shirts in the drawer to look at later.

What other secrets did my room hold?

I almost jumped when Mother appeared in my doorway. "Would you like some tea, Ava?"

I steadied my breath before I answered, willing my voice not to shake. "I'm a little tired." I closed the drawer slowly and carefully. She couldn't look! That would be terrible!

"Putting your things away?" Her gaze slid to the unopened suitcase.

"Just seeing what all I had."

She nodded, then stepped forward to pick up the paper flower I'd left on the dresser top.

My heart hammered so hard it was painful to take a breath.

"Did it fall off the wall?"

I took it from her before she might see the words. "It was on the floor."

She glanced around my room, her gaze resting on the heart pillow. "Take some time to lie down."

"Okay." I moved to the bed and sat down, needing to protect my pillow. Something in her expression unsettled me, like she wanted to take it away.

My body didn't relax until she left the hall. That had been close. Too close. I needed to be much more careful.

I wanted to close the door, lock it, move the dresser in front of it so she couldn't get in.

But I could not raise her suspicions. I had to protect the pillow. The phone inside. My notes. My journal. My flowers.

Maybe I should sleep. Then I could stay awake late at night, when I could work without fear.

Read everything. Contact Tucker.

And if Mother scared me in any way, I would call the woman on the card. Get help. She said I could.

I stretched out on the bed, placing my head on the heart pillow. I pinched it until I could feel the solid mass of the phone hidden inside.

Tonight, I'd talk to my boyfriend.

And read the flowers to learn more about who I was.

CHAPTER 8
Tucker

Gram forgave me for giving away my phone, but she made me spend my own money to replace it. It took all my saved allowance. After a stern reminder that we had to be careful with expenses if I was going to community college next year, Gram added a third line to our plan.

I didn't care. I would work ten jobs to make sure I could keep in contact with Ava.

I was careful about how I texted her. I did it late at night, when I could be the most certain Ava wouldn't get caught if she accidentally turned on the sound. But I heard nothing. I didn't know if Ava was still in the hospital. I didn't know if the phone had been found or confiscated.

What if she'd had another seizure and didn't remember it was in the pillow?

But I didn't stop. I sent Ava instructions on how to type. How to send a text. How to make a phone call, if she got that opportunity. I reminded her who I was. Who she was. I told her the story of how we met and what we'd done together.

It was two long days before it finally happened. My

new phone buzzed with the ringtone that meant my old phone had sent me a message.

Tucker? Are you there?

Over the next weeks, we kept in contact. She told me what her days were like, studying and cooking and reading her notes. Her mother had told her that the neighbor next door should be avoided, but one day an older woman with dark skin had walked onto her back balcony and smiled and waved to Ava in a wistful way. Ava hoped she could talk to her if she ever got a chance.

But that seemed unlikely. Her mother's paranoia had grown to the point that she never left Ava alone, taking her along on every errand.

I couldn't currently drive. In Texas, people with epilepsy had to wait three months after a seizure before their license was reinstated. Even though nothing had happened in the hospital, I'd had a bad one a few weeks before. So Bill drove me across town to scope out the situation.

The line of duplexes drooped and sagged. Bill offered to stop in front of them, but I waved him on. Ava was certain she couldn't get out. The window in her room didn't even open. I couldn't risk being seen for nothing.

She told me where they went grocery shopping, one of their few outings. Of course, they would have to go midafternoon on Wednesdays, when we had class.

But Bill and our friend Carlos were game. "We're seniors," Bill insisted. "We should have a skip day."

So the next Wednesday, Bill picked me up for my usual ride to school. We stopped to nab Carlos and spent the morning at the food trailers in SoCo, trying one item on every menu. By the time the afternoon rolled around,

Carlos was half sick, and Bill was regretting the chicken sandwich made with doughnuts.

Unlike my Neanderthal friends, I felt supercharged with energy, anxious to get to the grocery store and see Ava again. We waited at the Shelfmart in deep South Austin until Ava and her mother walked into the store. I didn't dare go up to them. If Ava's mother saw me, it would tip her off that we'd been in contact.

Ava looked more beautiful than I remembered. She wore a long gray skirt and a white shirt. The guys got stupid and loud, so I ditched them in the condom aisle where they were acting like morons.

I followed Ava at a distance, quickly turning corners, hoping she would see me and know I had made it like we planned.

She waited until her mother was tied up with the man behind the meat counter and said she was going to the bathroom.

I darted down a different aisle and raced for the back hallway. When I turned the corner, Ava walked straight into my arms and kissed me.

I held her so close. Her hair spilled over my arms, silky and long. I decided never to make fun of musicals again because I totally felt like singing.

She gazed up at me. "You're exactly as I remember."

"I'm so glad nothing happened to make you forget."

We had very little time, so we made the most of it, kissing and holding each other tight, things that weren't possible whispered over the phone or through texts.

Way too soon, she pulled away. "I have to go. This is risky. But I'm glad you did it."

"What do we do now?"

"I've been trying to figure out how to get my window to open. I have to be careful Mother doesn't notice."

"Let me know when you do. We'll sneak you out."

"We?"

"Me and my friends. You can meet them."

She nodded. "I have to go." She pressed one final kiss to my lips, then hurried toward the main part of the store.

I watched her retreating figure with a sense of loss. I needed more.

I sat with Gram after dinner a couple of weeks after the grocery store outing, staring at my phone, willing Ava to write me.

She had to wait until it was completely safe. If her mother caught her with the phone, it was toast.

Gram picked up the plates. "Are you going to be able to set that down long enough to help with dishes?"

I collected our glasses. "Yes, Gram."

As we washed our plates and set them to dry in the nonfunctioning dishwasher that now served as a drying rack, she asked, "You going to see her again?"

"She's been trying to sneak out, but every time she walks down the hall, her mother shows up to check on her. She's had to drink like ten cups of tea, pretending that's the reason she left her room."

"That mother sure does have a firm grip on her."

I passed her the dirty forks. "We did a video chat the other day so she could show me her window, but it's like it doesn't even have cracks around it to open."

"Did it have a latch?"

"Sure, but there was no way to lift the window. I saw it.

It was like the wall and the edges around the glass are one solid piece."

"Is it a rental?"

"I don't know. I'm not sure if Ava would know."

"Most rentals I've seen have been painted so many times that the window is plumb painted shut. But she should be able to cut through the paint with a box cutter, if she's got one." She passed me a glass and I rested it in the dishwasher.

"I didn't think of that."

"That's because our windows aren't painted shut." She chuckled. "I lived with your grandpa in a place like that off Riverside. If you wanted some fresh air, you best opened the door."

That night, I told Ava what Gram had said. She didn't have a box cutter, but she took a butcher knife to the window and slowly carved her way through decades of lacquer so it would open.

It took a week, but she got it done.

Since I couldn't drive, Bill came up with the idea for a double date. We waited for Ava to come up with a time she thought she could get away. It took patience and several false starts, but finally a couple of weeks after she freed the window, she gave us the all clear to come get her.

Bill and his girlfriend Sarah laughed and joked the whole way over. They called it "Mission: Impossible" and played the theme song to the movie on infinite repeat.

I tried to control my nerves.

When we got to Ava's street, we parked around the corner and I walked along the cracked sidewalk to her duplex. The early spring night was cool and dark. I zipped my hoodie and tried to look casual. We weren't completely sure she would be able to get out. Her last text said she was waiting for her mother to settle in for the night.

I got to the corner and hung out, pretending to read my phone.

It buzzed.

I'm out.

My heart leaped. I hurried up the street to her house. She appeared from the side, a shadow in a sweater and a long skirt. She spotted me and ran in my direction.

I took her hand, and we dashed to Bill's car.

I had her.

CHAPTER 9
Ava

I was out in the world without my mother.

Tucker held my hand as we ran across the damp grass, dodging a sprinkler. The spray caught us, and we stifled our laughs as we leaped over a small line of flowers and onto the sidewalk.

My notes told me I had friends once, when I lived in a different house, before the duplex. We'd go to a neighborhood park and hang out on the swings. Sometimes they would bring beer and I didn't like it, but I would take swigs to be as cool as them.

I scoured my references to that time of my life. Had I had a boyfriend before? Had anyone kissed me before Tucker? If they had, either I didn't write about it, or Mother found those notes and destroyed them.

But I was free again, walking down the sidewalk, headed toward a low gray car farther down the block.

"Are your friends in there?" I asked.

"Yes. You'll meet Bill and his girlfriend Sarah. One thing to know about Bill—if we run into anyone he's known a long time, they might call him Jill. It'll upset him, but it happens a lot."

"Why would anyone do that?"

"He was born Jill."

"He changed his name?"

"Bill knew he was a boy all along. Now that he's turned eighteen, he's living it."

"Okay. I'll make sure to call him Bill."

"He'll understand about not having a supportive family."

Would he? So it happened to others, too. "That's good."

He grinned. "Even so, I hope we can go on a date alone sometime."

"When you can drive?"

"Two weeks until I hit the magic three months."

We stopped beside the back door of a gray car. Two figures filled the front seat, locked in an embrace.

Tucker banged on the window, then opened the door. A light popped on. Tucker slid into the back seat and held out a hand to lead me inside.

A girl with a head full of intricate braids turned around. Her skin was the color of the woman next door, dark and beautiful. "I'm Sarah. This knucklehead is Bill. He thinks he's a comedian, but you're mainly going to groan at his bad jokes."

"Everyone's a critic," Bill said.

"We can't help it around you, bro," Tucker said.

"No respect, can't get any respect," Bill said, causing the others to laugh.

I could barely follow the conversation, new words coming at me fast. Knucklehead. Comedian. Critic.

Sarah waved her hand at me. "We'll try not to overwhelm you on the first night."

"No promises!" Bill called back. He moved the gearshift between him and Sarah, and the car shot forward.

I clutched Tucker's arm. My mother didn't drive like this, and I'd never been in a car with anyone else.

He turned the corner hard, a squealing sound coming from the tires.

"We should buckle you up," Tucker said. "It's by your shoulder."

I found the harness and brought it down to click into the base.

"Red light incoming," Sarah said.

Bill turned and gave her a big smile. "Thanks, hon."

She leaned in for a quick kiss.

Bill roared up to the light, then slammed the brakes again. The motion of the car made me shift forward against the seatbelt.

Tucker took my hand. "I swear I won't drive like a maniac."

"It's fine." My heart hammered painfully, but sitting here with two strangers, my hand gripping Tucker's, I felt electrically alive. Everything was new, the sights and colors, stores and cars and people on the sidewalks. I wanted to see it all.

As we crossed town, I got used to the crazy lurching of the car. Bill turned into a small parking lot and killed the engine in front of a tall statue of a boy in a green outfit.

"Peter Pan Mini Golf," Bill said. "Tucker, I have the libations hidden in a bag behind my seat. Can you get them?"

Tucker unearthed the bag from a pile of jackets, and we

scooted out of the car. Bill and Sarah were already halfway up a set of concrete stairs. "Nine holes or eighteen?" he called down.

"The way you suck, nine," Tucker replied.

I clutched his arm and leaned in close. "What are libations? And what are we doing with holes?"

Tucker slid an arm around my waist. "Do you know what golf is?"

I shook my head.

"You swing a metal stick called a club to knock balls into holes. He was asking how many holes we wanted to aim at."

"And libation?"

Tucker lifted the bag. "Drinks. But don't worry. Alcohol doesn't play nice with my meds or yours. We'll get cokes. Or bottled water. Whatever you want."

I was grateful to be with someone who understood. As we collected our golf clubs and chose different colored balls, the sheer number of people overwhelmed me.

Brightly painted statues were strewn around the outdoor space. A rabbit. A turtle. A huge blue whale.

Tucker squeezed my hand as we approached the first hole. It was surrounded with green ground and short walls.

I watched Bill, who passed a bottle to Sarah. He set his ball on the ground, then swung the club until it struck.

The ball rolled along the green and bounced off the wooden edge. It stopped a few inches from the hole.

"So close!" Sarah called. "I'm going to kick your butt."

I waited for her silver shoe to smack the back of Bill's jeans, but she didn't do that, only lining up like Bill had done.

By the time Tucker finished his turn, I felt reasonably sure I knew what to do.

I stood as they did and gripped the handle of the club.

Tucker came up behind me, fitting his body against mine.

"Aww, yeah," Bill called. "Bow chicka bow wow."

I had no idea why he was saying that, but the feel of Tucker's body behind mine was worth any terrible mistake I might make trying to get the ball in the hole.

"Hold it like this." Tucker shifted my hands on the handle. "When you swing, go about this high, and follow through with your body."

We moved together like one person, our weight shifting, and the club arced down and connected with the ball.

Through sheer luck, it bounced off the back wall and angled straight into the hole. Tucker released me as we jumped in the air with a shout.

"You did it!" He wrapped his arms around my waist.

Bill and Sarah let out whoops as well, but the entire scene blurred around me as I focused only on Tucker. His dark eyes locked on me, his wild hair outlined against the light behind him. His arms held my body against his, trapping the metal club between us.

His face lowered to mine. We'd kissed before, in the hospital and at the store, but now there were no disapproving nurses, no mother. And all the time we wanted.

I wrapped my arms around his neck, relaxing into his embrace. A perfect stillness held us separate from the noise and movements of everyone else. We were here. He was mine. And I belonged to him. Our kiss sealed us together like we were merging into one.

The happy goodness in my belly expanded and grew.

Before Tucker, I trusted no one and believed only the notes left to me in my own handwriting.

But Tucker understood how our bodies could fail. That pills kept us safe. He wanted me to understand the world, not hide from it.

With every message he sent, every song he told me to listen to, every website I read, he brought me more into his world. And it was a fun one, full of silly jokes and goofy videos, music that made my heart pound or sometimes made me cry.

He felt things deeply and when he shared all that he knew, I felt those emotions, too. I had no idea there was so much to understand and experience. My mother's world was so small. Four movies. A shelf of books. And the stories she thought were safe to tell.

But now I had Tucker and a universe to explore. And he'd found a way for us to do it together.

"Get a room!" Bill called. "You're holding up the line."

Tucker released me, and we glanced behind us. Another group was waiting for our hole.

Sarah laughed and knocked all the colored balls into the hole with her shoe. "Two points for everyone but Ava! She's in the lead!"

Bill scooped up the balls, and we headed to the next hole.

Tucker kept me close to him, and I matched his step. The night moved on, filled with laughter and cheers and the smell of beer and smoky air.

The fun wasn't being the first to get your ball in the hole. It was the conversations, the beautiful night, and Bill's terrible jokes. I laughed when the others laughed, and reveled in the cool spring night, the feeling of Tucker's body close to mine, and the camaraderie of other happy people all doing the same thing. Nobody upset Bill by calling him Jill. Nobody made fun of me for knowing nothing.

This was life outside of my mother's house. A world with Tucker.

I wanted more. I wanted it all.

I wanted to be eighteen.

CHAPTER 10
Tucker

My first real date with Ava was a perfect night of introducing her to all the things she'd missed. She became a teenager like the rest of us.

I'd already fallen for her, hard, but it was even easier to love this version of her. Without the rough edges of the hospital, trying to prove herself to every doctor and social worker, she was funny and light-hearted.

She thought my corny jokes were funny. She was astonished at my dumb quarter-behind-the-ear trick. All the dorky actions that made me weird at school were perfect to her. She encouraged me to dive deeper into being me.

Even Sarah, who was infinitely cooler than the rest of us, acknowledged that I'd found the crazy-shaped puzzle piece that fit me.

The next weekend, Bill and Sarah picked us up, but then dropped us off at the ghostly playscape at Zilker Park with a midnight picnic made by Gram.

We ate on a blanket beneath the labyrinth of stairs, slides, and bridges, our knees pressed close together.

For the first time, we were entirely alone.

"I wonder if I ever played here, or on any playscape," Ava said. The dim light of a distant street lamp glinted in her eyes as she looked at the apparatus all around us.

"I guess not all moms take their kids to play at parks."

"I don't have any notes about it. Maybe I was too young to write."

I picked up her hand and ran my thumb across her palm. I wanted to always be touching her. "Most of us quit playing at parks with our moms around fifth grade."

"How old are you in fifth?"

I forgot how some of the most common things were unknown to her. "Ten or so."

"Ten. I should have been able to write. I have been to parks before. I would sneak out to go with friends."

A hint of jealousy sliced through me. "How old were you then?"

"I'm not completely sure. I didn't put a date on everything. But I'm guessing thirteen."

"How did you meet those friends?"

"I don't know that either. I went to school when I was really young. Kindergarten. First grade. Mom only pulled me later."

"Do you ever ask her about it?"

"Sure, but I don't know if I trust her answers."

"That sucks. I hate that your mom is so hard to deal with." I wanted to ask about her dad, but Ava never brought him up. But then, I didn't talk much about my parents either. Some wounds didn't need poking.

She leaned in close to me, and I kissed her. She was becoming familiar, the shape of her lips, the brush of her hair on my cheeks. She always smelled of lemon shampoo.

There was no one to interrupt us. We were as alone as we'd ever been.

I cupped the back of her neck beneath her long fall of hair. I drew her closer so that our bodies touched. She settled against me.

Everything felt natural. Her hand moved to my shoulder, and her lips parted.

I could do this forever, although my body pushed forward with an urgency I had to ignore.

I figured Ava didn't have much experience, or if she did, she wouldn't remember it. I definitely didn't have a lot. I didn't know how to set a pace, how far to go, and when to make each move. I understood the mechanics of it, but not the steps, how to get there.

Ava leaned forward so far that I fell backward on the blanket. We knocked over the basket, spilling the plastic dishes.

She laughed, moving it all aside. "I saw something like this on one of the TV shows in the hospital. They knocked things off the table while they were kissing. My mom shut it off."

"I should log you into my Netflix account," I said. "There's plenty to see there."

"On the phone?" She rolled next to me and we lay on our sides, face to face.

"Sure. We could watch something together."

"Not during our real time," she said, leaning in again.

She was right, as always. We could watch things when we were apart, in our separate houses, separate lives.

Her long skirt tangled in my legs as we kissed. She dressed from another era, but that didn't matter to me. I ran my hands along her shoulder, her arm, her waist. She rolled on top of me, our bodies touching everywhere. There was no controlling my reaction to her.

If she noticed, she gave no indication, and her weight settled on top of me.

My pulse raced. I'd never been in this position with anyone.

A cold wind rushed beneath the playscape and sent her shivering. She snuggled in close, tucking her head into my neck.

I drew her tightly against me. My heart hammered hard, and I knew she could hear it. She fingered the pocket of my shirt over my chest. "We only have two months to wait."

I wondered what she meant. To go farther? Should I stop?

She went on. "I'm going to wake up that morning, my bag already packed, and I'm just going to walk out. I don't care about Mother's presents or cake or anything. I'm going to go right out the door, and she won't be able to do a thing about it."

Her birthday. That was what she meant.

"I'll be there. I'll pick you up." I wasn't sure what I would do with her. Gram encouraged our relationship, even with Ava sneaking out. But she wouldn't necessarily be keen on my girlfriend moving in.

It didn't matter. We would figure it out. We had some time.

"I'll keep dreaming about that day until it happens," Ava said.

I kissed her forehead. "Me, too."

My phone buzzed. It was Bill.

On our way back. I've already blown Sarah's curfew.

Our time was up again.

We kissed one more time, lingering and long, then picked up the scattered picnic.

Ava snuck out a few more times over the next weeks. We took walks. Ate pizza. Soaked up each other's presence. On my eighteenth birthday, Ava, Bill, Sarah, Carlos, and I sent balls skittering into pins at a twenty-four-hour bowling alley.

It worked, but she still lived in her mother's grip. She wasn't in school, had no job, no experience. She'd been kept from learning about money, budgets, rent, and basic survival. Even if she left when her birthday arrived, she wasn't sure how to fill her own prescription or what to do about health insurance, which she'd never heard of before I told her.

But I wanted to save her.

With no more seizures, I got my driver's license reinstated. I wouldn't get behind the wheel often because of the risk, but I wanted that right.

Gram handed me the keys a month before my high school graduation. I could tell she was worried. I assured her I would hit the hazard lights and pull over if I felt the tiniest bit weird, and I would take side streets rather than the freeways, just in case.

My urgency to see Ava whenever I wanted was more important than anything. She'd be eighteen in June, and she'd need me to help her build a life away from her mother.

The night I drove over to Ava's house by myself, I felt like the king of the world. I parked Gram's car around the corner and waited.

Ava didn't come out.

I texted her.

She didn't respond.

My heart hammered.

Had she been caught? Did she lose the phone?

I got out of the car, closing the door softly. I walked along the street, tiptoeing past the flower beds and avoiding the street lamps.

My steps slowed as I passed Ava's duplex. A shadow on the front porch shifted, and the wood floor squeaked. I froze, terrified that Ava's mother was outside and had seen me.

But a low, wavering voice said, "The mother suspects."

I peered at the shadow on the porch. It wasn't Ava's side, but the other one.

"Are you Grandma Flowers?" Ava had mentioned her many times since learning more about her from her old journal. The two had managed to smile and wave, but Ava's mother refused to let Ava talk to the woman.

She rose from her chair, her silhouette blocking the window behind her. "Ava called me that, back when I could see her. I have lived next door to that family for coming up on three years." She moved painfully down the steps, holding onto the rail.

I began to make her out in a long, loose dress.

When she came down the walk, the streetlight illuminated her big, kind eyes. "Let's take a walk, you and I."

"I'm supposed to meet Ava."

"You won't be seeing her tonight."

"Why not?"

"Let's move along, and I'll tell you what I know."

When we'd put some distance between us and the duplex, she spoke again. "I'm a night owl. I've seen you coming for her, and you should know, the last time her mother learned a boy was near her daughter, they moved."

My fists tightened. "She'd do that? Just move her?"

The old woman sighed. "The girl was beside herself when she arrived here, missing those friends of hers. I gave her some flowers. She didn't know she had a gift for tending them, but I could see she'd done it before."

We turned the corner. "What happened? Why can't Ava see you anymore?"

"I love that girl like the moon," she said. "We spent many long afternoons together. We read books and talked flowers. But I saw what was going on there, and I asked too many questions."

My mouth went dry. "What *is* going on?"

"Her mother wants Ava protected. So she keeps her away from the whole world. Nobody comes 'round to see her. She's like a bird in a cage." She shakes her head. "It's a tough go sometimes. I've seen her forget a few things. And I've seen her forget everything. It's like rolling the dice."

"So not every seizure is the same?"

"No. Some of them take everything away, even her ability to read. But most only take her memories. One day we'll be chatting about the roses, and the next she won't know a flower from a turnip."

"She's been taking medicine since the hospital," I said. "I've been talking to her."

"That's good," she said. "No young person should be locked away from the world."

"I'm going to get her out of there. She turns eighteen soon."

Grandma Flowers patted my back. "You stay the course, young man. She needs someone to rely on."

We turned and headed back.

"So she won't get out tonight?" I asked.

"They had an awful argument, so loud even I could

hear it," she said. "Ava was insisting she hadn't gone anywhere. Seems like she had some new song she'd been singing. Her mother controls her life. She knows when her girl has new ideas, new thoughts, new experiences."

The idea that I'd gotten Ava in trouble just by knowing her stuck in my throat, making it impossible to swallow. We'd have to be more careful.

My phone buzzed.

Stuck. Not sure I can make it out tonight. Tomorrow?

I quickly tapped out, *of course*.

Grandma Flowers waited, the streetlight bright on her gray curls. "You'll do right by her. I have faith."

"How long should I wait?"

"Only you will know that, child. But be careful. They don't own a lot of things. They could spirit away at any time. They did it before."

I thanked Grandma Flowers for her advice and hurried to my car.

Ava's eighteenth birthday couldn't come fast enough.

CHAPTER 11
Ava

Tucker agreed to wait at least a week before we saw each other again, to be safe.

Since our argument over the song, I'd been so careful to protect the secret of the window, volunteering to wash them myself, keeping my room as organized and clean as possible so that my mother would only give it a quick once-over and never look close.

But yesterday she'd wandered in with her paper towel and Windex.

And she'd seen the cuts around the edges of the frame.

Her eyes went wide, the paper towel fluttering to the floor. She pressed her fingers into the cracks where the paint had once sealed it shut.

I wanted to be fierce, to tell her I had a life of my own, and soon, she'd be no part of it. But the first sign of her wrath, eyebrows pointing toward her nose, mouth set tight, sent fear flooding through me. I'd been careful not to anger her now that I had a secret to hide. My notes told me she sometimes went wild, dumping drawers, clearing out closets, searching for my journals, my notes, anything that might be advising me to rebel.

As Mother lifted the window and leaned out, I pressed into the far corner of the room, wedged between my dresser and the paper flower wall.

"How many times have you left?" she asked, her voice low and menacing, like the angry dogs I sometimes saw on our walks.

I was so close. My birthday was mere weeks away.

I thought fast.

"Never. I only wanted fresh air." The lie was smooth, convincing, and without even a waver in my voice. The fear receded. I was strong.

Mother studied me, her eyes blazing. "I don't believe you."

My mind raced again, and the answer clicked into place. I could kill two birds with one stone, as Tucker sometimes said.

"One of the neighbors plays their music loud. I like it. So I opened the window to hear it. That's why I knew that song the other day."

Something relaxed in her, her shoulders shifting down. She stood straighter.

She believed me.

"I used to have a record player," she said, surprising me. "Then, in middle school, I used a cassette player until much later, when CDs became popular."

"I don't know what any of those are." I did, actually, but I couldn't admit that Bill's old car didn't have a hookup for his phone, so he sometimes played CDs. That vinyl was a thing again and Sarah's brother had an entire collection.

Perhaps I knew more than she did. We were locked up here together, after all.

"Do you have them now?" I asked.

"That was a long time ago." Mother picked up the paper towel and held it out. "You clean this while I get a hammer and nails."

She was going to lock me inside again.

I quickly cleaned the window, already formulating a message to Tucker in my mind. *I'm caught, and I'm stuck. But soon I'll be eighteen, and I'll walk out of here. I'll get a job, and we can see each other whenever we want.*

Tucker had plans. He was talking to some of Sarah's friends who were headed to community college and looking for roommates. When he found a place, we'd apply to grocery stores or restaurants nearby that might hire us both. The idea of seeing him any time I liked was the ultimate prize.

I would not mess up so close to freedom.

Mother returned with a hammer and pounded nails into the wood surrounding the window. She clearly had little experience with tools and almost cracked the glass. But when she was done, four crooked, bent nails held the pane in place. She checked, making sure it wouldn't lift, then left me alone in the room.

I wrote Tucker, saying I couldn't come.

But the loss of our real-life dates made my need of him stronger, until I couldn't stand it a minute more. Only a week later, I worked the nails loose, making the holes wide enough that I could slide them in and out.

And I texted asking him to come.

CHAPTER 12
Tucker

I was desperate to see Ava by the time she asked me to visit her. I wanted to tell her my latest news in person. I'd gotten a job. I would work as a grocery bagger at the Shelfmart up the road from my house.

I planned to sock away as much money as possible. I had spoken with the manager, and he assured me that once summer came, they'd be hiring several more people. I was confident that we could get a job for her, too.

To top it off, I'd been looking around for a place for her to stay, and one of Sarah's friends had found a house to rent after graduation. They were cramming a half-dozen beds in the rooms so they could afford it. I had pictures of the place, her new roommates, and the Shelfmart where I worked. Everything was falling into place.

I parked around the corner from her house that night, holding a pot of yellow daffodils. I crossed behind the line of duplexes until I reached the porch behind Ava's.

I flattened myself against the wall and texted her to let her know I was there.

The wait was excruciating.

Finally, I heard a rustling and saw her in the window, wiggling the nails out of their spots. I guess she saw me because she smiled.

Worth it. Worth every risk.

With painstaking slowness, she raised the window and leaned out.

"Hi, handsome," she whispered. She wore pale yellow pajamas, her hair in disarray. My throat tightened at seeing her in this new way, like she was headed to bed.

"Should we recite some *Romeo and Juliet*?" I'd been reading it in English Lit, and she loved hearing the story.

"Way too tragic," she said. "Our story has a happy ending."

I lifted the pot of daffodils.

"Love them," she said. "Put them on the back porch close to the middle, so Mother will think they belong to Grandma Flowers."

I did as she asked and came back to her window.

"I'm so happy to see your face," I said.

Ava glanced behind her. "Hold on a second."

I flattened myself against the wall in case her mother was coming. But after a moment, Ava returned. "She's in bed. Why don't you come up?"

Enter her room?

I reached up to grasp the bottom of the window, not sure I'd make it in.

"Find an empty pot to turn over," Ava whispered.

I searched around and found a good-sized one. With the extra step, I managed to get my shoulders through the window. Ava pulled me through, and I dropped softly onto a rug.

A single lamp by her bed cast a soft glow over a pink bedspread and a dresser. One wall was covered with flowers cut from colored paper. I spotted roses, tulips, daisies, and many more I didn't recognize. Some had faded, a testament to the years she'd been painstakingly taping them up, but others were bright. I walked along them as she carefully closed the window.

"When you mentioned paper flowers, I didn't imagine so many."

"They're my greatest secret. The more I have, the easier it is to hide what I'm doing." She lifted the leaf of one of the closest flowers. "Look closely."

On the back side were tiny words.

I used my phone as a light to read them.

You were born in 2000. Your father left. Marcus Anthony Roberts. He married your mother in 1997.

"Whoa. Are there words on all of them?"

"No, it's random. She's never caught them." She gazed proudly at the walls. "I wouldn't have known so much of my history after the hospital without them. She's changed my journal many times. I've gotten good at spotting which handwriting is mine and which is hers."

She lifted a yellow flower from a small table by her bed. "This one is for you."

I aimed my phone at it. Like the others, tiny words created the illusion of stray lines.

. . .

Tucker Giddings is beautiful, smart & perfect. I love him. Even if I lose my memories. My heart will remember. Always.

I lifted my gaze from the flower to her face. "You mean it?"

Her expression didn't waver. "I do."

"I love you too, Ava," I said. "Ever since the disco room."

We watched each other, her eyes glistening, until footsteps broke the quiet. A door closed down the hall.

"This way," she whispered, leading me to her closet. She had built a space between cardboard boxes, covered with a quilt.

I ducked into it and she pulled the quilt down over the gap.

"Ava?" Her mother, slightly muffled, just outside the door.

"Yes, Mom?" Ava's voice was thick with sleep. She faked it well.

Her door creaked, and I assumed her mother entered the room. "You left your light on."

"Oh, sorry." A small click.

"Goodnight."

"Goodnight." The door closed with a groan and a pop.

I waited. I held the flower, delicate and precious. I rolled it carefully so that it wouldn't get crumpled and slid it into the pocket of my shirt.

Time passed slowly as I waited. My back ached, hunched over in the tight space. At last, the quilt moved aside. "Tucker?" I could barely see Ava now that the room was dark.

"I'm here."

"She won't check again."

"You sure?"

"Yeah."

"Should I go?" I asked.

"Get in bed with me. Worst case, I throw a pillow over you."

In bed. "Okay."

My eyes adjusted to the low light as Ava pushed back the covers.

"You should probably take off your shoes," she said.

"So much for a quick getaway."

She giggled softly. "Come here."

I settled next to her, and she rested her head on my shoulder. A deep sigh escaped my chest. This was the most perfect thing I'd ever felt.

She curled in closer. "This is nice."

"Yeah."

"You said you had something to tell me that had to be in person."

"I do." I told her about the job and the house.

"You've thought of everything," she said.

"Not really. You'll have to get an ID at some point for the job. Do you have your birth certificate?"

"What's that?"

"A document that lists when you were born and who your parents are. It's something you need when you fill out forms for a job." There were a lot more steps than that, but I didn't want to overwhelm her with Social Security cards and all that.

I'd just been through it, and I knew the drill. I'd had to get almost everything reprinted since it was impossible to sort through all the stuff from my old house after my family died. There was so much emotion in old things. Even something as simple as a chair brought up the image of my mother sitting on it, lecturing me as she doctored my skinned knee. A toolbox was my father trying to show me how to line up the shaft of a screwdriver in a groove.

When I got the Shelfmart job, I hadn't been up for reliving my past to find the documents. It was easier to fill out forms and get replacements. It would be the same for Ava, although for different reasons. "Thank you," she whispered.

I turned to kiss her. It felt different lying this way, her hair a dark shadow across the white pillow.

After a moment, she pulled away. "Tucker, can I ask you something?"

"Always."

"How do you know if you're a virgin?"

"You mean me?"

"No, silly." She gave my chest a playful shove. "For girls. How do they know if they've had sex or not?"

My throat went dry. "I think you bleed the first time. There's something inside that breaks." I had a lot of second-hand knowledge, Bill telling me about how Sarah "bled like a murder scene" and they had to clean it off the back seat of his car. And some random bits from health class.

"Oh," she said. "That sounds painful."

"I don't know. I've never done it."

"You haven't?"

"I've had a lot of seizures at school," I said. "Although, even if I hadn't, I'm not sure I would have been anyone's first pick."

"You're my first pick."

My feelings for her turned ever so slowly in my chest.

"You think we could find out?" she asked.

"If you're a virgin?"

"Yes," she whispered. "I know that I met boys before. But I was a lot younger then. Maybe too young for that. But I want to know. It doesn't seem right not knowing if you're a virgin."

I hesitated. "I don't carry condoms around."

"I don't think I have VD," she said carefully. "The kind that Bill jokes about."

I was glad for the dark because my face must have turned ten shades of red. "That was Bill being a jerk."

"I don't think I have anything wrong with me."

"I'm sure you don't. That's not what I meant for the condoms. I mean, if we don't take care of things, you can get pregnant."

"Oh." She paused, her voice even softer when she spoke again. "When I was in the hospital, they asked about my period. When I had my last one."

My face burned again.

"I had no idea," she said. "I didn't even know what she meant. So, I asked the nurse what a period was. She said when I bled between my legs."

"Did your mother say anything?"

"She wasn't in the room. I was with the social worker and a nurse. You know, after I said Mother had hurt me. We were sorting all that out."

"What did the nurse say?"

"She went to my chart and said that I was on some sort of shot. It's one you only have to get every few months, so you can't get pregnant."

"I've heard about that," I said.

"Well, I'm on it. So, I can't get pregnant."

Her last word hung in the air.

She wanted to do this.

With me.

"Tucker? Can we do it, so I can find out?" Her eyes shone, catching the hint of light from the window. "You know, like an experiment. For *science*."

That made me grin. "Well, I can't say no if it's for science."

She pulled my face to hers. We kissed, and it was like no other kiss that came before. Until then, we'd always reserved something so that we wouldn't bend so far that we might break.

But now, we held nothing back. We kissed everything, touched everything, and when I felt inside her body, there was resistance.

"I think it's a yes," I told her.

"Really?" she sat up. Her shirt was off, and the feeble light from the window illuminated her body. She was letting me see this. Touch this. And soon more.

"I think so. But I don't have a ton of experience."

She pulled off my shirt. "Let's find out. I don't care if it hurts."

I scrambled out of my pants and underwear.

"Whoa," Ava said. "That's what goes in me?"

I glanced down. "We don't have to."

"No, I want to. It just seems like a lot."

I slid into bed beside her. "It's probably on the average side."

She laughed. "Is this what they're talking about when they say, 'Size matters'?"

I grinned. "I think so."

"Well, you're about to *matter* a lot."

I had to stifle my laugh. Ava could really be funny when she wanted.

She wiggled out of her pajama bottoms. "I guess these have to go."

I wasn't laughing anymore. My anticipation was so great, I wasn't sure how I would even hold back when I got there.

But this night would prove it. Ava and I were meant to be together.

CHAPTER 13

Ava

I watched Tucker in the moonlight, memorizing every part of him. His face was tight with concentration as his hands slid over my belly. Inside me, everything was quivering. I was nervous about this, but if he was right, at least I hadn't forgotten any other time this had happened. It felt so big, like giving over a part of myself.

I told him the truth on my flower, at least the truth as I knew it. My heart would remember. Even if a seizure took away my memory, it didn't erase how I felt. There were moments that went deeper than brain cells. They infused your entire body with emotion.

Like how I knew my bedroom was mine.

And how I knew Grandma Flowers was a good person, even when my mother told me to avoid her.

My arms would know Tucker because they felt right wrapped around his body. My lips would know because kissing him sent sparks through me that touched every layer of my skin. And my heart would definitely know because seeing him, or hearing his voice, or even reading his words on a tiny screen made it speed up.

No matter what happened, I would know him. Always. And some part of me would remember this night.

He watched my face. "You ready?"

I nodded. "Yes."

He shifted the mound of blankets in our way. I wasn't sure what I wanted. To be covered up? Who was I hiding from?

I kicked the covers to push them off the end, but I forgot something critical. One of the metal knobs attached to the bottom of the bed was loose.

The blanket caught on it, then knocked it off.

The heavy metal knob landed on the floor with an unexpectedly loud thud, then rolled in circles across the uneven hardwood floor.

A door opened down the hall. "Ava?" my mother called. "Did you fall out of bed?" Her footsteps slapped down the hall.

I sat up on the bed. "Oh, no. Go, Tucker, go!"

He paused by the closet as if trying to decide if he should hide by the box again. But then he rushed to the window and lifted the pane.

"Ava?" Mother cried, fear in her voice. "Are you okay?"

The door flew open. As the overhead light illuminated the room, Tucker froze by the half-open window. He was completely naked. I clutched the pillow to my chest.

Mother's face contorted in anger. "*You*. I can't believe it." She took him in, then me, her eyes blazing.

He snatched up a shirt to cover himself.

"You will pay for this," she told Tucker. She picked up my pajamas from the floor and threw them at me. "Get your clothes on. I'm calling the police."

"No, Mother," I scrambled into my top and pants. "I love him."

"You listen to me," her mother hissed. "I'm here to protect you. Protect you from boys like that."

"No," I cried. "It's not what you think!"

"I know exactly what this is," she said. She grabbed my arm and dragged me across the room.

Tucker had flung on his shirt and pants. "Let her go!" He lunged for me, but Mother stood firm between us.

"I won't give him up!" I cried. "You can't keep me here forever!"

Mother's grip was so tight on my arm that it hurt. "I'm calling the police. Unless you want to go to jail for rape, I suggest you get out of here right now."

"No," Tucker said. "I won't leave her."

"Your funeral." She dragged me out into the hall.

Tucker followed. "You already tried to have her declared medically incompetent," he said. "You're trying to control her life!"

"Don't talk to me about her life!" she shouted. "You haven't been here all these years. She forgets everything. She has to start completely over. I haven't had a day without fear for her in seventeen years!"

She opened a closet door and pulled out an old-fashioned phone with a spiral cord. She stuck the end into a jack in the wall.

I stared in astonishment. "We have a phone?"

"Of course I do." Mother slammed her fingers on three buttons.

9-1-1. She was calling the police.

I turned as far as I could, still locked in her tight grip. "Tucker, you've gotta get out of here. I'll find you again. I promise. I need you to go. I can't live with you getting in trouble for me."

"I don't trust her," he said. "I won't leave you."

And he didn't. Not when Mother locked the two of us in the bathroom to wait. And not when the police came. Not until they took him away, still shouting, "I love you, Ava Roberts!"

They left him in the squad car while they took a statement from Mother. I refused to say anything other than "NO!" when she said he raped me.

When they drove off, I collapsed on the floor by the living room windows. I wanted to run away. But where could I go? What could I do?

I shouldn't have stayed in the living room. It was a huge mistake. Mother ran inside my room and wedged something against the door so I couldn't get in.

I could hear her opening all my drawers, moving my furniture, throwing things to the floor.

When she finally came out, the cell phone was smashed, the cord snipped in two.

My only real link to him, to our friends. Gone.

Now I had nothing.

CHAPTER 14
Tucker

I sat in the cop car for what seemed like an eternity. I wondered what the charges would be. Trespassing. Rape. Since we hadn't done it, maybe only attempted rape. Either way, it was true that I was eighteen, and she was not. That might be statutory rape. I wasn't sure.

I wondered how much I'd screwed up my life. Would I go to jail? And even if I didn't, I had this arrest on my record. Would my college even take me now?

I'd blown everything.

Eventually, the cop came back to his car. We drove in silence. The second car didn't follow us, but peeled off in another direction.

"What's going to happen to me?" I asked the officer.

"We'll go downtown and notify your parents."

Gram. I would have to tell her. How much misery could one family heap on her? A dead son. A dead grandchild. Dead daughter-in-law. Her one remaining grandson winding up in jail.

The ride to the downtown facility took about twenty minutes. I recognized the tall brick building. I'd passed it on the freeway many times, sometimes joking with Bill that one of us would end up there at some point. And here I was.

I didn't know much about how this worked other than what I'd seen in movies. I figured I'd be fingerprinted and my mug shot taken. Big men with tattoos would push me around.

But when we entered, I was taken to a small office.

A lady was there. She didn't look too scary. The woman and the officer spoke outside the room, and I was left alone. I guessed they didn't see me as much of a threat.

After a minute, the woman returned.

"Let me go over your name and address and some other details, and then we'll call your parents," she said.

"Am I going to jail?" I asked.

"Let's get your family on the phone. We'll go over the situation with them."

"I'm eighteen," I said. "Do we have to involve them?"

She set down her pen and looked me in the eye. "Are you in high school?"

"Yes. I graduate in a few weeks."

"Then let's call your parents."

"I only have a grandmother," I said. "My parents died in a car crash when I was twelve. It was here in town. You could look it up. Melissa and James Giddings."

She folded her hands together. "I see. And your grandmother raised you?"

"She's lost everybody in her life but me." I lowered my head. "And now this."

The woman sat for long moments, looking at me. "Was that your girlfriend you were with?"

"Yes, ma'am."

"How long have you been together?"

"Almost four months. We met in the hospital. We both have epilepsy."

She let out a long gust of air. "Do you drive?"

"Yes. My car is back by her house."

"Do you have a friend or someone who could go get it for you?"

"Yeah. I could call one of them." Hope rose in my chest that she was going to let me go. It was a damn sad story. I couldn't help it. It was the only story I had.

"Well, here's the deal," she said. "What happened tonight is not that unusual. Some mom or dad doesn't like their daughter's boyfriend and tries to press statutory rape charges against him."

"We didn't—"

"Irrelevant." She picked up a pencil and tapped it on the desk. "The girl is seventeen. That's the age of consent in Texas, so you're fine on that count. But the mother could still get you on small charges, like trespassing or criminal mischief."

"Who decides that?"

"The prosecutor, but he won't even see the case if I don't put it in the system." She sat back in her chair. "You seem like a nice boy. I'm not really of the mind to muck up the record of a kid about to graduate when all he's done is choose a girl with a mother like that."

"She's terrible," I said.

She held up a hand to stop me. "You make your friend get your car. Do not go near that house, do you understand me? If that woman spots you and she calls the police again, I won't be able to help you. Do you understand?"

"I understand."

"You have to recognize when you're stuck. And until that girl turns eighteen and walks out of her mother's house, you're stuck. The two of you have to bide your time. Until then, you have to know this is a losing proposition."

I disagreed completely. Helping Ava was never the wrong thing. I had to stick by her all the way until she got her freedom. A seizure could cause her to lose everything. The most important thing to me was ensuring that she continued to be the person she wanted to be—fierce, independent, and eager to learn.

"Is it possible for me to ask you to do something for me?" I asked.

"And what would that be, Mr. Giddings?" She sounded incredulous that I would ask after she had gotten me off the hook.

"Ava is in danger with her mother. She filed an abuse report at the hospital a few months ago. If you could ask someone at the hospital to follow up on that, I promise I'll leave her alone until she's eighteen. I need her to be safe."

The woman's gaze on me was fierce. "I believe your heart thinks all this is true, but I've seen a lot of drama in my years, and I'm telling you—let this go. If the abuse charges had been ruled as credible in the hospital, CPS would have taken Ava already. I'll escort you downstairs."

I was angry, so angry. She wasn't listening. She didn't know.

Hot tears threatened to spill from my eyes, but I refused to let them fall. I would save her. I had promised myself that. Promised Ava.

The woman led me downstairs. I used my phone to call for a ride. Then I called Bill and asked him to have Sarah drive him over there to pick up my car and bring it to my house.

I texted Ava over and over again, from the minute I got outside, all night. She never answered.

I didn't sleep. Didn't tell Gram. I paced my room until noon. And then I decided that I had to go over there. It was worth the risk. I'd take jail over abandoning her when she needed me.

I drove over to her neighborhood and slowly rolled up to the duplex. But as soon as I saw it, I knew something was different. The windows didn't have curtains anymore. With a sinking feeling in the pit of my stomach, I parked and walked up the stairs to peek into the front window. They'd left in a hurry. The big furniture was there, a sofa and a bookshelf, but the closets and cabinets stood open, cleaned out.

I walked next door. When I knocked, Grandma Flowers came out on the porch.

"I reckoned I'd hear from you," she said. "They're gone."

"You know where they went?"

"I wish I did, child," she said.

"Did you see Ava when they left?"

"I did. She was crying."

My poor Ava. "She won't answer her phone."

"Her mama's got control," she said. "There was a whole lot of carrying on after the cops came. I saw you in that police car."

"What happened after I left?"

"They packed up," she said. "Doors slamming. By morning, they were all loaded up in a U-Haul."

"She can't just disappear," I said. "How will I find her?"

"If Ava has faith in you, then you must be up to the task."

Grandma Flowers asked me to stay, but I was too upset, too angry, too tired.

I drove home and collapsed on my bed. When I refused to eat or get up to go to class the next day, Gram came into my room. I didn't tell her everything that had happened, only that Ava's mother found out we were still talking and moved her away. I hadn't heard from her, and I didn't know if I ever would.

She stroked my hair like she had after the accident. I felt the losses compound on me. Mom. Dad. Stephen. Now Ava.

The world had taken more from me than I could bear.

CHAPTER 15
Ava

Mother and I spent a couple of days in a cheap hotel. She called about rentals, carefully removing the phone at night and sleeping in front of the door with it tucked beneath her pillow. She knew I would call Tucker if given a chance, and that I would run away if at all possible.

Eventually, she found a house for rent. It sat well back from a highway outside of town. The nearest neighbor was at least a mile away.

The tumble-down two-bedroom had a sagging porch and a leaky roof. But whoever lived here last planted roses, so I spent the first days after our arrival trying to prune and water them back to health.

I didn't bother to hang my paper flower wall. I wouldn't be there long enough.

All I had to do was wait three weeks until I was legally eighteen. Then I'd walk out of this house, and she could not force me back.

I'd find Tucker. He'd be in high school only a couple more weeks. I could go there and wait. He also had a job at a

Shelfmart. I wasn't completely sure which one, as I'd never been to it, but I could call any of them and figure it out. When I had the phone and it was so easy to get in touch with him, I hadn't thought to get addresses or numbers to find him some other way. I didn't even know Gram's first name.

But I could do it. Maybe even go to the hospital and talk to that social worker. I wrote her number in lots of random places before Mother found the business card and took it.

And when I found a way back to Tucker, our lives together would begin.

Until then, the rosebushes kept me sane.

Mother stepped out onto the porch. "Don't spend too much time out here. You'll burn."

"Don't talk to me," I said. "You're only going to be my mother for three more weeks." I'd been civil with her in the months since the hospital because I had a secret to hide. But now I no longer cared.

She crossed her arms over her chest in a faded orange dress, her hair swinging. She hadn't gotten it cut since the hospital. Probably, she was too afraid to be stuck in a hairdresser's chair when I might run away.

"Who is going to watch over you?" she asked, her voice shrill. "You don't know anything about the world."

"And whose fault is that?" I shot back. "You refuse to let me have a life!"

She sat down on the steps, gathering her skirt around her legs. The wind picked up, making her hair fly. I had mine sensibly tied back in a ponytail.

"Ava, I know you resent me. These years have been hard on both of us. But you have a very serious condition. It takes treatments that—" She cut off, and I glanced up, curious. Mother stared at the sky, her fingers trembling as they pressed against her mouth.

She seemed almost frightened. This was a big change from her usual stiff anger.

"Mom? What are you not telling me?"

I hadn't called her *Mother*. I had no idea why. "Mom" just came out.

Her gaze slid to me as she drew in a jagged breath. Her eyes were softer. "You called me Mom in the hospital when you first awakened."

Right. Before I figured out what she had done. Dumb mistake. I picked up the old scissors I was using to prune the rosebush and lopped off a dead, drooping bloom. It hit the earth with a thud and shattered into loose petals.

She was quiet a while, probably hoping we were about to have some big mother-daughter reconciliation. As if she hadn't just had the love of my life arrested and moved me away.

When she finally spoke, her voice was quiet. "If you have a seizure by yourself, no one will be there to reorient you to the world. That's what I've been here for. I try to keep you safe, try to keep your medical care continuous and thoughtful. Some doctors would try any random thing, without concern for the effect on you."

"Like what?"

"Like drugs that made you sleep all day. Or ones that caused you to cry nonstop. I have careful notes. You are my daughter. The best thing in my life. Every decision I make is for you."

"Sure, like having me declared medically incompetent."

"I don't think you're ready to be alone in the world."

Back to that. "Tucker will help me. And he won't keep

me from watching television. Or using the internet. Or having a phone."

She pushed a loose piece of hair behind her ear. "I do all of that to protect you."

I kept my eyes on the flowers. "I don't even know my own father."

"That was his choice," she said. "And we don't talk about him."

"Maybe I'll find him myself." I stole a glance at her to gauge her reaction.

Her look wasn't angry, though, just resigned. "You can certainly do that. But don't get your hopes up."

I stabbed my little shovel in the ground. "Are you going to tell me what I need to know when I go, or will I have to figure it out on my own?"

She flicked a beetle off the stair near her worn gray shoes. "I have a list of the meds we've tried. They all seem to fail eventually. You weren't a candidate for brain surgery."

"Do I have a regular doctor?"

"We go to the Austin Regional Clinic. Your records are there. And at the children's hospital."

I cut dead buds off the nearest bush, working to avoid getting stuck by thorns. "I never remember what causes them."

"There's no rhyme or reason. It's not hunger or tiredness. We checked vitamins and all that."

"Just random."

"Puberty made it worse, but clearly you're through that."

My cheeks burned at the reference to my night with Tucker. "You put me on the shot."

"Years ago. There is a school of thought that hormone

changes with menstrual cycles can trigger seizures. We couldn't afford to wait and see with your memory loss, so we went the preventative route."

This was the longest conversation we'd had since my memory was wiped in the hospital. I had no notes that we'd ever talked this way before. Only that I shouldn't trust her.

Should I trust what she was saying now?

Her face seemed relaxed, her fingers worrying a bit of string that had pulled loose on her skirt.

"So why no television? No friends? Why did you keep me away from Grandma Flowers?"

That made her tense right up. "You're very vulnerable, Ava. When your memory starts over, I have to be careful about what influences your personality. I wouldn't have allowed it in the hospital, but they were trying to take you from me after that stunt you pulled."

I wished they had but didn't say it aloud. "You were wrong about Grandma Flowers. She was nice to me. She showed me how to grow things." I plucked more forcefully, and my hand brushed against a barren stem. Thorns stabbed my arm, drawing blood.

"I was the one who showed you how to tend flowers. You've loved them since you were small. That neighbor was a meddling woman who couldn't mind her own business."

"She cared about me."

"I care about you!"

The line of blood welled up, but I ignored the sting. It was nothing compared to my huge, looming problems.

When I kept fiddling with the flowers, refusing to look at her, Mother stood. "When you're done there, I could use you to help me prop up the back porch. It's not safe to go down those stairs right now, and I'm tired of having to walk around."

She disappeared inside the house, and I pressed my hand against the bleeding cut. I had no interest in helping her. I was perfectly happy to stay here with my roses and their thorns.

CHAPTER 16
Tucker

How could a person simply disappear?

I banged on my keyboard for the hundredth time that afternoon.

I couldn't find her.

Gram stepped inside my room. "You okay?"

I pushed the laptop farther back on my desk. "She's nowhere. The hospital won't talk to me, not that they'd know anything. There's nobody with her name looking for a new apartment or a job anywhere on the internet. I don't know what else to do."

"It's hard, baby. I know." She came up behind me. "But I brought something that might cheer you up." She held a plastic suit bag out so I could see it, then unzipped it down the middle.

Inside was a black rented tux.

I pushed my chair away from her. "I'm not going."

Her hopeful expression fell. "To prom? You were so excited about it!"

"When I was taking Ava!"

Gram sat on the bed, the tux on her lap. "That was

always a long shot. You didn't know for sure she could get away that early in the evening."

"But at least I had hope. Now, there's nothing."

"Won't your friends miss you?"

"They won't miss my bad attitude." A pain struck my head, and I pressed my palms into both temples. Sometimes pressure helped.

"Another headache?"

"Just stress. This is stressful!"

"I know. I know." She stood. "It's a hard time. I thought prom might be a good distraction. I'll leave this in your closet in case you change your mind."

"I won't."

Of course, the minute Bill and Carlos caught wind of my refusal to go to prom, they went all out to convince me to change my mind. Carlos insisted I not leave him as the third wheel with Bill and Sarah, who were bound to get tossed from the dance for getting too friendly.

I'd abandoned them more than I should have for Ava, so eventually I gave in. We agreed that Bill and Sarah would drive Bill's car, and Carlos and I would go in Gram's. That way, if the whole thing sucked, the bored parties could leave.

Gram made everyone come to our house for pictures.

"Smile, Tucker!" she said, snapping shots with an actual camera rather than a phone.

Bill and Carlos acted like their usual moron selves, striking dumb poses and making Sarah laugh. Carlos played the role of my date, kicking up his foot with a big stupid grin while pinning a boutonniere on my lapel. They might be total dorks, but they were trying.

We stopped by the drive-through at Mickey D's the way we always said we would on prom night, ordering

Big Macs and Happy Meals in our fancy clothes. When we arrived at the dance, I had to admit, it was cool. Arches of balloons with yards of streamers covered the entrance to the hotel ballroom. Flashes popped in one corner where couples lined up for official pictures.

A long table along the side wall was covered with snacks and rows of bottled water.

Carlos smacked my arm. "Where's the punch bowl? How can anybody spike a bunch of bottles?"

Bill shoved him aside. "This isn't 1950."

"I wanted a punch bowl," Carlos grumbled.

A DJ surrounded by equipment played a hair band rock anthem, and my thoughts instantly turned to Ava. If she had been here, I could have requested "Highway to Hell" and it would have been the perfect joke.

Bill elbowed me. "We should dance. Beats standing around."

"No way," Carlos said. "You'll find me at the snacks."

"Oh no," I told him. "You dragged me here. We're doing this right."

We skirted clusters of dancers to find a spot in the middle. Bill started spinning Sarah in circles. Carlos shuffled self-consciously for a bit, then must have decided *screw it*, because he launched into a head-banging, arm-flailing spectacular.

A ripple of laughter went through the crowd at first, but then a few others found their 80s jam and followed his lead. I had enough of a lingering headache to avoid tossing my brain around, so I stepped aside from the fray, taking it easy while Carlos stole the limelight.

The next song slowed down. Bill brought Sarah in close. Carlos attempted to continue his head-banging, but it wasn't funny anymore.

I wandered back and nudged his arm. "Refuel."

He shrugged and followed me over to the snack table. We grabbed a plate of little fried somethings and found a piece of wall to lean against. Only a smattering of round tables filled the far corner, and they seemed to be taken up by hordes of girls, all chatting and watching the dance floor.

"So much fresh meat over there," Carlos said. "Maybe I'll make their day."

"You go right ahead. But I wouldn't call them meat if you want a chance."

"You still hung up on Ava?"

It took a lot of control not to shoot back an angry reply. Carlos had never had a girlfriend. He didn't know. "Yep."

"But look at them." He gestured with his plate.

"All yours, Romeo."

He handed me his food. "I'm going in."

I walked over to a trash can. The music picked up, but I stayed in the shadows. I was here. It was prom. I'd done the thing. If Carlos struck gold with some girl, I could consider my wingman duties complete.

I had Gram's car. I could drive by Ava's old duplex if I wanted. Maybe I would reclaim the flowers I brought Ava that last night. I doubt she was able to take them from the porch next door. Having some small thing of hers might make this night less horrible.

Carlos returned with not just one girl, but two. "Told you," he said. "This is Sheila." He took off for the dance floor with the other girl.

Sheila fiddled with the red wrist corsage that matched her bright dress. "Sorry. He sort of dragged me here."

"Carlos is like that," I said. "Didn't we take chemistry

together last year? Mr. Cameron relied on you to have the answers when nobody else did."

Her face brightened. "That's right! I remember you. The row by the wall." She let go of the corsage. "You didn't take physics?"

I shook my head. "I decided to coast senior year." It wasn't worth mentioning that my medication side effects last fall meant I couldn't have passed physics even if I'd given it a shot.

She stared out at the dance floor, the disco lights turning her dark curls into different colors. I thought once more of the night I met Ava with her white gauze. What color had her tape been?

I couldn't remember, and a panic sent heat through my chest. Blue? Yellow? Pink? I racked my brain, but I couldn't come up with it. Was I already forgetting her?

Sheila turned to me. "Are you okay?"

I realized I wasn't. The panic was growing, not receding. I felt woozy. "I have to sit down," I said to Sheila.

She took my arm and led me to the tables. "Here." She pulled out a chair.

I sank onto it. My headache raged. I hadn't brought anything for it. There were meds in Gram's car.

Sheila moved a chair next to me, and the other girls watched us with curiosity. "I remember you having to go to the nurse a lot," she said. "Is something wrong?"

I didn't want to say it. I barely knew this girl, and I was already a big enough freak.

I sat there for a moment, assessing myself. Legs: working. Eyes: fine. Head: rubbish. But the wooziness seemed to ebb.

The song ended, and the noise levels dropped. I drew in a ragged breath. Of course prom would get ruined in every way possible. First, no Ava. Now, these stupid brain blips that rendered me useless.

Sheila leaned closer. "Should I get someone?"

"No," I said. "I'm all right."

I stared at the floor, listening to my breath, making sure nothing more was going to happen. But when the next song began, a rap anthem with a punishing beat, every thump of the speakers made my head pulse with pain. "I'm going to go grab some Advil from my car," I told her. I almost added, "I'll be right back," but I didn't.

"You want me to walk with you?" Her face was pinched with worry.

"I'm fine. Thanks."

Carlos was out on the dance floor. So was Bill. I'd text them later, let them know I had to bail.

The cool air outside the hotel was pure bliss. So was the quiet.

I found Gram's car and sat behind the wheel a moment, assessing again. I seemed reasonably okay. I opened the glove box and grabbed the small med container. It still had pills from three different prescriptions in it. My history in little colored discs.

I knocked out two Advil and popped them in my mouth. I should have brought a bottle of water with me. I managed to dry swallow and sat another moment. Latecomers in glittery gowns and black tuxes passed by. No one noticed me in my dark car.

I sat back in the seat, resting my head. Laughter filtered in. Prom night, and here I was, managing symptoms and wishing for quiet.

I wondered where Ava might be. How far would her mother have taken her to escape me? No internet. No phone. Maybe no memory of me by now.

I swiped my jacket sleeve at my eye. The night had been fun for a moment. We had pictures and memories of Carlos head-banging to bring up at reunions. It was enough.

I started the engine. I didn't feel great, and occasionally the world seemed to swoop underneath me like I'd lost gravity.

But my eyes worked, and I knew the way home. So I drove.

When Gram looked up from her book as I came in, her eyes were sympathetic. "I'm glad you went."

I stripped off my bow tie as I passed through the living room. "Thanks for making me go. It was cool."

Then I lay on my bed and stared at the ceiling, reimagining every scene at prom, but this time, with Ava in them.

The weeks went on with no sign of Ava. I went to class, scarcely paying attention, and sat in the cafeteria with Bill and Carlos. The prom girl was working out for Carlos, so sometimes she and Sheila sat with all of us. Sheila kept her distance from me. I didn't blame her.

Graduation was a nightmare due to a debilitating headache. I had to take a serious drug to get through it but managed not to stumble on stage. That was about all I remembered.

Once school was out, my days became the same. I cut back my hours at Shelfmart, unable to keep a schedule. I worked on good days, but they were becoming fewer and fewer.

But every morning, I started the day with a search for Ava Roberts.

One morning, Gram entered my room with her coffee and peered at my screen.

"You're still looking?"

"Of course I am."

"Tucker, it's been three months."

"And she turned eighteen two months ago. Why didn't she walk out? Why didn't she come find me? I've put up a million signposts all over the internet. She only has to Google my name and I've got a whole website telling her how to find me."

Gram sat on my bed, the steam from her mug fogging her glasses. "I know how frustrating this must be. I wish I could help."

The dull ache in my forehead began to pulse. I pressed my hands into my eyes.

"How are the headaches?" Gram asked.

"About the same."

"You want me to call the neurologist again? It might be more cluster seizures."

"Why? So they can give me meds to make me stupider and slower than I already am?"

Gram set the mug on my desk and squeezed my shoulder. "This is a hard road. And with none of the meds working for you, you need to focus on managing your pain, not staring at a bright screen."

She was right about that. Just closing my eyes cut the ache in half. "But the screen is the only thing that might help me find her."

"I know, baby, I know."

My hospital time hadn't given me any answers, so we were still flying blind. Stress made it all worse.

Nothing had gone right since Ava left. Nothing.

"Why did all this crap have to happen to me?"

Gram increased the pressure of her hands on my shoulders. "I've asked myself the same thing a million times. The night of the accident, I thought I'd lose everybody I loved. My son. Your mother. Your brother. You."

"Don't tell me I'm lucky to have survived."

"I wouldn't. But I sure am lucky you did."

My computer dinged. Another hit on the word "Ava." But it was some other woman, fifty years old. She'd won a business award.

Looking at the screen again made my head buzz. My hand began to tremble.

"That's not good," Gram said. "Looks like a focal seizure to me. Into bed. You'll need to recover."

I didn't even argue. I fell back on my pillow, arms crossed over my face.

There was nothing left to fight for.

CHAPTER 17
Ava

This was going to be the best birthday yet.

Mom and I stood in front of the cake mixes, pondering the perfect flavor for my Sweet Sixteen cake.

"I think it should be pink!" I said.

"Anything my baby girl wants," Mom said. "We could get strawberry, which already comes in pink. Or we could get a vanilla one and add food coloring."

"I like vanilla best, but food coloring is expensive," I said. "We only have forty dollars to spend, and we would waste a whole dollar on the color."

"You already ran the numbers?"

I glanced through the basket. This was one of my strengths. "Eight ninety-six, ten forty-two..." I slid my hands over the boxes and jars. "Actually, we should have a few dollars to spare. We could get the pink!"

"Done," Mom said, dropping the vanilla cake mix and the bottle of food coloring into the basket. "You're so good with figures!"

She cupped my chin to look into my eyes. I saw the joy there. I was glad I made her so happy. We were a team. We could create a feast from two potatoes and a leek. Our time in the kitchen, making the most of our meager food supply, was one of the best parts of each day.

"I'm so proud of what a resourceful, level-headed girl you've become this time."

"This time?"

Mom's smile froze, and my belly quaked. I'd said something wrong. I spoke quickly to fix it. "Should I see if I can find some fruit on sale? If we save some money there, we might be able to get ice cream!"

Mom's smile returned. "That's a good idea. I'll go to the frozen section. There's a nice store brand."

"I'll meet you there!" I scurried toward the produce. We'd budgeted six dollars for fruit and vegetables. Surely I could find things on sale for less than that.

I passed the bulletin board near the front door, and a sign caught my eye.

Are you sixteen? Be a stocker at Shelfmart!

I was sixteen! I could be a stocker!

Earn up to $15 an hour.

Fifteen dollars an hour! That was four cake mixes! Two tubs of ice cream! Every hour!

We could buy more food. Get new clothes. Watch more movies than the four we had. I saw the titles in racks at the store. I loved how Mom laughed when the Munchkins showed up in *The Wizard of Oz*. There had to be more movies that could make her laugh.

A girl not much older than me walked up to the board and stapled a flier in an empty spot. She wore one of the red Shelfmart shirts. Her badge read "Natalia."

"Need some help?" she asked.

I pointed to the sign. "What's a stocker?"

"That's the people who unpack the deliveries and put the food on the shelves."

"Oh, I could do that!"

Natalia waved toward a tall man who stood behind the customer service counter. "Go talk to Frank. He's desperate for someone."

She pulled a paper out of one of the big envelopes hanging on the board. "You'll need an application. You can fill out this one, or you can do it online."

Online. I wasn't sure what that meant, but I'd ask Frank.

I took the paper and headed for the counter. No one was waiting, and Mom was way over in frozen foods, so I was safe to talk to him. What a surprise this would be if I got a job. She'd be so happy!

When I arrived at the counter, Frank leaned over with a big grin beneath a fuzzy mustache. "Hey, are you turning that in?"

I set it on the counter. "I haven't filled it out yet."

"How old are you?"

"I turned sixteen today."

His smile grew bigger. "Well, happy birthday!"

"Thank you. I think I could be a stocker."

"You in school?" Frank asked.

"I'm homeschooled."

"So you could work this shift right now?"

Wow. That was fast. "You mean right this very minute?"

Frank laughed. "No. I mean weekday mornings. I'm struggling to find someone for this shift."

"Sure."

Frank rubbed his mustache with his thumb. "I assume you haven't had a job before."

"No. But I'm responsible. Ask all the flowers I keep alive despite the summer heat."

He laughed again. I liked him. He was like a big, funny teddy bear.

He slid the paper back toward me. "I tell you what. Fill out this application and bring it back on Monday. And don't forget your ID for the tax forms. Since you just turned sixteen, I assume you don't have a driver's license. You have a permit?"

I thought fast. "Not yet. My mom will drive me. Or I can walk."

"Good. Bring your Social Security card and birth certificate."

I had no idea what those were, but Mom surely would.

"So I'm hired?"

"Sure. We'll try you out. See how it goes."

"Wow! Thank you!"

Frank laughed again. "See you Monday at eight sharp. Have a good birthday."

I backed away, holding the application to my chest. I had a job! Mom would be so proud.

I raced to the produce section, grabbed the cheapest apples I could find plus a bundle of spinach, and hurried to frozen foods, folding up the paper to hide in my pocket.

Mom's face looked hard, like the soldiers in *The Sound of Music*. "What took so long?"

THIS KISS

I swallowed. I had never lied to her before. "I was looking for fruit that was cheap enough to help us get ice cream."

Mom looked into my eyes for a moment. I held up the bag of apples.

Her face relaxed. "They look good. And see, the ice cream is on sale, too."

"Wow. For my birthday!"

"It's a sign."

We placed our treasures in the cart and rolled our way to the checkout line.

I'd done it.

That evening, Mom came out of the kitchen with my pink cake. On top was a tiny ceramic unicorn.

"I love it!" I said. "It's like a cake and a present in one."

"I know!" Mom said. "And since you love unicorns so much, I knew it would make you smile." She kissed the top of my head. "Happy sweet sixteen, my darling."

I waited until she sliced the pieces of cake and set them on the table. After a few bites, I decided to spring the news on her.

"Mom, I did something today that I think will help us buy more things."

"Did you find more coupons?"

"Even better. I got a job application at Shelfmart, and I talked to the manager, and he said I could start working on Monday!"

I couldn't wait to see her reaction.

But her face contorted into anger.

"Ava, what were you thinking?" she cried. "You can't work a job!"

"Why can't I?"

Mom stared at the table for a moment. Her foot tapped the floor. "Darling, you have a condition. You're sick."

"I am?" I asked. "What's wrong with me?" Did I need a spoonful of sugar to help the medicine go down? Would I die like the mother of the von Trapp children in *The Sound of Music*? My chest felt tight, like I couldn't breathe. Was I dying already?

Mom looked around the room, as if she was searching for the answer.

"Mom? Am I dying?"

"No!" she said, and her voice sounded high, like a squeaky toy I'd seen a dog chewing in a shopping cart once. "No, no, darling. You aren't dying."

"Then what is it?"

She held onto my hand, squeezing it tightly. Her face looked like the man who pretended to be the great and powerful Wizard of Oz. He had the same panic in his voice when he told Dorothy and her friends to pay no attention to the man behind the curtain.

He was like Mom.

My heart sank. If she was a lie like the wizard was a lie, then what would I do? I didn't have a lion or a scarecrow or a tin man to help me. Not even a dog. I didn't have anybody but her.

"You have something called seizures," Mom said finally. "One minute you're fine, and the next minute you fall down and go unconscious. It's happened since you were small."

Fear curled in my belly, hot and heavy. This sounded very bad. "Why haven't you told me before?"

"Because it hasn't happened in a while."

"If it doesn't happen anymore, then I can start working."

That expression came over her again. *Don't look behind the curtain.*

"No, no," she said. "It doesn't happen because I keep your life very easy and simple. At the store—it would be too much. You can't do it. You just can't."

She smiled at me, but it didn't reach her eyes. "Darling, we're doing fine. We don't have a lot, but we have a house and food and clothes. We have each other. It's a good life."

I didn't believe her. Dorothy got to go on an adventure. So did Mary Poppins. Why couldn't I?

This job was supposed to be mine. Frank said I could start on Monday. I wasn't afraid like the Cowardly Lion. Why was Mom?

"I thought it would help," I said. "I thought you'd be happy."

"Of course I'm happy, darling. What a brave, thoughtful girl you are. But it's not possible for you to work. You need to be at home with me. Where you're safe."

"But what will I tell Frank?"

"You'll tell him your mother said no. You're sorry, but you can't do it."

I returned to my cake, but I couldn't make a single bite go down.

Mom had something to hide. I could see it in how she looked around.

There was something hidden behind her curtain.

I needed to find out the truth.

So, I did a terrible thing that night. It was wicked, like

when the nuns took the parts out of the car in *The Sound of Music*. But I did it anyway.

I made Mom go to sleep.

When I had trouble at night with my whirring thoughts, Mom would give me a pill from the cabinet. It always worked on me within minutes.

I couldn't make her take the pill without her knowing, so I had to find a way to make her take it secretly.

I asked to watch two movies that night for my birthday. While *It's a Wonderful Life* played, I went to the kitchen to make some tea.

I found the pills and dropped one in the hot liquid to see if it would dissolve like the cubes of sugar. It floated to the top and changed color. I stirred and stirred, but it didn't dissolve.

I took it back out and tried to cut it up with a knife. This worked a little, shaving off small bits. I got out a spoon. I used the back of it to smash the pill. It crumbled into dust.

I was wicked. So wicked. Worse than the witch who made Dorothy sleep in the poppies.

I put the dust of the sleepy pill into her tea. I didn't know if it would work. But it was worth a try.

I gave her the mug and waited until ZuZu said the ringing of the bell meant an angel had gotten wings. Mom was clearly sleepy.

I quietly switched the movie to *Mary Poppins*, keeping the sound low. I avoided *The Wizard of Oz*, sure that the wickedness in that movie would make Mom see mine.

I needed her to be very asleep so I could go to her room. I knew that nothing important would be hidden anywhere else in the house. I never went into her room alone. If there was something I shouldn't see, she would put it there.

When her head fell back on the cushions, I covered her with a blanket so she would be cozy and less likely to startle awake. I turned the sound even lower.

I tiptoed inside her room and flipped on the light. My senses tingled with the certainty that an explanation for her reaction was here somewhere. She was hiding something from me, and because of it, I would not be able to go to Shelfmart on Monday and start working. Was I really sick? Or dying? I had to know.

I searched quickly through her drawers, lifting up all the clothes, especially ones I never saw her wear. I found nothing.

I opened her closet door. In the bottom corners were several boxes, but they only held a few odds and ends of things that were broken or we no longer used. In the corner by her bed was a small table covered in a blanket. On it she kept some books, a candle, and an alarm clock. I lifted the quilt.

Beneath the table was a large cardboard box, the flaps tucked down. I dragged it out.

Inside was some kind of machine in a beige box. Tucked along one side was a folder filled with papers. I pulled it out and glanced inside. My name was on the first one! There were notes and pages. All of them were about me!

I couldn't look at them now. I quickly closed the box back up and moved it back under the table.

I took the folder to my room. For a moment, I couldn't figure out where to put it so she wouldn't see. But then I stuck it in the bottom of one of my drawers.

When I got back to the living room, I sat carefully on

the cushions, but Mom startled awake. She rubbed her eyes. "I sure crashed. It must've been the sugar from the cake."

"Sugar does that?"

"Sometimes," she said. "It's called a sugar crash. The sugar gets your body all energetic, and then once you've used it all, you get really tired."

"Interesting."

My heart was pumping so hard I could swear she'd be able to hear it.

But I had done it.

Waiting all the way to the end of the movie to find out what was inside that folder was excruciating. I didn't get a sugar crash whatsoever. I was electrically awake.

When Mom finally went to bed, I waited for her to go to sleep. After the house had been quiet a good while, I sneaked to my dresser and opened the drawer. The folder might be nothing. But I had to know.

I sat on the bed and spread out the pages. The first one seemed to be from a hospital. Mom was right. I did have a condition. It was called epilepsy. It caused amnesia. I didn't know what amnesia meant, but by the time I read the description of my condition, I understood. A seizure could make me lose my memories.

The room spun, moments from my life that hadn't made sense rushing at me and aligning with this new information. Why I couldn't remember being small. There were dresses in the back of my closet that didn't fit me, but I had no idea when they might have ever been worn.

I felt sick. I wanted my mother. I wanted her to hold me close on the sofa. For us to watch the Munchkins and laugh at their dances.

I wanted to stop knowing, but I couldn't.

And there was so much more. The other pages were filled with small text and long words. I didn't understand any of it, and the dictionary was in the other room. I kept going.

I stopped when I found a piece of paper that looked like it had been torn out of a notebook. It said the year was 2016, and I, Ava Roberts, had just turned sixteen years old.

But that couldn't be right. I turned sixteen years old today. And it was now 2018. I read the date every time we drove by the bank on the way to the grocery store. A flashing sign said the day, time, and temperature.

My stomach tightened. Nothing made sense. I had to keep going. The notebook paper also said I had epilepsy, like the hospital pages. It said not to trust my mother. And it told me to keep a note on my belly at all times so that I would know the handwriting I could trust. The handwriting on this page.

Handwriting. The word made my belly buzz with fear.

A heavy piece of paper listed my name, and Mom's name, and another name as my father. Marcus Anthony Roberts.

Where was he?

It listed my birth date. Today was not my birthday at all! I turned eighteen three months ago! Mom had lied, big time. She'd made me a cake to fool me.

My eyes smarted with hot tears and my belly heaved. Why had she done this?

I stayed up all night reading. Not only the folder, but also other things I found. Another page told me that I hid notes in my room. The first one said to look beneath a dresser drawer, but when I looked, nothing was there.

This must be an old note. And if Mom had read it, she would have taken what was there already. I just knew it.

But maybe there were notes in other places, ones I didn't mention here.

I searched my room like I had never known to search before. Under my bed. In my closet. At last I found a page taped to the bottom of a box. I read it quickly.

Don't trust Mother. Trust only this handwriting.

My belly quivered as I searched for more. Another was tucked in my closet in the space where the bar met the wall. This one was longer. It told me about the paper flowers. That they held a secret.

The note said they hung on the wall, but they must have been taken down, as the paper flowers I knew about filled a drawer. They were old and faded, bent and torn. I examined them carefully. There were roses, tulips, daffodils. All flowers I'd learned about with Mom as we worked on them in the yard.

Then I saw it. Some of the colored flowers had words on the back, so tiny as to be almost impossible to read.

As I searched and read, I realized everything I'd ever known was a lie. We had not always lived in the country. We had been to other places. I read about a woman named Grandma Flowers who lived next door.

I'd once lived a life totally different from this one.

I had planned to run away at eighteen, but never got that chance. I don't know what happened, or why I failed, but it must have been Mom—Mother.

I read about a boy named Tucker. He had been special to me. One flower said:

Tonight, you will give Tucker a flower that tells him you love him. Look for the yellow daffodil that will tell you what he said back.

. . .

I sorted through the dozens of flowers strewn over my floor. I had five or six yellow daffodils, but none of them told me what I wanted to know. Who was this Tucker? And what had he said when I told him I loved him?

Could he help me? Was he out there looking for me?

My heart hammered in a way I'd never felt before. I wasn't dying. I was more alive than I'd ever been. I could feel the blood in my body, running hot and telling me to go, go, go.

I had to start my own adventure. Maybe I did have a scarecrow and a tin man out there somewhere. Maybe Tucker was one of many people my mother kept from me. A history she didn't let me learn.

I began packing. The flowers. The folder. What clothes would fit in my duffel bag.

I would not confront my mother. She had a power over me I did not understand. She scared me. I realized how little I knew about anything. But my eyes were open.

I would have to leave my mother behind. She'd recognize if I was scared, or if I had an expression on my face like the wizard. I was now the girl hiding behind the curtain.

I put on my best shoes, my favorite dress, and a jacket. I crept through the house while my mother slept. As the sun spread its rosy light on the fields, I slipped out the back door.

Then I ran.

CHAPTER 18
Tucker

The day I learned about Ava's escape started out the same as every other.

I got up, and like every morning for one hundred and eight days, I typed *Ava Roberts* into a Google search.

I was used to the links that always came up. The doctor. The actress. The microbiologist.

But, on this Saturday, something spectacular happened.

A police alert. Ava Roberts, a special-needs adult, aged eighteen, was reported missing by her mother.

I jumped out of my chair. She had gotten away.

How?

I circled my room, punching at the air. This was great.

But where was she?

Gram came to my door. "What's got you in such a fuss?"

"Ava ran away. They were living out in the country near Wimberley."

Gram peered at the screen. "Do they know where she's gone?"

"No. But I have to find her."

"Do you think she lost her memory?"

"She must have. She would have left on her birthday months ago if she remembered me. We always talked about what to do. They weren't so far away that she couldn't have gotten to me."

She nods. "You have any clues where she might be now?"

"I'm going to see Grandma Flowers. Maybe Ava will find her way back to the duplex."

"Okay, baby. When should I run you over there?"

I hadn't been able to drive since things went downhill after graduation. "I'll take the bus."

"You have your emblem on?"

I pulled the engraved medical alert medallion out from under my shirt.

"You sure you don't want me to drive?" Gram's mouth drooped with worry.

I hugged her. "Everything is about to turn around. I know it." When I pulled away, I could see she was not convinced. But as always, she let me go. There would be no stopping me.

When I got to the old duplex, the porch was still covered with pots. A family with little kids lived in Ava's old side, their toys strewn all over their half of the front lawn.

I knocked on Grandma Flowers's door.

When she saw me, her face lit up with a smile. "Oh gracious, boy, I didn't expect to see you again." She touched her hair, covered in a tight pink cap. "I wasn't planning on visitors." She fussed with her floral house coat.

"You look great. I wanted you to know that Ava ran away. Her mom has the police looking for her. I thought she might come back here. She leaves notes for herself. She might have written this address somewhere."

Grandma Flowers nodded. "That's good. I hope she returns to me. Come and sit a spell. Do you think she might come today?"

"It just happened. I don't know what notes she's found, if any."

"I'm glad you're here." We sat on her back porch, and she poured me a glass of orange juice. "Can I fix you some toast?"

"No, thank you. Can you tell me anything else about Ava?" I asked. "Or about her mother? I want to know everything, so I can guess where she might go."

She patted my hand. "I should have made you stay that morning they left, even though you were in distress. There were things I should have said. Let me go get something."

I sipped the juice while she disappeared through the squeaky screen door. It was early in the morning, and the dew clung to the sparse grass beyond the balcony. I remembered the yellow daffodils I'd brought Ava and glanced around the collection of pots. I hadn't been able to collect them on prom night like I thought I would. They might be in the back.

But no, they had been moved to the front, now only a bit of leaf, since the plant would shrink down to a bulb in its off season. I liked that something of ours was still here. It was proof that we'd existed, that Ava wasn't some long-ago dream.

Grandma Flowers returned with a stack of paperback books, worn and yellowed from age.

"What are these?" I asked. The top book was *The Color Purple* by Alice Walker. The next was Ralph Ellison's *Invis-*

ible Man. I'd read that in a literature class. I spotted a Toni Morrison, then a mystery with a woman running on the cover.

Grandma Flowers picked that one up. "She liked all kinds."

"Were these Ava's?"

"No, but she read them. Before her mother decided I was a bad influence."

I held *The Invisible Man*. I liked that she and I had this in common, even though she might not remember any of it.

"I'm not just showing off my collection," Grandma Flowers said. "Open one up and pay attention to the highlighted words."

I flipped to the first page and kept turning until I saw the first streak of yellow. It was the word *available*, but only the first three letters were highlighted.

Ava.

"Mmm hmm," Grandma Flowers said. "She always started by finding her name in the text, so she would know the message was for her."

My heart pounded. I didn't have to go very far before I found more highlighted words, single random selections.

Your

Mother

Wants

You

To

Stay

Stupid

Find

Your

Notes

So
You
Can
Be
Yourself
Find
The
Paper
Flowers
Trust
Only
Your
Own
Hand
Writing

I looked up. "You knew?"

"Not right away. I rarely open these books. But after one of her bad seizures, I pulled them out. Thought she'd like to read them again, since she loved them the first time."

"And you found this."

"I was shocked. I confronted her mother." Grandma Flowers rested her hands on the table, her brown fingers tightly locked together like a fervent prayer. "I shouldn't have. She cut me off, forbade Ava from seeing me."

"But you were right next door."

"She had a good grip on that girl. The next time I saw her, she didn't even know who I was."

"How long ago was that?"

"Over a year ago. Before you met her."

I picked up another book. The messages were similar. Warnings to herself. Locations of her notes.

"Do you know if Ava took meds for her seizures?"

"Not that I ever saw. But that doesn't mean anything. I only saw the child when she was outside."

"When we met in the hospital, Ava told me she thought her mother wanted to keep her from knowing about her old self. It was her way of making sure she didn't have bad influences."

Grandma Flowers shook her head. "Seems like the worst influence is her own kin."

I could agree with that. "Even if I find her, she may not remember anything from when we knew her. She could be so lost."

"I imagine if anybody can help her, you can. What are you going to do next?"

"I'm going back to the hospital where we met. If she ends up in an emergency room and still knows her name, they'll get her records from there. I went there when she first left, so I know the staff won't tell me anything about her, but I can make sure they know I'm looking for her."

"Good thinking. You keep on doing that and you'll find her."

I left my number with Grandma Flowers and set about searching all over again. Now that Ava was eighteen, maybe I could make more headway.

CHAPTER 19
Ava

Every car that passed as I walked along the road made my fear rise another notch. I hurried along the highway that Mother and I drove to go to the grocery store. When I made it to the tangle of streets and houses and stores, I relaxed. Mother would wake up soon, but I needed to talk to Frank at the grocery store.

I had a job there, and he would pay me money. Maybe if I started working today instead of Monday, I could get money right away to buy food.

It was a terrible idea, since Mother would look for me there. But it was the only idea I had.

The store was quiet at this early hour, so I went straight to the customer service desk.

It was closed. A sign on the counter said it would open at 8 a.m.

What time was it now? I had no idea.

A boy who seemed close to my age approached the counter, pushing a stack of boxes on a rolling cart. *Stocker*. Maybe I could learn something from him. He seemed friendly, a flop of hair falling over his forehead. He wore the red Shelfmart shirt.

I reached out a hand to stop him. "I'm about to start working here. I was hoping someone could walk me around."

He shrugged. "Sure. What are you going to be doing? Cashier?"

"Stocker."

He had wires hanging out of his ears, but he took them out and stuck them in his pocket. I wondered what they did.

So much to learn.

"You must be replacing Phil," he said.

"I'm not sure," I said carefully. "I talked to the manager yesterday."

"Justine or Frank?" he asked.

"Frank," I said.

"Frank's a card," he said. "You'll like working for him."

I didn't know what he meant by Frank being a card. Cards were something you use when you played a game with clubs and aces. But I didn't say that. I had my wizard face on.

"That's good," I said.

"The pallets are all in the back. New stuff gets delivered every day. You'll have a section. Phil was in dry goods. I reckon they'll put you there too, since you're kind of small to be lugging heavy stock."

I looked down at myself. I was certainly small compared to him.

"You want somewhere to put that bag?" he asked. "It looks heavy."

I adjusted the duffel bag on my shoulder. I didn't want

to let it out of my sight. It was the only thing I possessed, my life and my memories.

"It's okay," I said. "I'm fine."

"Maybe you're stronger than I thought." He grinned, and my heart flipped.

I pressed my hand to my chest. I'd only felt that funny flutter when Rolf kisses Liesl after singing "Sixteen Going on Seventeen." I didn't know real people could make it happen.

We walked along with his cart. He led me through the store, pointing out the aisles that had cereal, pasta, and other things I knew well.

"I've been coming to this store all my life," I said. Then I realized, no, I hadn't. But I couldn't change it now.

"Cool," he said. "Then you will know where most everything is already."

"I do."

"Well, let's head to the back for a minute. I can leave my cart here. I'll show you around. When did you say you were starting?"

"Monday." I didn't mention that I wanted to start sooner. I knew this boy couldn't tell me it was okay. It had to be Frank. The manager made the decisions.

"And you're here on a Saturday," he said. "You're going to show all of us up."

I had no idea what that meant. But he said it with a smile, so I smiled back.

"Frank is going to love you," he said. "He's better than my old boss, Penny."

"What happened to her?"

"She moved to a different store."

"There's more than one Shelfmart?"

He laughed. "You kidding me?"

I laughed too, but my head was spinning. There was more than one store, and people could move to others and keep their jobs. If I moved to another Shelfmart, Mom wouldn't know where I was. Working here was so risky. She'd come here first when she realized I was gone.

"Do you sometimes work at one of the other stores?" I asked.

"No, generally we pick one and stay there."

"How do I pick a different one?"

"It wouldn't be too hard to move if you wanted. That's what Phil did. He moved to San Antonio. Penny would take you at hers, I bet, if you can put up with her."

I had put up with Mother. How bad could this woman be?

"How do I talk to Penny?"

"Hold on, I probably have her number."

We stopped by the swinging doors behind the meat counter, which was still dark and empty since it was so early. He pulled a small, shiny object out of his pocket.

I'd seen other people carrying them in the store, but I had never fully understood what they were. Some people held them to their ears, while other people stared at them in their hands. When he touched it, a screen lit up like a tiny TV.

I wanted to ask about it, but I knew better. They were common. He would know I wasn't normal if I let on that I didn't know.

"I have it here in my phone," he said. "You want me to send it to yours?"

A phone. That was a phone.

"I'll write it down," I said. "My phone is... broken."

"I hear you," he said. "Dropped mine a couple weeks ago and had to get a new one. It was a pain in the butt."

I had no idea why that would hurt his backside, but I stayed quiet. I pulled my diary out of the bag. A pen was tucked inside it. "What was the number?"

He gave me several digits. "She's Penny St. Martin," he said. "You can tell her I sent you."

"And you are?"

He pointed to his badge, and my face flushed hot that I hadn't looked at it.

"James," he said. "She'll remember me."

"Thank you, James."

I had a plan again. But even though I knew the numbers, and I'd seen a phone, I had no idea how to call this Penny person.

We moved through the swinging doors. A huge open room was filled with stacks of boxes. Several more Shelfmart workers loaded items onto carts.

James droned on about the delivery doors and how to watch your back with the night stockers. I tried to pay attention, but really, I thought hard about all the places I knew. The Shelfmart. The gas station. There were other buildings around them. I knew of the bank, although we never went there. I didn't have money for something like the phone James had.

I could ask to use his. It would be embarrassing. But what if Penny St. Martin found out I didn't know about phones? Would James tell her? Would they laugh at me? And if they did, would she still let me work there?

No, I had to find another way. Someone who wouldn't tell Penny.

The employee who gave me the application had said I could do it online, whatever that meant. Maybe I could send a new application to Penny online.

"Where can I do online?" I asked James, interrupting him mid-sentence.

His eyebrows lifted, but he didn't look mad. "I guess I got boring, rambling on about stockrooms. You don't have internet at home?"

"I don't."

"You could go over to the library. They have computers you can use."

"I don't think I've ever been to the library."

He laughed. "I don't step foot inside it myself."

Oh. Was it a bad place to go? Dangerous? I would have to risk it. "Where is the library?"

"Really close if you walk out the back door." He pointed to a double door on the far wall. "You just have to cross the field. If you take the road, it's a long way around."

This was good. The library was somewhere I'd never been. Possibly dangerous. But somewhere Mother wouldn't look. Would she call the police? Would they come find me? I didn't know. I'd have to do it. I had no other choice.

It was time to get out of this Shelfmart, where she'd certainly come first.

I thanked James for his help and promised to find him again unless I transferred to Penny's store. I'd learned a lot in the last hour. Mother had taught me so very little.

And that was when she wasn't lying.

The truth washed over me again. I was eighteen years old. Years of my life had been lost because she didn't let me remember them. Everything I knew was wrong. Tears pricked my eyes, but I refused to let them fall. I had to be like Dorothy and find my own way back to Kansas, whatever that might be for me.

When I stepped outside, panic threatened to engulf me. Even though it was the back side of the store, more employees in red shirts were pulling up. They might see me.

Mother would get help, sound all the alarms. Sometimes there were "Find this child" pictures on milk cartons. Would she put mine on one? She thought I was helpless. That I couldn't make it without her.

But I would.

I pulled the hood of my jacket over my hair. I walked quickly with my head down.

The building James meant had to be the one beyond the trees. There was a little path to it. As I got closer, I spotted a sign that said, "Wimberley Village Library."

But when I got to the door, it was locked. A sign said it wouldn't open until nine.

I had no idea what time it was, but I could wait.

I sat on the concrete porch by the door, hidden by bushes, and sorted through the papers I had. The hospital records were still a mystery. Maybe I could go there for help. Maybe the hospital was close enough to walk to.

Then my notes. *Trust only this handwriting.* The only handwriting I would see now would be mine. Maybe I could cross out the words that didn't match and salvage my notebook.

The door behind me clicked. A woman in a bright blue dress opened it and spotted me.

"Not too often we have someone breaking down our door so early on a Saturday morning," she said.

I scrambled to my feet. "I need to do an application online. Or I could call Penny St. Martin on a phone. I need to transfer to a different Shelfmart."

Her face shifted to confusion. "You don't have a phone

at home?"

I could do this. Take everything I'd learned from James and convince her to help. "I dropped my cell phone, and it broke. I need to call Penny, the manager of a different Shelfmart, because I'm supposed to start a job there."

She straightened. "Oh. Well, we don't really have a public phone, but there's no harm in you making a quick call, if you need to." She led me inside, stopping at the end of a long counter. She turned a strange boxy object toward me and lifted the top section to hand to me. "You have to dial nine before the number."

It wasn't anything like the shiny thing James had held, but I recalled something like it in the movies I'd seen. People held this part to their head. I lifted it there. The woman moved farther down the long counter.

A set of buttons with numbers on them must be how I put in the digits James gave me.

I would figure this out.

After opening my notebook to Penny's number, I pressed the first digit, and the woman said, "Don't forget to dial nine first."

I swallowed hard. I didn't know how to get rid of the number I'd already done.

I needed help. I had to admit it. "Do you mind showing me how to do this?"

The woman looked me in the eye. "No landline at home?"

"No."

"Gotta love Gen Z. Okay." She stepped close and took the phone from me. She set down the top part of the phone and picked it up again, pressing it to her ear.

"You dial nine, otherwise you're calling within the library. Then you punch in the numbers here." She turned my paper to look, then tapped out the numbers. When she was done, she handed the top of the phone to me. "Ask for the person you want to speak to. The manager probably won't answer the phone. Somebody else will."

I nodded and pressed the phone to my ear.

A voice came on the line. "Thank you for calling your friendly neighborhood Shelfmart. If you know your party's extension, enter it now."

Party? Extension? How did I enter?

The woman watched my face and then took the receiver.

"Oh, these automated systems. If you press zero, you get a person."

She pressed the zero, then spoke. "Is your manager, Penny St. Martin, there?" She nodded. "I think they're getting her." She passed the phone to me. "Good luck."

I didn't want her to go. She was the only thing that had gotten me this far.

A woman's voice spoke into my ear. "This is Penny."

Time to do this. "My name is Ava Roberts. Frank at the Shelfmart where you used to be hired me as a stocker, but James said you might need someone at your store."

"James is a good kid. I always need more stockers. What shifts can you work?"

I had no idea what a shift was, so I said, "I can work anytime."

"That's great. I lost a day stocker. You're not in school?"

"No. I'm eighteen." It felt strange to say it. Only yesterday I'd been sixteen.

"Great. Can you be here this afternoon? We'll get the paperwork done and you can officially start tomorrow."

"I will. Where is the store?"

She gave me an address, and I carefully wrote it in my notebook.

"Thank you," I said. "Tell Frank I'm sorry."

"Don't worry about it. We trade people all the time."

The phone clicked, then made a strange, even sound. I guessed the call was over.

I held the phone for a moment, my body feeling like sparks were firing inside. I'd done a big thing. I had a job. That had to be the hardest part. I'd get paid money. I could shop. Now, I had to find a place to live. It sounded like this store was really far. Mother would never find me.

I set the top of the phone back in its resting place. The woman who helped me drifted back over.

"Did it work?"

"It did," I smiled. "I have a job there. I need to figure out how to get there. I don't have a car. I suppose I could walk."

She turned my notebook around. "That's in Austin proper. Way too far to walk. We can look up a bus schedule."

"Does the bus cost money?" I hadn't thought to steal any from my mother, not that she'd have any. We spent it at the store.

Her crystal-gray eyes searched my face. "You're in a real tough spot, aren't you?"

"I am." Before I could stop myself, words tumbled out in a rush. "My mother didn't want me to have a job. I had to give her a sleepy pill to escape. I don't know how to get online and this was the first time I've ever used a phone."

The woman pressed her hand to her throat. "Do you have any other family in town?"

"No. It's only me and my mother. But she was lying to me. Something bad is happening. I just can't remember."

"Come here, child." She led me behind the counter and sat me in a chair. "How old are you?"

"Eighteen." I pulled out the folder and showed her my birth certificate. "I didn't know I was eighteen until last night. She told me I was sixteen. I think she did it so I wouldn't run away."

"Good Lord."

The woman glanced around the room. I wasn't sure what she was looking for.

"Should I call the police?" she asked.

"What will they do?"

"Ask you questions. Try to help."

My body trembled. "Aren't police for jail?"

"Your mother has probably already called them." The woman bit her lip. "There's a women's shelter in Austin. Let's see if they'll take you in. They can help you straighten all this out."

"What's a shelter?"

"They help women in trouble. Let me look up their number."

A long-held breath escaped from my chest. A place where people didn't know me, but still, they'd help. I had no idea such a thing could exist.

After an hour or so, a taxi came for me. The woman at the library said I wouldn't have to pay for it. After a long ride, we stopped at the biggest house I'd ever seen. There was a locked gate outside. Mother couldn't get to me here.

A kind, gray-haired woman let me in and told me to wait on a sofa, and someone would get me settled.

While I sat waiting in the living room, women walked in and out, some of them plopping beside me to talk. Some were angry. Others were sad. They told me stories of men who hurt them. Boyfriends. Husbands. Fathers. Compared to them with their bruises and broken arms and endless tears, I wasn't sure my life had been so bad.

Eventually, a woman in jeans and a T-shirt, with short curly hair and bare feet, sat by me on the sofa. "Ava, right?" Her voice was soothing, like a trickle of water.

"Ava Roberts. I'm eighteen." I opened my folder.

"I'm Sheila. The police are here for you."

I snapped the folder shut and held it to my chest. "I didn't do anything wrong." My voice sounded strange.

"You did not. You did nothing wrong. And I plan to send them away, but I need to talk to you first."

She wasn't sending me back to Mother. I drew in a shaking breath. "What's going to happen to me?"

"You're going to stay here for right now. But your mother marked you as a special needs person who should be returned. What is she talking about?"

I opened my folder again to show her the hospital papers. "I have epilepsy. She wouldn't let me get a job because she said I was sick. But I got a job. I'm supposed to start working for Penny St. Martin at Shelfmart tomorrow. But she said I couldn't. But she also said I was sixteen. But I'm not sixteen. I'm eighteen. She lied. I don't know how a phone works. I don't know anything."

Shiela squeezed my arm. "That's okay. You're going to be just fine. We'll get you to a doctor right away. I'll take you to Shelfmart. We'll get your new job handled. Don't worry, Ava. You're an adult, and you can find your way."

"But the police are here."

"Can I borrow these papers for a minute? I'll explain things to them. It will be okay."

Could I trust her? I looked into her eyes. They were brown and kind, with creases in the corners. She reminded me of Mary Poppins, but only in the eyes.

"Okay." I passed her the folder.

"I'll be right back."

I sat on the sofa, waiting. A woman in a chair in the corner watched me. "Mothers are hell, girl. Good on you."

Sheila came back and told me the police were gone, and I would not be returning to my mother for now. They would not let my mother know where I was. I could return to her in my own time, if I chose.

She showed me a room with both low beds and high beds. I got assigned washing dishes and putting away the dinner food. These were things I knew how to do, and I was happy to help.

Some of the women had children, so as the days passed, sometimes I did their chores for them, too. I didn't mind. I liked the noise and the talking and the TV with way more than four movies.

I started my job at Shelfmart. I couldn't figure out why James said Penny was so terrible. She let me work the hours I wanted, and I enjoyed arranging the colorful bags of chips and cookies and treats Mother never had the money to buy. I learned to ride the bus and navigate the different schedules. I could go anywhere.

The world was so big!

I asked Sheila if it would be okay if I got a phone. There was one at the shelter that everyone could use, but to have my own in my pocket seemed like the ultimate independence.

She suggested one where you only pay for the minutes that you use, since the other kind was expensive and required credit cards and an address to send the bills.

So I got one. Penny was the first person to get my number. Then I gave it to Sheila.

As soon as I put together enough money, Sheila said

she would help me find a place to live. She showed me how to make a budget for how much I could pay for rent, bills, and fun things.

I saw a doctor, and he confirmed I had epilepsy. He told me I'd been in the hospital when I was seventeen and had started new meds. They were very important because they would prevent the seizures that would make me lose my memory. If I didn't take them, I could have a seizure at any time and forget who I was.

When I picked up the pills at the Shelfmart pharmacy, I didn't recognize them. Mother gave me sleepy pills and vitamins. But never these. And they were expensive. I didn't have to pay for them because Sheila got me on some sort of medical assistance plan. But why hadn't Mother gotten assistance?

Maybe she hadn't wanted me to take them. If I knew I was eighteen, I would have left her. My anger burned hot. More lies. She hadn't kept me safe at all.

I had the pharmacist check to see if I had taken this medicine before. He said yes, he'd found a prescription from a year ago. But it stopped being refilled.

No medicine, no protection.

Mother let it happen.

She wasn't the man behind the curtain.

She was the wicked witch.

Obviously, my old boyfriend hadn't been any help. No one had helped me. And no one would now. I had to take this road on my own.

I couldn't dwell on Tucker or Grandma Flowers or the friends I mentioned in my notes. I lived for today. For my job. For the women I helped at the shelter. The only thing I really knew for sure was to stay far away from Mother.

CHAPTER 20
Tucker

I couldn't find Ava.

She never visited Grandma Flowers. The hospital put me off a second time. I went to the places we'd been, bowling and mini golf and parks, as if somehow she'd be there.

But of course, she wasn't.

The internet revealed nothing more. Besides, looking at computer screens had gotten difficult, causing migraines I couldn't control. Pretty regularly, I had the sort of seizure that laid me low for days. I rarely went to my community college classes, and Shelfmart quit scheduling me.

I stayed in bed, the windows blacked out, wishing my head would fall off because it wouldn't stop hurting. Both Bill and Carlos kept intense hours between work and school, so my world shrank. Sometimes, if I was feeling up for it, the three of us would sit on my front porch and talk. Video games were a thing of the past. Even movies were hard.

Over time, their visits became rare. They might be my best buds, but we had nothing in common anymore. Their lives would move on, classes and girlfriends and futures. Mine was stuck.

As the weather turned cool, Gram went in and out of my room, fetching me washcloths and grilled cheese sandwiches and pain meds that had no effect.

On one of those days, Bill texted a million times, but even the phone screen was too bright to read. Finally, he showed up at my house without bothering to ask if he should.

"Be careful with him," Gram said as she led him into my room. "He's had a bad time."

I couldn't even chastise her for saying it. Opening my eyes was like shoving a knife into the sockets.

Bill sat on the edge of my bed. "Man, it's dark in here. Did you turn into a vampire?"

"Something like that. What the hell are you doing here?"

"I saw Ava."

I bolted upright, the pain lost in my jolt of pure energy. "What? Where?"

"Get this. She works at a Shelfmart in North Austin. I saw her yesterday stocking shelves like it's no big deal that she dropped off the face of the earth for six months."

"What did you do?"

"I walked up and said hey."

"Did she recognize you?"

"No. She asked who I was, and I said she used to double date with a friend of mine."

"What did she say?"

"She said, 'That's a lie. I don't date.'"

I winced. "What else?"

"I asked for her number."

"Did you get it?"

"No. She wouldn't give it to me."

I rolled to the edge of my bed and stood. I had to get well. Like now. I needed to go to that Shelfmart. I grabbed the pain meds on my desk and took a triple dose. "Tell me exactly which Shelfmart it was."

"The one we went to that time to buy beer. Where we almost got away with it."

"I remember." I moved too quickly, and my head felt like it stayed behind. Regardless, I was going.

"Dude, you don't look good."

"I've been laid out for a few days." I sat on my desk chair, fumbling for my shoes.

"Still not able to drive?"

"Not since graduation."

"You want me to take you over there?"

I struggled with my tennis shoes, then dropped them and stuck my feet into some loafers. "Yeah. What time was she working when you saw her?"

"Like three in the afternoon."

"Sounds like she does a regular day shift." Ava hadn't known Bill yesterday, which means her memory had been reset since she knew *us*. But maybe being at a Shelfmart meant some part of her wanted our old plan, working together at the grocery store. This gave me a lot of hope, like the flower she gave me on that last night:

I love him. Even if I lose my memories. My heart will remember. Always.

"What time is it?" I asked.

"About two." He glanced at his watch. "You sure

you're up for this right now? You're not exactly Prince Charming at the moment."

"This is Ava we're talking about," I said.

Bill looked doubtful. "You know, she may not even know who you are."

"She'll know me."

"With her heart?" Bill knew about the flower. I had it on my desk.

He probably hadn't meant to make it sound like a sneer, but it did.

Regardless, I took the comment seriously. "With her heart."

I couldn't afford to doubt it. I had to believe that when we saw each other, she would remember me and know what we'd shared.

I'd get her back. She was everything to me. The losses in my life had led to the disco room and to her. She'd trusted me after that memory reset when everyone else was the enemy. We matched somewhere deep down, beyond memory, beneath both of our medical conditions. We were a team from the inside out.

My life only made sense with her in it. I was positive she'd feel the same way.

CHAPTER 21
Ava

I was busy stacking boxes of Ritz Crackers on the shelf when the boy who'd claimed I used to date his friend showed up a second time.

Now he had the friend.

This guy was different, sickly and pale. I wanted to send him to the vitamin aisle. He needed some sun.

"Ava, don't you remember me?" he asked over and over. "Don't you remember what we had together?"

I peered at him from the side of my eye. He had wild brown hair and might have been cute if he hadn't reminded me of the zombies from *The Walking Dead*. The women at the shelter loved *The Walking Dead*. They had fights over who was hotter—Rick or Daryl. Nobody liked Negan. Negan was too close to where many of them had been.

I made sure my voice sounded like the women I'd met, the ones who had to tell the bad men to shove off. "I don't know either of you, and I've got my own problems. So get lost."

"Let me help you," sick-boy said.

Right. I continued unpacking cracker boxes. *Like Mother helped. No thanks.*

The women at the shelter had told me all the things to watch out for in men. Promises they couldn't keep. Crappy pickup lines. They'd pressure you for sex, for money, for a place to crash. They would tell lies that they would protect you, be there for you, but before you knew it, you'd be a baby mama with a repo'd car and bad credit.

I wanted nothing to do with them. I had seen what men could do.

They still stood there, looming over me in the cracker aisle.

My anger sharpened. "I said, piss off." To make sure they did, I picked up my empty boxes and carted them to the back. The sickly one tried to follow me, but I punched the code to the locked door and headed up the stairs to the break room, making sure he didn't get through. I watched from the window overlooking the store as they talked to each other. The sickly one kept waving his arms at the other. Finally, they left.

I really did want everybody to leave me alone. I already had enough problems to deal with. Turned out I couldn't stay at the shelter indefinitely. And my Shelfmart job didn't pay enough money for rent anywhere without a roommate.

I had about three weeks to figure out my next move before I ended up on the street.

Being on your own wasn't everything it was cracked up to be.

I was saved by a Podunk diner.

Sheila showed me how to look online for roommates, but instead I spotted a new job where I would get tips.

Big Harry, the owner, said he liked the look of me and made me a waitress. His diner was known for its "heart attack on a plate"—chicken fried steak, fried 'taters, and fried okra.

I took all the hours he'd give me. The tips were good, and I made three times what I did at the grocery store. I found a crappy one-bedroom apartment and for the first time in my life, I got to come home to silence.

I hadn't worked at Big Harry's even a week when that boy showed up. The sick-looking one. I asked how the hell he found me again, and he said I shouldn't use my real name to answer public job postings online.

I told him *he* shouldn't be stalking me on the internet, and how was I supposed to get a job if I didn't use my name when I responded to a job ad?

Then he said something that stopped me cold. He said my mother could find me, and she was bad news.

How could he know that?

I felt sick. Big Harry saw how distressed I was and kicked him out.

But I remembered the name he gave me. He hadn't told me last time, or I hadn't heard it, but he got through to me today.

Tucker.

The name of the boy on my flowers.

Part of my lost history.

CHAPTER 22
Tucker

Ava Roberts was going to be the death of me.

I sat on a bench outside the diner, smarting from getting thrown out like a common criminal. I was tempted to march right back in there and demand she listen to me.

First, she posted her damn name on the internet like it wasn't important to lie low. She had an evil, psycho mother who was capable of doing terrible things. Ava hadn't even let me tell her what she needed to know.

She looked so different. Her expression was hard, like she'd seen too much. She didn't wear her hair soft and loose, but in tight coils on her head. Black T-shirt. Black jeans. She clearly didn't trust anybody. I had no idea what had shaped her experiences this time, but they couldn't have been good.

A happy couple walked up to the door of the diner and entered without a worry in the world. It wasn't fair. I wasn't welcome. I couldn't even sit at a table and watch Ava work. That would be better than the hell I'd lived since her mother moved her.

I understood that she didn't remember me, even

though I told Bill she would. Obviously, her memory had been reset. Obviously, she'd lost the phone I gave her, and maybe even her journals and flowers were gone.

I had to get through to her somehow. At the grocery store, she acted like we were trying to con her. And at the restaurant, she seemed to think I was stalking her.

Well, maybe I was. But not in a bad way.

Another group came out of the diner, and I couldn't take sitting there any longer. I launched off the bench and headed to the bus stop. I kept my head down, kicking at rocks, hating the world and everything that had gone wrong in it.

We couldn't exactly have a meeting of the souls if she was so closed off she wouldn't even accept a warning from someone who—I just had to say it—knew her better than she knew herself.

She could reject me if she wanted. But I wouldn't let her forget that her mother was out there.

I'd go back to the diner when that big gorilla of a man wasn't around. Maybe I could catch her before she went in. If I couldn't get to her, I'd ask someone else to go over there and talk some sense into her.

I didn't have much else to worry about, anyway.

Shelfmart let me go completely. I didn't have a job to go back to, even if I did get better. I was here today only because I'd tripled the pain meds again. I couldn't keep doing that. Gram would notice.

Life was going great. Just friggin' great.

But I wasn't quitting on Ava.

She might not remember my face, or my words, or what we did. But if we could spend time together, we'd figure it out all over again. She'd come back to me, even if she was different. With her memory restart, the events that shaped her weren't the same, including the ones she shared with me. But we would connect again. I knew it.

I could carry her memories for her, if she'd let me. I'd written up everything that had ever happened to us. The hospital. The dates. The night we almost went all the way together. I had pictures, anecdotes, mementos.

I'd written down everything she knew about her mother, her neighbors, any note she'd mentioned. I arranged it all into a timeline of her life story, ready to give to her.

But right now, I couldn't get near her.

CHAPTER 23
Ava

Tucker was right.

Mother found me.

She probably saw the online post too.

I was so stupid.

So. Stupid.

I was wiping down the counter to the bar in the back of the diner when the door opened mid-afternoon. I recognized her hair and flowered dress right off and ducked down next to the sink.

Harry had been replacing a keg when he saw me hit the floor. "What's going on, Lil' Ava?"

I pointed up.

Harry stood and grunted. "I see the resemblance."

I tried to keep my breathing steady as footsteps approached the bar.

My mother's voice was strong and sharp. "I'm looking for Ava Roberts."

I squished myself between the ice vat and an empty keg, pulling a damp towel onto my head for good measure.

Harry glanced down, then leaned over the bar, his big belly hanging over his black jeans.

"Nobody named Ava here."

"She answered a job ad for your restaurant."

So, Mother could use the internet. I knew now that the machine in the box in her room had been a computer. She must have fired it up after I ran away.

"I might recollect someone by that name posting," Harry said easily. "But she never showed."

A silence ensued. I peeked up at Harry and his gaze was boring into her, his elbows braced on the bar.

"Might I have a look around, then?" Mother asked.

Shoot. If she moved to the side, she'd be able to see me. The counter didn't fill the entire wall, so if you walked to the end, you could easily glance behind it.

"Certainly," Harry said.

I kicked out my boot to smack his ankle. He didn't even flinch.

I covered my face with the towel, which reeked of beer and lime juice. She couldn't do anything to me, not really. I was an adult with a job and my own apartment. I had nothing to fear.

Still, I did. She knew secrets about me. That I had seizures. Could she make one happen? I didn't know.

I risked another peek and saw Big Harry gesturing toward the opposite end of the counter. Charles, one of our regulars who kept a semi-permanent residence on one of the stools, stumbled off his chair.

He headed over to the juke box and dropped in several coins. A corny country song came on, and he moved out of my sight.

Harry winked down at me.

"Can I have this dance?" Charles asked, and I knew the

sudden gasp was my mother. "Come on, darling. It's my favorite song."

Rapid footsteps headed in the direction of the door. The light brightened, then dimmed again.

"Is she gone?" I asked.

Harry nodded. "You're safe."

I stood, eyes on the door, terrified she'd return.

"You owe her something?" Harry asked.

"She's my mother."

"I figured. So you don't owe her nothin'."

Tears pricked my eyes. "Exactly."

Charles sank back onto his stool. "I scared her off," he said.

Harry pulled a tall draught from the keg and slid it over to him. "Thank you kindly for your service."

I would have to be a lot more careful. I couldn't trust anybody. I was like this big target anyone could bring down. What would happen if I lost my memory alone in my apartment? I wouldn't even know I worked here. I wouldn't know anything.

I felt sick. Big Harry told me to go home for the day. The restaurant was dead anyway.

Paranoia took over. What if I had a seizure in my apartment right now?

I worked like my life depended on it.

I printed the words "trust only this handwriting" on my belly, like my old notes told me to do.

I wrote down everything I had learned.

About the shelter.

About the things the women taught me.

Men can't be trusted.

Don't become a baby mama.

Don't let anyone hurt you.

I wrote about Big Harry's and how he kept me safe. I described my apartment. I wrote out everything from all the backs of the paper flowers I'd brought from my room at my mother's house. Then I collected my birth certificate and medical records, everything I had.

I took the whole stack to a print shop and had the originals bound in a spiral, plus an extra copy made. I took the second book to Sheila. I said if I ever ended up at the shelter again, she should use it to help me figure out who I was. She said she would.

She sent me home with a DVD of a movie called *Memento*. Said I might learn something. I watched it three times and bawled my head off. How could he live like that? If his mind drifted even for a moment, he forgot everything all over again.

But at least he knew his name, his childhood, his purpose. I wasn't sure which was worse, his condition or mine.

The next afternoon, I collected some tips and went to the tattoo parlor down the street from Big Harry's. I got my warning inked onto the inside of my wrist, based on the words I scrawled on a sheet of paper for the artist to use. *Trust only this handwriting. Find the book. Remember your life.*

Then I had them tattoo my name and birthdate on my hip, upside down, so I could read it myself. On the other hip, we added *Mother is bad*.

Nobody could erase them now.

I hoped Mother never found me again. She scared me.

Maybe my brain couldn't remember everything she'd done or why, but the part of me that controlled my survival instinct knew to stay far, far away.

CHAPTER 24
Tucker

I had to watch out for Ava. I spent a lot of time at a twenty-four-hour laundromat in a strip mall across the street from the diner where she worked. I wanted to catch her without the big brute of an owner knowing.

The first time I managed to get to her, it was late, after midnight. A misty rain had fallen, and the streets were quiet and wet.

I tried not to scare her as I closed in from behind. She walked with a tough stride and carried her keys with the ends sticking out of her fist like she would attack someone with them. She was dressed in ripped jeans and a shirt with the sleeves cut off. Her hair was twisted into two tight balls high on her head.

"I can tell you more about who you used to be," I called out.

She stopped and turned around. "Oh, it's you."

"Tucker," I said.

"I remember."

My heart beat faster. "Remember what?"

"Your name. You said it last time."

I shoved aside my disappointment. "Are you willing to talk to me yet?"

"Nope." She started walking again.

I hurried to catch up. "I met you in the children's hospital. We were in the disco room, where they run strobes to set off seizures."

"Why would they do that? It takes away your memory!"

"It doesn't do that to everybody. I have seizures all the time, and I'm fine."

"That doesn't sound fine." Her eyes glanced my way, then back to the sidewalk. I could barely keep up with her. But this version of her wasn't completely unfamiliar to me. She was Survivor Ava, the one who had kissed me once just to make her mother mad.

This was an Ava I admired. I wanted us to be on the same side.

"We started seeing each other in secret. Your mother kept you locked in your house. We had to sneak you out."

"That sounds dangerous."

"We were in love."

She stopped at that. "Were we?"

We faced each other under a streetlight.

"Yes. I arranged a place for you to live. A job. We were waiting until you turned eighteen so we could be together."

"I ran away a few months after my eighteenth birthday. I didn't know I had a plan." Her posture relaxed. I saw the other Ava I knew. The softer, gentler one. I loved her both ways. My feelings rushed at me so hard, I almost staggered back.

I held out my hand, realized she would never take it,

and let it drop to my side. "We only had three weeks to wait. But we got caught."

"What did my mother do?"

"She had me arrested and moved you overnight. And either you had another seizure on your own, or else she..." I hesitated. It was a big thing to accuse someone of.

"I forgot everything." Ava pressed her hand to her forehead. "It was terrible. I have a diary. When it first happened, I couldn't read or write. It took months to be able to function." Her eyes lifted to mine. "Did you look for me?"

"Every day. I searched for you *every* day."

"We were outside of town."

"Wimberley. I saw the police report the moment your mother called it in."

"She came to see me a few days ago."

"Your mother?"

Ava turned and started walking again. "Yes. She found the diner. Big Harry sent her packing. Told her he didn't hire anybody named Ava."

I quickened my step beside her. "You think she believed him?"

"I think she got freaked out by one of our customers and fled." She smiled, the first genuine one I'd seen on this new Ava.

"Grandma Flowers wants to see you too," I said.

"The old woman with the pots?"

"That's her."

"I bought a couple of plants when I got my apartment," she said. "I killed them in a week. I've forgotten everything."

"She'll teach you again."

Ava shook her head. "The past is the past. Better left on old notes."

"But your paper flowers. You don't keep them?"

She shrugged. "I've learned what I need to know. And sure, I'll keep them around in case there's a next time. But I'm not interested in reliving any part of those days." She hesitated. "Not *any* part."

She couldn't mean that. "I can't see you again?"

We stopped walking, and she stared into the sky. The mist grew heavier. We were wet and cold, but she stood there, strong and unrelenting.

"I don't want to get bogged down by what I used to be. Mother forced me to start fresh. I'm ready to own it."

She took off toward a cluster of apartment buildings.

Crap. She was going to ditch me.

"Ava?"

She stopped but didn't turn around.

"If you change your mind, go see Grandma Flowers. She's still in the duplex on Brodie. Do you have the address anywhere?"

"Yeah. I found it."

"Go there. She knows how to find me."

She adjusted the strap to her bag. "Don't hold your breath."

Then she was inside the locked gate to her complex and out of my reach.

CHAPTER 25
Ava

Big Harry and the people at his diner became my family. We worked till midnight, hung out for hours after closing, and slept late. This was all fine by me. Eating, sleeping, and breathing around people I could trust became my most critical survival skill.

Thanksgiving passed. Then Christmas. I spent the holidays with random people from work, vaping and making fun of people who got sentimental about jolly old dudes in red suits and peace on earth, good will toward blah, blah, blah.

I might have looked like a tough girl on the outside with my black clothes and bad attitude, but inside I grew very careful. All the underage servers would sneak alcohol from the bar, but I stuck to Sprite with a slice of lime in it and maybe a splash of colored syrup for show.

I took my medication religiously. My life was a time bomb. If this medicine failed, or if I forgot to take it, I'd have to start all over again. That was the last thing I could handle now that I was on my own.

Tucker didn't give up when I failed to visit Grandma

Flowers and contact him. He showed up at unexpected times.

I would often grab a sandwich at a shop down the street from Big Harry's before I went on shift, and sometimes he would be there to buy me a cookie. Other times he'd pass me a book or a movie to watch. Small things like that. I couldn't fault him, so I accepted his brief, gift-driven attention.

One day in February, I spotted him waiting on a bench near the diner. When I got close, he stood and held out a giant bouquet of yellow daffodils.

"Do not tell me you brought me a Valentine."

He kept them extended, even though I didn't take them. "Nope. Daffodils were our flower, and today is an important day."

I cocked out a hip. "Let me guess, some anniversary. When we met?"

"Nailed it. One year since we first saw each other in the hospital," he said. "I know you don't remember it, but I do. So I wanted to commemorate it."

The flowers made me feel funny inside, like someone was about to punch me. I didn't like it.

I pushed the bouquet into his chest. "I can't take those. Everyone I work with will laugh at me."

"I figured you'd say that." He shifted the flowers into the crook of one elbow and handed me a small piece of cardboard inside a clear sleeve.

It read, "For Ava from Tucker. One year."

I flipped it over. On the other side, slid between the cardboard and the plastic sleeve, was a single yellow daffodil, pressed flat and dried.

"That one will fit in your pocket," he said. "No one will see it."

The uncomfortable feeling inside my chest increased. My eyes burned. But I took his sentimental offering and shoved it into my back pocket.

"Well, thanks. Thanks for remembering what I can't." I turned toward the diner.

"Ava," he said. "Can I say one more thing?"

I twisted around. "What's that?"

"You said something important to me on the last night I saw you before your mother moved you away."

I sighed. The past. Always the past. "All right. What did I say?"

"That your heart would remember. Even if it seemed like you forgot me, your heart would know mine."

He was probably right. It accounted for this terrible sick feeling. My heart was clenching or revolting, or maybe even imploding.

Like hell would I admit this to him, though.

Instead, the part of me most interested in escaping said, "Sounds like the old Ava was full of shit."

After my last show of cruel Ava, Tucker didn't come by for a while. But about a month after the daffodils, I spotted him on the bench.

He had another bouquet. Roses this time.

I paused a few feet away. "So, what silly romantic date have I forgotten this time?"

He was dressed up in khaki pants and a white button-down shirt that he had obviously ironed.

"Go on, tell me. We got married or something."

He laughed. "No, nothing like that. Today was our first official date, one year ago. I wanted to take you out by myself, but I was having seizures, so I couldn't drive. My friend Bill and his girlfriend came, and you climbed out of your window."

"What did we do on this date?"

"We played mini golf at Peter Pan."

"Were we seriously that cheesy?"

"With a capital C. And we had a picnic at Zilker Park."

I smacked my hand to my head. "So we got even worse."

He laughed. "At least we didn't go on a Ferris wheel. All the cheesiest movies have the couple on a Ferris wheel."

"I don't even know what that is."

"It's a ride. A big wheel with seats. You find them at carnivals."

"Never heard of a carnival, either."

"They have a bunch of rides, and you buy tickets to go on them. They have games of skill, like popping balloons with darts to win a prize."

"Sounds ridiculous."

"Most people find them fun. There's one pretty much year-round on the south side of town. Would you like to go?"

"No."

He couldn't hide the way his face fell. What did he expect? I'd been putting him off since he found me.

"Okay. Well, here are the roses for our first date. You can give them out to customers. Might get you better tips." He shoved them at me and walked away.

I watched him go, his head down.

Damn it, Tucker.

He needed to let me go. I wasn't going to put anyone else near my time bomb. Eventually, a seizure would come, and it would obliterate everyone. With all the seizures he talked about, he had enough problems of his own. He didn't need mine.

For a few days, I felt bad about what I'd said to Tucker. He'd been nothing but nice to me. It wasn't his fault my stomach dropped every time I saw him.

I kept the roses. I hid them in Big Harry's office. Big H saw me sneaking out with them, but he didn't say anything.

Weeks passed without Tucker showing up. I worried he was gone for good. Or that a seizure had gotten him. I pictured him collapsed in the street, rushed to the hospital. I had no way of contacting him. No phone number. No email.

I guessed I could go see Grandma Flowers.

Stupid past. I didn't want it. My life was fine.

Then one day, there he was, back on the bench outside the diner.

I sat down next to him. "What have you got for me today?"

He handed me an envelope. Inside were several pieces of paper, full from top to bottom with typewritten words.

"What is this, a story?"

"Sort of. It's everything I know about you. Everything you told me. How we met. What we used to do. You mentioned before that you had put together a book of your old stuff. The flowers from your wall and all that. I thought this could go in there. Information. Nothing more."

I'd already started reading. Disco room. AC/DC. His family.

God. His parents and brother were dead.

I looked up at him, our eyes meeting. That uncomfortable feeling filled my chest again. This time, I accepted it as part of being near him. It wasn't going to kill me. "I'm sorry about your family," I said.

"I still have Gram. She's great. She loves you."

My chest tightened a little more. There were others out in the world who cared about me, people I didn't even know. This Gram. And Grandma Flowers. I had refused to meet them.

Maybe I was wrong.

I returned to the pages. I read about my seizure and how he had worried about me. I had kissed him when I saw him again, even though I didn't know who he was. His first kiss. Maybe mine.

In those pages, I recognized the Ava he knew. The fighter. The survivor. Kicking butts and taking names. He was right there with me, following along. He helped me. He'd been on my side.

That soft spot opened up again, and I had to harden it. I shoved the papers back in the envelope. "I have to get to work, but I'll read this. If I think it's got information I should keep, I'll put in my book."

That was really, truly the best I could do with the outrageous war going on inside my body. He gave me a nod as I walked away.

I didn't know that much about him. I didn't even know if he had a job or people to hang out with or anything other than his gram.

I was a crappy friend. I would try to do better next time he showed.

That night I didn't stay at Big Harry's to hang out after closing. I said I had a headache and went home. I wanted to read the rest of Tucker's story. I started from the beginning and read all the way to the end.

He was right. Our story had been epic. We'd taken risks. And, in the end, when he should have walked away, he stayed. He'd gotten arrested for me. He tried to save me. Then, even when I disappeared, he didn't give up.

And now, despite how I had hurt him by insisting that my heart remembered nothing, that he had been erased, still, he came. Quietly, patiently, and with care.

He left his phone number on the pages.

Maybe I would go to that carnival.

CHAPTER 26
Tucker

I definitely didn't expect the text message that arrived one afternoon from an unknown number. I stared at it a moment, because it took a minute for the words to connect with who might've said them.

What do you wear to a carnival?

I hadn't smiled that big in almost a year.

I texted her back.

Me: Something colorful.

Ava: Everything I own is black.

Me: Then maybe I'll have to bring you something.

And I did. Gram and I drove to the mall, and I picked out a bright shirt the color of daffodils. Maybe I was hitting the flower symbol too hard, but I sensed that there was no going small with Ava. We needed big gestures to cling to, since all the details had been stripped away.

When I got to Ava's apartment, she took one look at the shirt and said, "No way."

"Afraid it'll destroy your image as a brooding Goth woman of the night?"

"It's like wearing the sun."

I folded up the shirt and set it on the overturned keg that served as a side table. I didn't care if she wore it or not. It was mainly a joke.

Ava's furniture consisted entirely of repurposed trash. Two obviously scavenged lawn chairs looked like they'd been through a tornado. Four wood crates stood against a wall, arranged so that they made a semi-functional bookshelf. A big upholstered chair in an orange and brown floral pattern was something not even a grandma could love.

I pointed at the array of neon signs on the wall.

"I like what you've done with the place."

She laughed. "Bar chic."

"Aren't those supposed to be marketing beer or something?"

"They are. In my apartment."

She stuffed her phone into her pocket and picked up the yellow shirt. "All right. I've gotten past my initial reaction. I suppose when at the carnival, do as the carnival people do."

"You don't have to wear it. It was just for fun."

She held it up. "I suppose I could try on a new skin."

My throat caught as she pulled off her black shirt with the arms cut out. Beneath it, she wore a black bra that would probably show through the yellow.

But this Ava didn't care about stuff like that. The new shirt fit perfectly. It also changed her completely.

Her brown hair was twisted into tight balls behind either ear, pieces sticking out like pinwheels. When she wore all black, the effect was badass. But with the sunny yellow shirt, it came off as playful and cute.

"I have to go check this out." She disappeared down the hall.

I sat on the orange chair and waited. I wondered if she would accept anything from me for her place. Gram's was crammed with stuff from my parents' old house. I had even more in storage. Suddenly, it seemed ridiculous to leave all the furniture, dishes, and appliances in there to rot. I would talk to Gram about it.

Ava returned. "You turned me into a flower. I'm used to being an angel of death."

"Ava Roberts, I'll take you any way you come. Sunshine or doom."

She twisted from side to side, tugging on the hem.

"I like it. I didn't think I would, but I do. Come on, let's go ride a cliché."

We took the bus down south, since I still couldn't drive. Having Ava back made me want to get a job again.

Fact was, I didn't even know what I could do. Lots of doors were closed to me with my migraines off the rails. I'd spent as much time in a dark room in recent months as I had out in the world. My ability to be at the carnival was courtesy of hoarded pain meds and sheer grit.

Hell, I didn't even know what company would take me in my condition. Gram had saved my parents' life insurance money for college, but I wasn't using it. It wouldn't last forever at any rate. Having Ava in my life made me want to figure everything out, make new dreams again.

We walked the last half-mile to the parking lot where the carnival was set up.

The colored lights shone on Ava's hair. "I haven't seen that much neon since Big Harry took me to one of the restaurant conventions. The parking lot is glowing."

"I think that's by design. They want you to see the adventure that awaits from miles away."

"An adventure. In a parking lot." Ava's voice expressed the disdain I remembered from our early hospital days.

"I think anything can be an adventure."

"All right, sunshine boy. Show me a good time."

I bought us a strip of tickets for the rides. We ventured onto the Hammerhead, which was a long rod with a capsule on either end. Each one could hold four people. Ava and I squeezed into our side, exchanging glances when we spotted the two girls opposite us. We had only buckled in, but one of them was already screaming.

"Is this a preview of coming horror?" Ava asked.

I didn't answer. It was hard to talk over the sounds of the girl.

"We already rode it once," her friend yelled. "She's planning ahead."

Ava leaned in next to my ear. "Ridiculous."

This was the closest we'd been since I found her again. I wondered what had made her change her mind and contact me.

I didn't dare ask. For now, we would ride.

If I had thought to worry that any part of the carnival was bad for our conditions, my fear was quickly put to rest. Ava was hooked. The most intense rides thrilled her, so we tried them all. The Shaker. The Spinning Cups. The Tilt-a-Whirl.

"My guts are scrambled!" she said. "It's the best feeling ever!"

"I know. It's like you've taken on the devil and won."

"Huh. You're exactly right. It's like I've survived something terrible, and I'm elated that it didn't kill me."

We wandered through the lines of booths on the Midway.

"These games look rigged," she said.

"A lot of people would agree with you. But I'm the master of Whack-a-Mole."

"The master of what?"

"Whack-a-Mole. It's a game. I'll show you."

We both sat in the semi-circle of stools.

Ava picked up her rubbery hammer. "Do I whack you with this?"

I laughed. "No. Those five circles will have moles pop up randomly. You're supposed to whack them."

She practiced her swings, slamming the mallet down on the empty holes. "I might like this a lot."

I passed tickets to the operator. Another couple sat down on the other seats.

Ava watched them, her hammer on her shoulder. The girl picked up her mallet and pretended to whack her date. He laughed and leaned over to kiss her.

As she studied them, I wondered if she was trying to compare their behavior to ours. A relationship might not come naturally to her.

The lights blinked on, and the first moles popped up.

Ava let out a shriek and smacked her first mole. I paid little attention to the game, content to watch her. She had her full concentration on the circles, smacking the mallet as hard as possible.

The buzzer sounded.

"How did I do?" she asked.

Our scores lit up the display.

"Looks like the bright yellow lady wins!" the man said.

"What? Me?" She tried to stand up with the mallet,

plunking back down on the seat when she came to the end of the tether. "Oh!"

"What would you like?" He gestured to the stuffed animals hanging from a beam above the game.

"I don't know!" Her glee was so childlike, so pure, that several people stopped to see what she chose.

She selected a soft brown bear and clutched it to her chest. "I've never had a bear."

The man bowed. "Then enjoy this one."

We walked away, Ava holding the bear out in front of her. "At least I don't think I've ever had one."

"You told me once that your dad mailed you one for your birthday," I said. "Your mother trashed it, but you rescued it. It disappeared later."

"She probably erased my memory just so I wouldn't know about it anymore." Her tone was bitter. Did she think her mother could do that? I flashed to that final night, her mother calling the cops, locking them in the bathroom.

Yeah. Maybe.

"You were eight when you got that bear. That was probably a lot of memory erases ago."

She bumped her shoulder into mine. "You really do know everything about me."

"Everything you ever shared."

She held my gaze a moment, and I didn't let it go. She needed to remember who I was to her. Who I wanted to be.

"Okay, Mr. Loser of Whack-a-Mole. Does this big win make *me* the master?"

"Seems I've met my match."

Our hands collided, and she accepted mine. My heart

squeezed. For the first time in a year, I got to hold Ava's hand.

"What's that?" she asked, pointing ahead.

"It's a Fun House."

"That sounds amazing!" She hurried toward it, pulling me along.

Her behavior was a complete turnaround from anything I'd seen since she went away. This was working. She was coming back to me.

I handed over tickets, and we stomped up the metal ramp.

"Ack!" she said when the floor started slanting at a sideways angle. And "Ack!" again when we approached a room full of mirrors, distorting us in every direction.

"This is wild!" she said.

We approached a turning tunnel with spiral walls.

"This is really disorienting," she said.

I hadn't even thought of that. The Fun House was a horrible choice and now we were deep into it. I wasn't photosensitive, so flashing lights didn't bother me. But she certainly was.

"Close your eyes," I said. "I'll lead you."

She did as I suggested, and I walked her down the tube. We turned a corner.

And it happened.

A strobe light.

My hands moved fast, clapping over her eyes.

"It's so bright and blinky!" she said. "Let me see!"

"No, Ava, it's a strobe!"

The strobe turned off, only to activate again when we moved.

"Shit! Somebody shut that off!" I shouted.

"It's okay!" Ava said.

"No, it's not." I shouted, again and again, for someone to turn it off. But the circus music drowned me out, not that an employee was anywhere close.

"Okay, Ava, walk forward. Keep your eyes shut tight."

"I don't feel very well. I'm not sure I can walk." She stumbled.

I had to release her eyes to catch her.

"Keep your eyes closed, Ava." I scooped her up in my arms.

Thankfully, she was small enough for me to carry, and I pushed through a black curtain and out into the night air.

I hauled her to a bench and sat down, keeping her and the bear in my lap.

"Ava?" My chest was so tight I could barely breathe.

She was quiet, too quiet.

Was it a seizure? She wasn't stiff. Nothing was pulsing.

But still, she didn't come around.

This was my fault.

I should have known there would be a strobe in a Fun House. I understood carnivals. She didn't. This was on me. I hadn't protected her at all.

"Ava?"

I wasn't sure what was wrong. Her face wasn't blue. As I held her, she seemed to breathe.

"Ava?"

Her head turned to the side and moved in a short, jerky pulse.

Damn it, a seizure. Damn it. Damn it. Damn it.

"Ava?" I wasn't sure how long to wait before I called for help.

A few curious passers-by watched us, probably assuming we were having a lovers' moment.

Her head got heavy and flopped against my arm, and then she said, "Owww."

I was so relieved, I felt like crying. This was nothing like the one in the hospital. Short. Only her head was affected.

"Are you back?"

She lifted her hands to her hair. "My head is going to fall off. It feels like death."

"I know that feeling."

I still wasn't sure she knew me. I had no idea how she came out of seizures. This was only a partial one. Her whole body hadn't been involved. I had them all the time. But I'd missed the ending of the only one of Ava's I'd seen, that first time in the disco room.

"What's your name?" I asked.

She thumped my chest. "Ava, you dummy. You were saying it nonstop."

"What's my name?"

She gazed up at me. "I haven't forgotten anything. You're Tucker, and you brought me here with promises of a Ferris wheel."

I relaxed and squeezed her against me. "Okay. So it didn't happen."

"I guess the medicine worked. Stopped it from going all the way."

"That's what it's supposed to do."

She slid off my lap. "I have a killer headache."

"We can go."

"No, I have some pain meds in my bag. Let me take them and see. I don't want to miss that Ferris wheel."

I smoothed her hair where it had partially fallen from her twists. "Okay."

"Go get me a Coke, boyfriend," she said.

My breath caught. She hadn't spoken to me like that since I found her again.

"I'll be right back."

I didn't go so far that I couldn't keep her in my sight. She sat, clutching her bear, until I returned. After a drink and her meds, we got in line for the Ferris wheel. She leaned against me as we waited out the pain.

Despite my stupid, awful mistake, we'd faced the devil and won.

CHAPTER 27
Ava

Seizures definitely sucked.

My headache eased as we waited in line for the Ferris wheel. The blinking lights set at intervals on the giant circle made my heart race with anxiety, but these were obviously something my broken brain could handle.

Unlike that strobe.

Now I knew what Superman felt like. Strobes were my Kryptonite. Anybody could bring me down with them. Tucker had covered my eyes, but what if I got a good hard dose? Would the medicine still help?

I'd have to ask the doctor.

By the time we loaded into a seat that rocked back and forth, a long belt buckled over our laps, my head felt better. The night was crisp, and as we rose in steady increments into the sky, I snuggled closer to Tucker.

He liked this and put his arm around me to pull me tight.

My chest loosened, and my shoulders relaxed. I had no idea I'd been holding myself so stiffly until this moment. Had I been this way since my escape?

Probably so.

We made it to the tippy top, and the wheel stopped again to load another couple.

Up here, the air felt clear, and despite the garish lights below, a star or two peeped between the clouds. We leaned back, and the seat rocked gently as we stared into the night.

"I hear the stars have names," I said. "If I ever knew them, they've long been erased."

Tucker extended an arm to point above us. "The star most people talk about is the North Star. It's used for navigation. It's bright enough to see even in tough conditions."

"Like sitting on top of a carnival?"

"Like that."

One other bright ball stood out. I pointed to it. "What's that star?"

"It's actually not a star at all. It's a planet. Venus."

"So planets glow too?"

"No, we're seeing a reflection of our sun's light on its atmosphere."

"You're speaking Greek."

"The atmosphere is made of the gases surrounding a planet."

I sighed. "I don't even know what I don't know."

Tucker turned to me, his eyes reflecting the shifting colors of the neon bar attached to the wheel. "You don't have to know everything to enjoy the stars."

I wiggled down in the seat to make it easier to stare up. The Ferris wheel moved another slot, and now we were one position past the top. "I don't feel anything when I look at the stars, so maybe I never learned much about them."

"I can't imagine your mother pointing them out."

"You met her?"

"Sure. In the hospital. She tried to get me kicked out. Then the night she had me arrested."

"Oh, right. She definitely doesn't love *you*."

"Now that's an understatement."

I pulled the bear closer to me. "Do you know anything else about my dad? I didn't read about the bear in any of my notes. Not even in yours."

"I'm sorry I left it out. But you used to have a note about him. His name was Marcus, I think."

"Yes, Marcus Anthony Roberts. He's on my birth certificate."

"You only mentioned the bear. Sometimes when you'd hear a sad song, you'd say that maybe you sensed how it felt when he left."

I squeezed the bear more tightly. "Do you think he sent other things that Mother kept from me?"

"Probably. That was the only thing you caught, or at least the only one you wrote a note to yourself about."

"Or at least a note she didn't destroy."

"That, too." He shook his head. "She's a piece of work."

"She doesn't have a job. How does she get money to rent the house or buy food?"

"Sounds like your dad paid child support."

I sat up suddenly, causing the chair to rock. "You mean my dad has been involved all along?"

"Unless your mom was independently wealthy. Did she ever go to the bank?"

"No. We passed one on the way to the store, but we never stopped."

"Did you see where her money came from?"

I thought for a moment. "We sometimes went to the

counter at the grocery store and she passed the man a piece of paper. He gave her cash. I guess that was a check. It wasn't a paycheck, like I get now, with typed numbers. It was handwritten. So I guess it was a check from Dad?"

"Sounds like it."

"So, he didn't abandon me."

Tucker reached for my hand and squeezed it. "Have you searched for him?"

His hand was warm on mine, so I kept it there. "Sure. He lives in Houston."

"Are you going to contact him?"

"Why? He ditched me."

"Maybe your mother lied to him, too."

Had she? Could he have wanted me all this time?

The wheel moved again, but this time it did not stop, picking up speed. We reached the bottom, and it began another ascent. I clutched Tucker's hand. "Is it supposed to do this?"

He squeezed my fingers. "Yes, once it's loaded all the passengers."

The breeze from our movement ruffled Tucker's hair and sent wispy bits of my own into my face. I pushed them back and caught Tucker watching me. "You okay?" he asked.

"I'm fine. It's kind of a rush. Not wild like the other rides. But still a rush."

"We're up pretty high. You feel exposed sitting in a seat like this."

He lifted our joined hands to his lips and pressed a soft kiss onto my knuckles. "Headache gone?"

I nodded. "You get them a lot, right?"

"Not at the moment. My life is about as perfect as it gets."

Our eyes held. The wind rushed against us, the seat shifting forward and back as we made the circle again. The noise of the crowd grew as we reached the bottom, then faded as we rose into the sky.

I didn't know where to look, what to think, how to feel. The night was perfect and beautiful. Tucker was warm and close. He'd protected me. But my life was no different from what it had been when I first turned him down.

I was a walking disaster. He'd seen it first-hand when we met, and again tonight.

The Ferris wheel slowed down and soon it stopped, beginning the process of letting riders off and loading the next.

Tucker squeezed my hand. "Ava, I'm so glad you came here with me. I'm sorry I didn't think about the strobe."

I leaned my head on his shoulder. "No, no. It's fine. You helped me. I hadn't even known strobes existed. Now I know to avoid them."

"I couldn't bear it if anything happened to you again."

"You saw me seize. But... doesn't it happen to you?"

"It's different. I don't lose my memory. But also, it's only minor ones. They add up to the headaches, though."

"You can't take medicine like I do?"

He huffed out a breath. "I've taken most of them. My version of epilepsy isn't as treatable as yours."

"I guess they both suck in their own way."

He brought my hand to his lips again. "But we're here."

The wheel shifted to another slot. Soon we'd be escorted off. I didn't want this part of the night to end.

"Tucker..." But as soon as I said it, my confidence fled. I had to glance away.

He held my hand to his lips. "You okay?"

"I'm sorry I was so harsh when you first started coming around. I didn't know." Well, I had. But I'd wanted to avoid the messy feelings.

"I knew there was a risk that you would have forgotten me. I was willing to work hard to get you back."

We dropped another slot. Only three now until we would get off.

"Why? What's so special about me?"

"Everything. I've known it since the day in the disco room."

"But what is it about *us*?"

He sat back against the wooden seat. "I'm braver and stronger when I'm near you. I plan ahead. I dream again. My condition becomes just a part of me. I think—nothing can be all bad when I'm with Ava."

Wow. "I guess you're going to kiss me, then?"

Tucker grinned. "It's been a long time since I've gotten to do that."

"I'm not sure I know what I'm doing. Obviously, we've kissed before. But I don't exactly remember how."

"I like getting to be your first kiss all over again."

"Well, get it over with. I want to catch up." I'd seen movies. I knew what to do. I closed my eyes and tilted up my chin, waiting.

For a moment, nothing happened. I was about to open my eyes when Tucker released my hand and drew me closer to him.

When his lips met mine, I almost gasped at the rush of emotion that poured forth. Tears sprung to the corners of my eyes. My belly warmed over. And a deep sense of contentment washed over my entire body.

I relaxed against him, and my lips parted. Our kiss went deeper, our mouths remembering each other in ways

I couldn't have predicted. I clutched the collar of his shirt, wanting him closer. A new, unexpected need shot through me like stars bursting into shimmering sparks.

The wheel lurched forward, and a low voice said, "Step to your right!"

We were at the bottom. Tucker's eyes met mine. "We're back," he said.

I didn't know if he meant back to the bottom, or back together, or back to where we should have been.

I could only say, "Yes, we are."

CHAPTER 28
Tucker

Life after the carnival felt miraculous compared to the time we spent apart. I brought Ava to meet Gram, something we hadn't been able to do in the before times.

Afterward, Gram remarked that Ava seemed very different from how I described her a year ago.

"She is," I told her. "But whether she dresses in long skirts or all in black, and whether she's easygoing or intense, she still feels like the same person to me."

Gram nodded. "We all grow and change. Your grandfather was a different man at age sixty than he was at twenty-five, but our love was the same."

"Exactly."

I continued to go see Ava outside the diner. On one of those nights, a couple of weeks after the carnival, she suggested we go to her apartment and cook. She was trying to get back into making her own food.

"Just nothing from when I lived at home," she said. "Something about tasting those things takes me back to that horrible time."

"Did you have a lot of variety? It might be hard to avoid it all."

She shrugged. "We didn't have a lot of money. We made things we could stretch. Soups. Stews. Stuff with potatoes and ramen noodles."

"My grandmother has the best lasagna recipe," I said. "Even if you've had lasagna before, you've never had *this* lasagna."

She tilted her head. "I've heard the word lasagna. And I know it's an Italian food because I've seen the Olive Garden commercials. We don't serve it at the diner, and I never made it with Mother."

"Then it's settled. I'll grab the ingredients, and we can make it at your place. You have things like pans and baking dishes?" I couldn't assume anything.

She laughed. "I have a pot. And a couple of plates."

"No problem. I'll bring what I need."

"It's a date." She glanced at the diner door. "I'm late, and Big Harry is a brute."

"Don't I know it."

She leaned in for a super-fast kiss, and my heart sped up. It was so easy, so natural, but after a year without it, this kiss, and every kiss, felt like a miracle.

As I headed to the bus stop, I suddenly understood the urge of people in old-fashioned movies to jump in the air and click their heels.

I sure felt like it. I glanced around. There were a few people wandering First Street. Who cared? I jumped in the air, and wouldn't you know it, my heels connected.

Someone behind me whooped, and I waved.

Yes, this day was a good one.

Gram was meeting some of her friends the night Ava and I chose for the lasagna dinner, so she dropped me off at Ava's apartment rather than having me lug all my kitchenware on the bus.

I wanted to drive again, but that seemed completely out of reach.

"I can come and fetch you after," she said as I opened the door.

"No need. I've got this."

Her smile got tight. "Call me if you don't feel well."

"I'll be fine. I really will, Gram."

I knew she was glad to see me out of my room. But at the same time, she also knew how bad things were. My migraine meds were nearly empty, but we couldn't refill them for another two weeks. Because of the way I was hoarding and over-ingesting them on Ava days, she was worried.

I was too. But this was more important.

When Ava opened her door, I smiled at seeing her wearing all black, as usual. Her hair was down today though, so she looked more like the Ava I once knew.

"I only have that one shirt that isn't black, and I wore it on our last date," she said flatly.

I leaned in to brush my lips against hers. "You look perfect."

Her brows drew together as if she wasn't sure she could believe the compliment. "Let's check out your kitchen skills," she said.

I followed her through the ramshackle apartment with its lawn chairs and crates. I pictured my family's old coffee table there. And the gliding rocker Mom loved. I should get them soon. I wanted those things for her. I wanted to imagine the two lives I loved coming together, even without me.

I slid the paper bag onto the counter and began pulling

out the contents. Gram and I had assumed nothing. I had a pan for browning the meat. A spatula. The big pot for making sauce, and later, boiling the noodles. A large bowl to mix the cheeses.

I slid a cutting board and knife toward her. "You can cut up the tomatoes." I passed her the bag.

She dug out the tomatoes and took them to the sink to be rinsed, while I arranged the spices along the counter. Soon, her kitchen smelled of the aromatic sauce.

"It'll be a while before we need to do the next step." I took her hand. "Want to listen to music?"

"Sure."

We settled on the floor by the wall near the kitchen. "I brought songs we liked back in the day. I know your amnesia is complete, but I thought it would be interesting for you to hear them. See if it makes you feel anything."

"Like a big ol' Ava experiment."

I hesitated. "Or you can choose. I have a subscription. We can make a new list."

"No, it's cool. Hit me with our greatest hits."

I passed her one of my earbuds and pulled up my Ava playlist. I didn't want to start with "Highway to Hell," even though it matched her current personality. I went with Lizzo.

Her eyes lit up. "I love this one. The first time I heard it playing at the shelter, I knew it was my jam."

Of course. Many of the songs were so popular that she would've heard them since her memory reset. I didn't know why I thought this would work. And it's not like I needed the help of her old memories. Things were going pretty great.

But when she jumped up to dance, there was something I noticed immediately. Parts of Ava hadn't changed.

The way she moved, the way she held out her elbows and closed her fists, was the same as before. She closed her eyes and angled her head exactly as she had in the art room over a year ago. I knew it. Ava was still Ava.

The song ended, and she opened her eyes and drew in a breath, as if she might ask me to play it again, but then she paused.

The first notes of the next song had already begun, and she plunked down onto the carpet.

This one was Taylor Swift, one of the obscure songs from the *1989* album that never got much airplay. We had listened to it over and over again when she was stuck with her mother.

She placed her elbows on her crossed legs, concentrating.

After a moment, she pressed her hands to her cheeks, her eyes glistening. "It's Taylor Swift, isn't it? What's happening?" She wiped a finger under her eyes and stared at the wetness.

"We listened to this album a lot on the nights we couldn't get together."

"What's it called?"

"'You Are in Love.'"

"It's the sappiest thing I've ever heard."

Oh. I reached to move the playlist forward, but she stopped me. "I want to hear the rest of it."

We kept listening, and it got hard for me not to tear up, too. As great a song as it was when we were a couple, it had become tragic for me in the months I couldn't find her, then the period when she wouldn't see me.

"You can't tell anyone at work that I'm a secret Swiftie. It'll destroy my reputation." Her voice shook.

"I won't."

"Here I am, crying like a lovesick schoolgirl." She wiped her eyes. "I'm supposed to be a badass bitch."

I slipped my arm around her shoulders. "Songs are supposed to make us feel something."

"What am I going to do about you? I'm not supposed to feel this emotional! I'm supposed to avoid feelings. Repel them. Make fun of them."

"Maybe there's more to you than you've let yourself be since you left your mom."

She laid her head on my shoulder. "Maybe."

We stayed like that for quite a while, but when she lifted her face to mine, I knew exactly what she wanted. We were on our third Taylor Swift song, back in that sacred space we'd always found in those moments we stole together last year.

Connected. In tune with each other. Like gravity existed to draw us together.

Her lips were as I remembered, soft and inquisitive. She kissed like she was always asking a question. What now? What next? How is this possible?

I wanted to drown in it. Drown in her. Something settled inside me. I unclenched, like I no longer had to hold myself so tight.

The kiss went on for two more songs before another Lizzo worked its way into the playlist and broke us apart, laughing.

"She's the best," Ava said.

"You always loved her."

"Still do." Her gaze met mine. "I didn't have the guts to ask something at the carnival."

"Ask me anything."

She sat away from me, leaning against the wall. Her

hair was filled with static electricity, and it fanned out around her head.

"When we were together before, did we ever…" She looked down and bit her lip.

I knew what she meant. "No. We were about to on the last night. But your mom caught us."

"Okay. I read your story about that night. But I didn't know if maybe you didn't want to write out that part. An admission of guilt or whatever."

I shook my head. "I would've said it. You were so determined to know if you were a virgin that night."

"And you felt like I was."

"I mean, you're talking to someone who was barely eighteen and pretty inexperienced. But it seemed like you were."

She glanced in the kitchen. "And how much longer will the sauce take?"

My heart hammered at what she was suggesting. "Some people let it simmer for hours before they declare it ready."

She held my gaze. "Then we should let it simmer for hours."

This time when she kissed me, with a determination that matched the final fateful night we were together, the ground swooped out from me. Maybe something was unclenching in her, too.

She stood up and took my hand. "Okay, let's do this thing."

I stood beside her. "Are you sure? We're still new this time."

She punched my chest. "Are you saying no? You've waited over a year."

"Hell no, I'm not saying no."

"Then come on." She pulled me down the hall. "And am I to understand you didn't get any more experience in the time we were apart?" Her voice was light and kidding, but I stopped dead in my tracks.

"Ava, there is no question to me that you are the only one I'll ever want."

She faced me in the hall. "How can you know that? How can anyone know that?"

I gripped her hands. "Some of us just do."

She watched me for another long moment, as if trying to decide if what I said could possibly be true.

"Well, Mr. Mush. Mr. Romance. Mr. Lovestruck, let's figure this thing out together."

CHAPTER 29
Ava

I didn't feel nervous as I brought Tucker into my bedroom. I figured that this time I had more knowledge about what was about to happen than I might've before.

After my time at the shelter and all the life experience explained to me by the women there, I had a pretty good grasp of how things would go.

It was a good deal different from movies and TV shows. I knew that much.

Tucker cared a lot. That was important, at least according to Alicia and Tara and Yvonne. Most men didn't.

I lead a visibly nervous Tucker into my bedroom, but decided to leave the light off. A fair amount of lamplight from the parking lot spilled through the edges of the blinds, which didn't quite fit the window.

I didn't feel any more self-conscious about my bedroom than the other parts of my apartment. I knew it was meager, but I was proud of what I'd managed to put together.

In the half-light, the shadowy forms of my bed, which

was only a mattress and box spring, and a small dresser I had scavenged didn't seem quite so bad.

The bed was covered with a soft velour blanket I'd picked up on sale at Target. It was one of my favorite possessions, actually. Sitting on it was like resting on a cloud.

Tucker and I sat side by side on the edge, our thighs pressed against each other.

"It's just like the first time you kissed me," Tucker said.

"At the hospital?"

"Yeah."

I grinned at him, although I wasn't sure he could see it in the dim light. "So, it sounds like I've been the one making all the bold moves."

He laughed. "Maybe."

Now that we were here, I felt a little anxious. "I'm still on that shot that I talked about in your story. The night we were supposed to do this."

He nodded. "Okay. Good."

This felt awkward. Maybe I shouldn't have pushed him. Maybe he wasn't ready.

If Marguerite and Bethany were right, this whole thing wasn't worth the effort. There would be a lot of grunting and pushing and being all sticky later.

I was about to call it off, but then Tucker closed the gap to draw me close. Warmth rushed through my body, leaving me tingling.

He kissed my hair, then close to my ear, then my jaw. Finally, he moved to my mouth.

Something about this kiss felt different. It wasn't light and hurried, like the ones outside the diner, or when we would say goodbye after meeting with Gram.

And it wasn't new and unfamiliar, like at the carnival.

This kiss hit differently, deeper down. This was a kiss of someone I knew loved me, even if I wasn't quite ready to love him back. He'd known me all along, and now I had begun to know him, too.

It was a kiss of trust. And longevity. Of new beginnings.

As he pressed his lips to mine, I realized I knew this kiss. This exact one. It was a kiss of wanting more. Of contentment. Security.

He teased my lips open with his tongue, and we pulled closer together, our bodies connected as we sat side by side.

He tasted like mint gum, which made me smile. Tucker always planned ahead. He was thoughtful. Patient.

But as the kiss went on, something flared. Something bright and down low, a spark igniting in what had been a dark, hidden part of me.

His fingers brushed the loose hair at the back of my neck and the tingles became intense, like lightning flew from his fingers.

I sucked in a breath, but Tucker wasn't hesitant any longer. He dragged me close. He shivered lightly, and I realized he was feeling the same thing. We were going through this together.

There had only been one woman at the shelter who spoke of love in a wistful way. Missy had been engaged once, years before the string of problems that brought her to the shelter with a newborn.

Her first great love had died in a motorcycle accident. When the other women insisted relationships led only to ruin, she spoke of her feelings in reverent tones. He had been her everything, tender and caring. From the way she described him, it seemed like they'd experienced everything as one person.

Now I understood what she meant.

Tucker's hand slid beneath the bottom of my shirt, and I sucked in a breath at the intensity of my reaction.

I wanted more of this. So much more. I pressed against him, urging him on. Now that we were here, Tucker was no longer tentative at all. His hand slid up my rib cage to cup the cotton bra.

When his thumb crossed over the flimsy fabric, a tiny unexpected sound came out of me. It was half groan, half sigh.

Pleasure splintered through me, cutting through everything I had tried to become. There was no negativity. No bitterness. No sharp edges. The stiff, angry person I had fashioned since learning Mother's secret fell away like broken shells.

Tucker slipped his thumb beneath the elastic edge of the bra, coming in contact with new skin. I didn't think these feelings could get any stronger, but they broke wide open. I gasped against his mouth. "Tucker!"

He stilled. "Is this okay?"

"Yes. Don't stop."

He smiled again. "You forgot that I already know what you like."

He was right about that. His hand slowly slid over my bare skin, and I gasped again. My whole body felt on fire. The shelter women had steered me wrong on this. Nobody had talked about how incredible this was.

"Tucker?"

He shifted his mouth to my jaw, sending kisses along the way to my ear. "Yes, Ava?"

"Do you feel like I do? Like your body is on fire?"

His voice near my ear sent a shudder through my body. "More."

He released me. I wanted to beg him to go back to where he'd been, but he grabbed the bottom of my shirt and pulled it over my head. Yes. This was better. I almost told him about my bra, but he'd already realized there was no latch in the back and tugged it away to fall with my shirt.

Being exposed to him was so hot. The need to keep going pulsed low in my body. I wanted to get there, but then I wanted this exploration to last forever, too.

Tucker took his time, giving every exposed part of me slow, easy attention. But when he bent down, replacing his hands with his mouth, I saw sparks in my vision.

There was no need for me to control any of this. Tucker knew exactly what he was doing. And he knew me. It was just like he said.

His hair tickled my neck. He pressed me down on the bed, not stopping what he was doing. As he made his way down to my belly. I could scarcely catch my breath.

He stood and slid my legs around so that I was lying fully on the bed. The snap of my jeans popped in the quiet, then the slide of the zipper.

My heart hammered hard. I watched him move in the half-light and tangled my fingers in his hair.

He glanced up at me with a grin, his eyes shining.

My jeans slid down my legs and landed on the floor.

I hadn't planned for this, so my underwear was plain white cotton from Target. I didn't look anything like the women in movies or TV shows, all tanned skin and lace.

But the moment Tucker started edging the panties down, my mind was erased of anything but his touch.

The world narrowed to this space. He lifted my hips to

remove the last piece of my clothing. His thumb moved down there, and I sucked in a breath with the aching rush that overwhelmed all my other senses.

When he slid a finger more deeply inside, I gasped, my body arching. Whatever I felt before was nothing compared to the explosion of pleasure and emotion that burst through me.

Scenes flashed through my head, unbidden. Tucker smiling at me. Tucker with the daffodils. Tucker walking away, both sad and determined during the time I wouldn't see him.

The hope in his face whenever I did talk to him.

His concern for me at the carnival.

It all mixed together. The fierce pleasure. The feverish need. His tender care.

Then his mouth was on me, and all thoughts were obliterated. I grasped the blanket with both hands. My body had a mind of its own as it pushed against him.

Even though I was flooded with every kind of pleasure, I still felt like I was reaching for something, straining toward some unknown place I'd never been.

Then it happened. Something inside me clenched, then tightened. I felt as though I was spiraling on the inside. I drew in a breath that was deeper than I had ever breathed before.

I hovered, suspended in this strange inky blackness, the insides of me tight. Then everything let go at once.

I heard my voice saying, "Oh my God, oh my God, oh my God, oh my God," mixed in with Tucker's name and strange unintelligible sounds.

But that was vague and in the distance. My body didn't feel like a body. It rippled like I imagined waves would on an ocean. Pulse after pulse after pulse, radiating out, starting from within me and seeking the width and breadth of the universe.

I couldn't breathe. I couldn't feel my body. I was all waves, signaling out like a radio, as if I was communing with the night sky.

Then gradually, it dissipated, like the glitter bomb Nadia set off once at the diner by accident. For a second, it had caught in the air drafts from the ceiling fans, then slowly it rained down until it littered the floor. And oh, how Big Harry had shouted at her.

I lay there *feeling* rather than *seeing* the sparkles fall and land around me on the bed. Tucker hovered over me, watching my face. "You all right?" he asked.

I didn't have speech yet. I nodded. I reached out to squeeze his arm.

He lay beside me for a moment, and I realized he was still fully dressed while I was completely naked. This struck me as hilarious, and my voice returned and I laughed.

Tucker grinned at me. "This is funny?"

"Did that part happen before? How could I have forgotten?"

He shook his head. "We didn't get a lot of opportunity to be this alone with so much time."

"So, you think it's my first?"

"Seems probable."

"I think I would've left a note about this." I rested the back of my hand on my forehead. "Of course, if there was a note about this, Mother would've taken it for sure."

"She can't get you here." Tucker ran the back of his hand along my arm.

I reached out to brush his hair off his forehead. "Can we do the rest? With you involved this time?"

He chuckled. "I think I was pretty involved there."

"I mean with your other body parts."

He rolled off the bed, shucking his clothes.

I watched him, seeing all of him for the first time.

He was lean, but not skinny. And while he wasn't tricked out like the male models who did TikTok dances or the ones who starred in movies, his muscles were wiry and strong. His arms were defined, his chest wide and tight.

I hadn't watched porn even though I knew it existed, so when the rest of him came out, I sat up. "So that's it!"

He laughed again. "That's it."

"But it's so long."

"You said something similar last time."

"Is that going to hurt?"

"It might a little."

"Okay. I had my turn. Let's do this."

But even though I said those things, he didn't rush me. His touch skimmed over my body, revisiting the highlights from earlier.

It wasn't as intense this time, but it calmed and relaxed me. The feeling was sweet, like smelling flowers. Or the last strokes when you brush your hair, and it's smooth and easy.

He rolled over me, bracing on his elbows. "You sure?"

"I'm sure."

He shifted my legs and pressed down.

This going into me was nothing like what happened before. My body resisted, and I took a deep breath to relax.

And he was right. There was a pinch, and the feeling of something filling me in a way I had never known.

But then he moved inside me, and the pleasure was like touching something silky, like a satin pillowcase gliding through your fingertips.

As he moved, I felt connected to him, as though everything that had come before had led to this.

Emotions sprinkled over me like a fresh rain.

I held onto his neck, tangling my fingers in his hair.

His eyes were closed with concentration, and his muscles shifted as he moved over me.

I felt on the verge of tears again, like when I heard the song. There would be more of this, so much more of it. The days ahead laid out like a path of flowers. Time with Tucker. Laughing. Cooking. Talking And doing more of this.

As he said my name, everything in his body tightening, I knew exactly what he was feeling.

His eyes squeezed shut and I knew, even with my lost memory, that he looked more beautiful than I'd ever seen him be before.

I let out a small sob, so relieved that we had gotten here. He had been right all along. I was just too scared to listen. Too broken by what had happened before.

His eyes opened, and the wonder with which he looked at me made my whole body tingle, so much like the time that the sparkles fell from the sky that I washed over with pure joy.

"You were right," I managed to get out. "You were absolutely right."

He rolled beside me and drew me against him. "We made it, Ava."

I buried my face in his neck.

I had come home.

Tucker and I saw each other often after that. I made Big Harry stop threatening to kick him out. Gram would sometimes come to the diner, too, and she and Tucker liked to eat there when the crowd was light.

He turned nineteen, then I did. We had parties, real ones, for actual birthdays, not fake ones making me think I wasn't my actual age.

I had a family again.

But it was Big Harry who said I should go to college. We sat behind his bar during a slow day, rolling silverware.

"You're young, Ava. Go to school. Learn some things."

I placed a knife, fork, and spoon in a red napkin. "Right. Just so I can have a seizure and erase my expensive education."

"And I could die of a heart attack in five minutes. Still have to roll this silverware."

I aimed a knife at his bushy beard like I might stab him for saying it. He was officially my favorite person, next to Tucker. And Gram.

"What could I do?" I spread out another napkin.

"I dunno. Be a nurse. A teacher."

"Right. Because both of those are a great fit if I forget everything."

"You said your hands remember things your head forgets, right?"

"Yeah. I learned that the first time I cut an onion." The knife had moved almost on its own.

"Those were some sweet slices."

"All right, so what does that get me? Car repair?"

"You could play a musical instrument."

I had never thought to do that. We didn't have any at

Mother's house out in Wimberley, so I assumed I'd never had lessons.

"What about painting? Can you draw?" Big Harry slid another bin of clean silverware between us. The job never ended.

"No. I tried that. I like taking pictures with my phone, though." I pulled it out of my pocket to show him shots of downtown, the bar, and the lights over Second Street.

"Those are good. So why not do photography?"

"Tuition? I'm barely getting by already."

"I tell you what. You sign up at Austin Community College, and I'll pay for the first semester."

Huh. I didn't expect that. "So you're not as poor as you let on."

"Maybe. Maybe not."

Harry didn't have a wife. No family. He lived in a trailer behind the building. Even so, he shouldn't spend his money on me.

"I see those gears turning, Li'l Ava," he said. "I mean it. Sign up. I'll pay."

"You know I'll have to work fewer hours. You'll need another part-time server."

"Missy asked for more hours. She'll take them."

I dropped another silverware roll on the stack. "You've got it all figured out."

"Yup."

I told Tucker about Harry's offer that night. He said I should go for it. He was having a hard time that evening, so we stayed over at his gram's. He couldn't look at screens or really have much light at all, so we lay on his bed in the dark, listening to quiet music while I worked out the details in my mind.

It took some effort to enroll. I had no education paperwork to show I'd ever been to school or learned anything. A friendly lady at ACC combed through everything she could access and said it appeared I stopped attending school in seventh grade, and that my mother stopped filing homeschool exemptions a few years later.

So, I'd have to take some classes in math and English first, then pass the GED. She was able to sign me up for a non-credit photography class, though.

Life sped up. I went to classes and earned my GED. Big Harry paid for two semesters, but then I got a student loan to keep going.

I continued to work at the diner and saw Tucker on his good days. My mother didn't find me again, and I felt content. Nobody had a perfect life, but this one was about as good as I could expect.

CHAPTER 30
Tucker

I saw Ava less than I liked, still dealing with debilitating headaches and micro-seizures that kept me in bed more days than not. I hadn't involved Ava in my troubles, preferring to skip the pain meds on days she worked at the diner and doubling up on the days we could see each other.

Bill figured out I was seeing Ava and suggested another double date for old time's sake, but this time I was the one with the busy life. I had a full-time job of dealing with my health condition, and what few good hours I had, I gave to Ava.

Gram finally caught on to what I was doing and gave me a fierce lecture. We made an appointment with my neurologist, but after yet another pointless conversation with no real answers, Gram tracked down a new doctor in Houston.

Dr. Vicks was everything my old neurologist wasn't. Sharp, kind, thoughtful. When we reviewed my history, her head tilted, black braids touching one shoulder. I could tell she was really listening.

"There's no need to repeat these tests," she said. "You have a recent MRI and EEG. Now that you've aged out of Dell Children's Hospital, it's considerably less pleasant on an adult epilepsy ward."

"And no disco room," I said.

Dr. Vicks looked up from her iPad. "Disco room?"

"Oh, there's a space at the children's hospital for the teens to hang out while they are wired."

"That's fun." She scrolled through screens of reports. "We have plenty of data on the parts of your brain that are affected. I see you were deemed ineligible for surgery."

Gram spoke. "Too many parts affected."

"I'm surprised you haven't been offered a VNS. As far as lifestyle and side effects, they are minimal. It's not a perfect solution, but a decent shot at one. Good enough to install."

"But he has more migraines than actual seizures," Gram said.

"It's all the same in this case," Dr. Vicks said. "His migraines are actually the postictal results of seizures that aren't visible."

"Oh." Gram and I looked at each other.

Dr. Vicks explained that they'd wrap a wire around one of the nerves in my neck that went up to my brain. It would connect to a small box under the skin of my chest and send a light electric shock to my brain every sixty seconds. If I felt a seizure coming on, I could pass a magnet on a wrist strap over the box to send a stronger zap to try and stop it. But otherwise, it would do the work on its own since my seizures were mainly invisible.

It sounded wild to me, but Dr. Vicks said it was a good option for patients who didn't respond to medicine.

As Gram drove us out of town, she asked, "So, what do you think?"

"One night in the hospital? Could solve my problems? I'm in." I was elated. "I'm only mad my old doc never suggested it. Think about it! I could go to college! Think of all the classes I avoided in high school because the meds made me brain-dead."

"If it doesn't work, you'll have that contraption in you for the rest of your life," Gram said. "And it's surgery every time you need a new battery."

"But, I'll be one step closer to transforming into a cyborg."

Gram shook her head, but she laughed. "We'll have to stay in Houston a few days. Will you be able to separate yourself from your girl?"

"I'm thinking of bringing her with us, if she wants to come."

"Sure. I'm happy to turn over some of the nursemaid duties to her."

The city zoomed by as we drove down the freeway. "Her dad lives here in Houston. I think I can convince her to see him."

"Is that a good idea? She never speaks of him."

"Not often. But when she does, she gets this wistful look."

Gram nodded, her gray curls bouncing. "So what's your plan?"

"I have his address. I was thinking of driving by his house. Get an idea of what his life is like."

"You have your map pulled up?"

I angled my phone toward her. "It's about twenty minutes out of the way. Houston is huge."

"I'm game if you are."

I navigated her through the highway interchanges. Houston was a maze of toll roads and interstates. We finally exited and drove along normal city streets before turning into a neighborhood bordered by a fancy stone wall.

"My, my," she said, ducking her head for a better look at the tall, lush trees that lined the road.

"It's something, all right." The Houston we'd seen so far had been industrial and gray. Houses were packed together like cracker boxes on a shelf. But this neighborhood took its time. Each home was unique, spread apart, and lush with greenery.

"Older neighborhoods keep their trees," Gram said. "Looks like Ava's dad does all right."

I glanced back down at the phone. "It's up ahead on the left."

Gram slowed down as we approached the house Marcus Roberts bought nine years ago, according to the real estate records. The brick two-story had a wide porch with a swing. Bright flowers led up the walk.

"Children live here," Gram said, gesturing to the lawn. A pink bike lay in the grass.

"You think Ava has a sister?" I had no idea what Ava would think of that.

"He might have remarried, and she's a stepdaughter."

"True." I snapped a quick photo of the front of the house, in case Ava wanted to see. She might have already Google Mapped it, but being here was an entirely different thing.

We drove on, and I helped Gram get back to the highway.

"You going to tell Ava you found him?"

"Sure. I don't keep secrets from her."

"That's good." Her eyes held mine for a moment, then she refocused on the road.

"Are you really okay with her coming?"

"It's fine. Just don't expect any quality time. You're going to be in recovery."

She was right. But I wanted Ava there. "I sure hope it works."

"Me too, baby. Me too."

CHAPTER 31
Ava

When Tucker came over after his trip to Houston, I was sitting on the floor of my apartment surrounded by photographs.

"Look here." I pointed to an image of him leaning against the giant blue shoe at the mini golf course. "The saturation is good."

"I like the new printer. Are you going to start charging?"

"Big Harry said I could put cards out if I wanted to drum up customers. I've been taking pictures of the regulars for a while now. Should I wait until I graduate, though?"

"I don't think many photographers go to school in the first place. You're already ahead." Tucker kneeled in front of an image of Charles reaching for a frothy-headed beer, a stream of colored light from the neon landing on the mug like it was the Holy Grail.

He lifted it to examine more closely. "This is good."

"You think so? My professor says I have the eye."

"You do."

I stacked the prints to store in my portfolio. I had so little documentation of my life that photography seemed the perfect occupation. And the more I could photograph, the more I'd get back after any memory resets, should the worst happen.

I only had a crappy old digital SLR I bought used, and the lens was rubbish, but my professor insisted that great art could be made with a box and a pinhole. The equipment was not the point.

Still, I was saving my tips for something better. It wasn't easy, paying rent and going to school. But I was doing it.

For the first time, I was pursuing a dream, learning something on my own. And as both Big Harry and my neurologist had pointed out, even if I lost my episodic memory, a skill like this would stick. As soon as I reacquainted myself with the camera functions, I'd be able to quickly re-establish my ability to capture a great image.

When I set the portfolio aside, I realized Tucker hadn't moved. "What's up?" I asked, scooting closer so that our knees touched.

"I want you to see something," he said, opening the photo app on his phone and turning the screen to me.

I took it from him. "A house. Pretty fancy. Not good lighting, though. It would have been an awesome shot about two hours later."

"It's your dad's house."

My belly dropped. "You mean Marcus?"

"Yeah. When Gram and I were in Houston, we drove by it."

I peered closer. "They grow flowers. That's good. It's a nice house." I passed the phone back. "What's your point?"

"I'm going to have surgery in Houston in a few weeks."

"You're what?"

"It's a good thing." He took my hands in his. "The new doc says there's this thing called a VNS they can attach to me and it might prevent the seizures."

"Really?" I'd never heard of anything like that.

"It's something they do for people who can't take meds."

"Is it safe?"

"They do it on little kids, even."

I moved closer, climbing onto his lap and straddling his waist to face him. My fingers ran through his hair. He smelled of gardenia bath wash. Gram's. He must have run out of his. "I don't like the thought of someone cutting on you."

"Hand me your camera," he said, and I twisted around to lift it from the floor.

He turned it over in his hand. "How does this thing work?"

"Photo or video?"

"Video."

I flipped it on and adjusted the settings for the light in the apartment. "What's it for?"

He took it from me and held it out, the lens pointed toward us. "Is it rolling?"

I pressed the button to start the recording. "It is now."

He turned to the camera. "I'm Tucker. The weird one. And this is Ava. She's too good for me."

I punched his ribs, but he only laughed. "We are about to embark on a great journey into the depths of my screwy brain." I punched him again, and he could barely stop laughing enough to talk. "Hey, I'm trying to save this for posterity."

I pressed my face into his shoulder. What was he up to?

"In a few weeks hence, I will begin my transformation into Tucker Prime, part human, part machine."

I couldn't stand it anymore. I grabbed his arm and angled the camera toward me. "I'm sure we're completely out of focus and this footage is so shaky it will look like we're living through an earthquake."

He turned the camera back to his face and said in a shaky voice, as if it really were an earthquake, "Thisssss isss the lassst will and tesssstament of Tucker Giddingsss."

"Get on with it," I said, but my anxiety had eased. Tucker was always good for that.

"Before my transformation into a cyborg and a life of robotic crime, I wanted proof that I was once a loving and doting boyfriend." He kissed my hair. "And that we are definitely going to be together forever."

He lowered the camera. "And… cut." He set the camera on the carpet.

"You're nuts," I told him. "Was that for me to remember you by if you die in surgery?"

He pulled me close. "I won't die. I'm excited. And I'd like you to come. I don't have an exact date yet. I can work around your classes if you think Harry will let you off."

"I'll skip classes. You're more important."

"It's outpatient. And maybe one night in a hotel if I'm not up for the drive back."

"You'd ride in a car the day they cut you?"

"It'll be tiny cuts. You'll barely see them after they heal." He cradled me against his chest. "I'll be fine, Ava. This is my best chance at knocking this problem out."

"What if it doesn't work?"

"Then it doesn't work. But it's a shot."

"Why does anything have to change?" I pressed my face into his chest, trying to stop myself from trembling. Trusting someone was hard for me. I was so vulnerable. And now Tucker wanted to take this big risk.

"Because I want a life again, like when we were first together. Remember how I drove a car and took you on dates? We stayed out late and sent messages half the night."

Of course, I remembered none of that, but I knew what he meant. "Okay. I'll come. But do what's best for you. I can miss a class. The professor thinks I'm God's gift to photography already."

He laughed and the rumble of it set my soul at ease. He squeezed me inside his embrace. "You're God's gift to everything."

"Tell that to those idiots who don't tip their server."

We sat there a moment, holding each other. I sensed he had something else to say.

"What?" I asked.

"I was thinking. If we're in Houston..."

I pulled away to stare at the bar signs on the wall. "I don't know."

"We know where he lives."

"I can't simply drop in. Hey, Pops, remember me? The kid you ditched?"

"There was a pink bike there. Wouldn't you like to know if you have a sister? She might be worth more than a dad."

A sister.

I had no real concept of blood ties. Just a mother who'd wrecked me, bound me to her through a condition I couldn't control.

"I'll think about it."

Tucker pulled me back into his embrace. "I once had a dad. Your mother—she's a mess. I don't blame you for never wanting to see her. But if I could see my dad again—" His voice broke, and my chest tightened. Tucker rarely talked about his family.

"But your dad didn't leave you when he could have stayed." I brushed his hair back from his forehead.

"I know. But he wasn't the perfect dad. He was really athletic, and so was my brother. They played football together. Watched games. Real 1950s stuff."

"What about you?"

"I wasn't particularly big on sports, although he often took Stephen and I bowling. I was a gamer nerd. I spent all my time on my consoles." His fingers tweaked one of the pinwheels in my hair. "For a long time, Dad wasn't into video games at all. Thought it rotted our heads. I felt like he disapproved of me, like I couldn't do anything right because I wasn't on some sports team."

"You're not exactly selling me on dads here."

"Hold on. Something changed him when I was ten or so. I guess he realized he was spending more time with Stephen than me. I don't know. Maybe Mom guilted him or something."

"So, he played video games with you?" I tried to picture young Tucker, the version I saw in pictures at Gram's house.

"He did. And he actually liked the racing games. Mario Kart and all that. We'd play for hours until Mom made us stop for dinner."

"He figured out a way to be your dad, too. Not just Stephen's."

"He did. And I let go of all the years I felt he wasn't a

real dad to me. Let myself be his kid again, at least while I had him."

I blew out a long breath. "You've made your point. Let me think about it."

That weekend Josefina, a girl from my photography class, called me in a panic. Her cousin Rita was having her quinceañera, a super fancy fifteenth birthday party. Since Josefina was studying photography, she'd been roped into taking the pictures.

She was terrified she'd miss something important, like the last doll or the rose ceremony. Would I please, please be her backup? I could use the photos in my portfolio if I ever wanted to book events.

I instantly said yes. My professor had told us that building a portfolio was the most important step in preparing to charge money for taking pictures. As much as I loved Big Harry and our crew at his diner, I did not want to be a waitress forever.

I arrived at the church as fifteen-year-old Rita waited by the back door to be escorted inside with her parents. Josefina circled the family, snapping away.

I immediately began photographing Rita. Her bright blue dress tufted out around her like a bell, thousands of ruffles aligned in perfect rows.

When Josefina spotted me, her shoulders relaxed. "Thank God you made it, Ava. I'm already exhausted, and I've only done the preparation pictures!"

"Where do you want me?"

Josefina stationed me along the side wall of the church for the religious part of the ceremony. Rita's parents led her to the altar to be blessed. The words were all in Spanish, but I picked up a few of them. I concentrated on the lighting, snapping the solemn faces.

The tone of the event completely changed after everyone moved to the adjacent banquet hall. Several young couples were announced as they entered, like royalty in old movies. Josefina leaned in as Rita stood alone in a spotlight. "Rita wanted to walk in with her girlfriend as escort, but her family wouldn't let her."

"Why not?"

"Appearances." Josefina shook her head. "The abuelas would have had a fit. At least her parents haven't stopped them from dating. That's something. Still wrecking her big day, though."

"Is the girlfriend here?"

"No. It was too hard. Oh, time for the tiara."

We parted again, wildly snapping images as the mother approached Rita to place a crown on her head. I had never seen anything as beautiful and elaborate as their dresses and hair.

An elderly woman moved forward with a pair of high-heeled shoes that matched Rita's blue dress. I quickly zoomed in on them, bright and sparkling in the woman's wrinkled hands.

Rita lifted her hem and stepped out of her flat white shoes to wear the heels instead. I understood now. This was her transition into womanhood.

Her father approached, and the DJ played a slow, languid song in Spanish. The two of them danced alone across the room. Many of the women brought out handkerchiefs to dab their eyes.

I took a dozen shots, then lowered my camera. The father smiled down at his daughter. Despite whatever problems they were having with the decision not to allow her girlfriend to escort her, in this moment, he seemed happy and proud. She gazed up at him with shining eyes, and my stomach knotted.

So this is what Tucker had meant about his dad. About family. You can have problems and still find ways to love each other.

While loading the images on my computer that night to review my shots, I couldn't stop thinking about the quinceañera. It wasn't just the father-daughter dance. It was all the family. *Abuelos*, grandparents. *Tías y tíos*, aunts and uncles. And so many cousins. All those people, related to you, there to celebrate your birthday. I'd never seen anything like it.

The only family Tucker and I had was his gram. I had no idea if the father I met—if he would even talk to me—would be worthy of a moment like I'd seen.

But maybe I had other people out there connected to me. Mother must have had parents. My father, too. A whole trove of aunts, uncles, and cousins could be wondering what happened to me.

My mother didn't know where I was, and I didn't want her, anyway. Even grandparents and cousins on her side might be risky, as they'd clue her in to my whereabouts.

My father might be better. Until Tucker's push, I'd chosen not to try.

But I wanted the answer to why he left. I would ask him if Mother drove him away. Maybe she kept him from me through some sort of threat, and he was miserable, too. I wanted to watch his face for the truth or the lie.

Maybe we could be like Rita and her father. Despite the conflict, the past upset, we could find a way to be family. Maybe like Tucker and his dad, we could find something in common.

Tucker sat beside me as I wrote an email to the address listed on Dad's business website. I kept it simple. No accusations. Nothing about Mother. Just that I was living on my own. And I would be in Houston soon. Was he willing to meet?

When I thought I had it right, I hit *send*.

We expected it to be hours or even days before we heard back, so we were both shocked when a *ping* sounded only minutes later.

It was him. Marcus Roberts.

I glanced over at Tucker. "I don't know if I can read it."

"Should I look at it first?"

I nodded and leaned against his shoulder, watching his face.

He clicked it open and his eyes moved from side to side as he read.

Then he smiled.

I sat up. "What?"

"He asks when you can come."

My eyes burned as I took the laptop to see the words for myself.

My dearest sweet Ava,

I've been waiting for this day for so long. I tried to find you when you turned eighteen, but your mother only ever sent me a PO Box for the checks. Then you ran away. I'm happy to initiate this any way you like. Email. A phone call. And by all means,

please come to visit. I can absolutely see you the weekend you are in Houston. Nothing is more important.
 Dad

He'd been waiting.
 I squeezed Tucker's hand, unable to speak.
 I was going to meet my father.
 My *dad*.

CHAPTER 32
Tucker

I never imagined the first road trip I took with a girl would involve Gram driving the car, but here we were.

Ava had never been outside of Austin, at least not in her current memory, so she was fascinated by all the scenes we took for granted. She sat in the front passenger seat, pointing out everything from billboards to pump jacks.

Her chatter filled the car. "How many miles have we gone? How long would it take if we were walking?"

Gram and I kept catching each other's gaze in the rearview mirror. It was amusing.

Then Ava gasped and spread her hands on her side window. "Are those *cows*?"

"It's a rule!" Gram said. "If you see cows, you must announce that you see cows."

"We're going to be talking a lot about cows," I said.

Ava's nose pressed to the glass, her pinwheel hair making her look twelve years old. "Why are some white and others brown?"

Gram grabbed the favorite line before I got a chance. "The brown ones are for chocolate milk."

Ava turned to me in the back seat, her eyes wide. "I had no idea!" She resumed looking out the window. "But what if they're half and half?"

Gram busted out in a snort-laugh, and I had to hold my shaking belly.

Ava crossed her arms over her chest. "You two are pulling my leg, aren't you?"

Gram smacked the steering wheel, the air conditioning blowing her fine gray hair from her face. "My father told me the same story when I was a girl."

"And Gram told me," I said.

"All right. If it's an old family joke." She grinned back at me, but her eyes told me her real thoughts. She hadn't had family jokes. She had a father who took off, and a mother who'd tried to prevent her from ever leaving home.

I leaned forward and squeezed her shoulder. "This trip is going to be great."

"For me, maybe," she said. "You're getting cut open."

I shook my head. "You keep reminding me."

"This is going to be a whole new beginning for Tucker," Gram said. "I can feel it."

I hoped she was right.

The surgery part was a blur. Check-in, meeting the surgeon, the smiles of the nurses. I could only take one person back with me for prep, but I couldn't choose between Gram and Ava.

Ava insisted they could take turns. She sent Gram for the pre-surgery shift while she retouched images on her laptop in the waiting area. She'd come for post-op.

The installation would take less than two hours, but

then there was recovery. If all went well, I would be at the hotel by evening, and we'd spend the night to make sure I was ready for the ride back. Gram had insisted.

Ava would have to meet her dad without me, but she said that was for the best. Having another person there might stifle the conversation.

When they told me to count backwards from ten, the last thing I pictured before everything went black was Ava.

"Everything went great." The voice was disembodied at first, a sound in the white haze, then my vision cleared. I recognized the surgeon. "I'm going to fetch you some company. She can be with you now."

I tried to nod, but my head wouldn't move.

"You're still coming out of it," a nurse said. "You'll be sleepy."

If she said anything else, I didn't know it. The next thing I knew, I was in the curtained area where I'd been prepped, and Ava sat on a chair beside me.

"I see peepers," she said. "You've been out a while."

I couldn't think of anything clever to say. My head felt full of cobwebs.

"I have water and crackers here for you if you're starving," she said. "The nurse left them. Five-star food if I ever saw it." She held up a cup and a package of Goldfish.

"Maybe in a minute." The words sounded like a frog croaking.

"Sounds like you could use the water." She moved in close, angling the straw at my mouth. The cool, wet drink was like sipping from a mountain stream.

And Ava was here. I didn't care what I'd been through. This was heaven.

Ava set the cup down. "They said everything is all hooked up. They won't turn it on until you get back to your doctor in Austin, though."

A nurse slid back the curtain. "You're awake! Let's look you over and see when you might be ready to roll out of here."

She inflated a cuff on my arm, but I kept my eyes on Ava. This was almost certainly the first day of the next, best part of my life.

CHAPTER 33
Ava

Tucker's recovery went perfectly, and he was discharged right on time. After making sure he and Gram were settled at the hotel, I arranged for a ride to a Mexican restaurant my father had chosen.

He had a headshot on his company website, so I felt reasonably sure I could spot him. We bore only a passing resemblance. Maybe something about our eyes or nose.

The restaurant was quiet, caught in the lull between lunch and dinner. Colored flags fluttered in the air conditioning as I searched for him.

One man sat alone in the center of the sea of square tables. He matched the photograph, his dark hair peppered with gray, cut short in a corporate style. He dressed on the high end of casual in a pale blue polo shirt and khaki pants. He could've been anyone's middle-aged father. However, he was mine.

I wound my way through the tables and headed for him. He noticed me and stood. I extended a hand as I got near. Rather than call him the wrong thing, Dad or Marcus or Mr. Roberts, I simply said, "Hello."

He clasped my hand in both of his, like an embrace. "Ava. What a lovely young woman you've become."

He pulled out my chair. I sat, feeling off balance, my stomach quivering. Nothing about him felt familiar.

"So how is work with the oil company?" I had prepared opening questions. I wasn't sure exactly how we might break the awkwardness.

"Good. I like it. Helps me prepare for college bills."

My heart plummeted. The other daughters. I'd learned since the first email that he had two of them. Ones who didn't forget him.

"What are their names again?" I tried to make my voice normal, but it still wavered.

My father must've heard that note and shifted his gaze. "My oldest daughter is Amanda. She's hoping to go to Tulane when she graduates high school."

My heart thundered down to my belly. *I* was his oldest daughter. Not Amanda.

"And the other?"

"Jennifer. She's twelve."

Jennifer and Amanda. The sisters I'd never met.

"Your name is on my birth certificate," I said. "But, given the circumstances, I wanted to confirm with you personally that you are my biological father."

He sat straighter, his hands on the table going still. "Did your mother suggest that?"

"No, I don't have a reason to question it, other than the fact that..." I hesitated. "You left us."

He didn't answer right away, his fingers drumming lightly on the wood surface.

"Your mother and I were married and very much in love when you were conceived. I have no reason to doubt that you are mine."

The server chose that moment to approach with her bouncy walk and bright smile. "Can I get you two something to drink?"

"Just water," I said.

"Me too."

"Chips? Salsa? Appetizers?"

"No, thank you." I accepted both of the menus and flattened them on the table.

By the time she walked away, my father had composed himself.

"I'm not proud of what I did, but I tried to stay in contact with you."

"How?"

"I sent a gift every year on your birthday. All the way until the police called, saying you were missing."

Years of gifts, and I had none. My anger at my mother burned hot.

"Why did the police call you?"

"Your mother thought I'd kidnapped you."

She did? "I ran away."

He fingered the corner of a menu. "That's what I was told. You went to a shelter."

"They took me in. I had no one to help me." I lifted my chin, a challenge.

"They told me not to come," he said.

"Would you have?"

He hesitated.

"I thought not," I said.

"That's not fair, Ava—"

I cut him off. "You know what's not fair? Having to fend for yourself after you've been forced to live alone with a crazy woman. When I ran away, I didn't even know how to use a telephone!"

He looked beyond me, running his fingers through his hair. I recognized the gesture. I did it, too. This fueled my anger.

"I'd like to know why I have no relationship with any family. No grandparents. No aunts or uncles. Don't I have anyone?"

He cleared his throat. "Your mother had two brothers. They're probably still around somewhere. She ran away from home when she was seventeen. I met her about a year later. My parents died when I was thirty, before you were born. I am an only child."

He was tense, like he was trying to evade the hard stuff. I could read his expression as well as my own.

"Your mother moved in with me rather fast. Neither of us had any money, and it was economical to share a place while I got my engineering degree. She told me about life with her family, and it wasn't pretty. There was a lot of abuse. She'd been desperate to get away."

He held my gaze for a moment, slate blue and intense. The world tilted for a moment as it seemed I was staring into a mirror, his eyes were such a match for mine.

"I'm not surprised that she was on her own with you after I left. I didn't want to abandon her. But she made me leave."

"I don't believe that. There was this one movie we watched. *The Sound of Music*. And many times when the man sang to Maria, she would escape to the bathroom. I didn't understand it when I lived with her, but now I know. That was all about you."

His nervous hands stilled. "She never indicated that to me."

"What ended things?"

"You were in kindergarten when I moved out. It was a

rough year for you. You had your first seizure when you were four. It wasn't clear right away that your memory was impacted. You forgot things, but you were small. It wasn't until you were in school and we had specific things that we knew you'd learned that we realized the seizures were stealing your memory. You still knew letters and shapes, but lost all the stories you'd been told. Books we read to you were forgotten. But you were little. It was pretty muddy."

I wanted to write this down, or record it, but I could only pay fierce attention, hoping I'd remember it all.

"I was determined to get you the best help I could. We went to a lot of doctors and even flew to other cities. I wanted to keep you in school, give you as normal a life as possible. Your mother didn't. She wanted you home with her. She was terribly afraid something would happen to you."

The woman set our drinks on the table, but we waved her away before she could interrupt us again.

"Was I on any medications then?"

"Several. And some of them were, frankly, horrifying. We looked into brain surgery. Your mother was opposed. There came a time when it made sense to let one parent's vision take precedence over the other. I had to work. I couldn't go to every single one of the appointments and hear exactly what was being said. Your mother wasn't always truthful. She only listened to what she wanted to hear. Mainly that her little girl needed her mother and should stay home."

"None of that sounds like a reason to abandon us."

"You're right." He set his elbows on the table, bracing his head with his hands. I almost felt sorry that I was making him so frustrated and upset.

But Survival Ava said, *No, forget it. You have over a decade of upset to make up for.*

His voice dropped a notch. "I'm listening to myself tell the story, and it sounds horrible. But it was different to be there. To feel as though you had no voice, and your wife was going to do things her way, even when I felt strongly that she was wrong. We fought all the time. We yelled and carried on. It upset you a lot."

I clutched my napkin, shredding the edges. "You left me with her."

"Nobody loves you more than her."

"Least of all you."

"That's fair. Absolutely fair. I moved out. I came to see you every weekend. But you were getting worse. I'd be talking to you and you'd freeze up, look away, and quit responding. Your mother talked in circles about your care. And then one day, when you were six years old, I came over for the weekend and you didn't know who I was. You clung to your mother, asking who the scary man was."

"And so you decided to quit tormenting me, right?" My anger rose like a pot boiling. I couldn't bring it down. My napkin tore in two.

"No, I didn't give up then. I had private consultations with your doctors away from your mother. The best course of action was to find a medication that would stop the seizures, and that was what they were working on. For all my faulting her, it seemed your mother was doing the right thing."

"When did you stop coming completely?"

"When I got this." He removed a small note from his pocket. He unfolded it and flattened it on the table.

It was a stick-figure drawing that showed a woman and a girl smiling.

Underneath it, in childlike handwriting, were the words: *I am happy with mommy. Please don't scare me anymore. Ava.*

I dragged the paper closer. I'd read my old notes. I knew my handwriting, the quirks of my language, and how hard I pushed down on a pen.

But for this, I would have been very young. I couldn't compare the handwriting to my wrist, but I did anyway. I pulled up my shirt sleeve, exposing the tattoo.

"What is that?" my father asked, but I ignored him for the moment.

The comparison was useless. Crayon versus pen. There was no way to tell if I'd written this myself, or if my mother had sent it on her own. I pulled my sleeve back down.

"The woman that you left me with would make up stories after I lost my memory. She would put them in my diary. She would make me think they were my ideas and thoughts."

I pushed the paper back at him.

"I have no idea if I wrote that or not. But given my mother's history, I think there's a good chance she did this. But like you said, I was getting upset around you. You saw that with your own eyes. Who's to say who's right?"

"Did you ever confront your mother about what she was doing?"

"Are you kidding? I was helpless and scared. When I realized I was old enough to leave, not sixteen like she'd told me, I ran away. I have an amazing boyfriend. He's known me since before I left her. He helped me piece together my life through pictures and stories and accounts by other people."

He rotated the glass of water between his hands. "Ava, if you want me to be here for you now, I can do that."

"Why would I want that? I already figured everything out!"

He stared at the folded paper. He'd been led astray, sure. Either by my mother or me, or a combination of the two of us. But he should've known. He should've tried harder.

"I want to leave that door open. Amanda and Jennifer know about you. I have pictures of you still. So if you ever—"

My anger dissolved in the light of this news. "You have pictures of me? As a girl?"

"Of course I do. Baby photos. Right up until," he looked down at the paper. "Up until this. Your mother never sent any. To me, you were always six years old."

"I would love to see them. I have no idea what I looked like as a child."

He pulled out his wallet.

"I have this one on me." He tugged out a small photo, somewhat faded and rough around the edges.

I examined it. A young version of myself stared up at me. My dark hair was short and curled beneath my chin. I wore a red headband that matched the long-sleeved shirt beneath my dress. My smile was huge and genuine.

"Kindergarten," he said. "The last good days. I wanted to hold that image of you in my heart."

My eyes pricked as a rush of emotion coursed through me. He still carried my picture.

"I know you could have used me there. In hindsight, I see my mistake was enormous. I made sure you always had a home. I sent your mother money every month."

"What I needed was you."

"I see that. I wish I could go back and change things."

"I think she kept me sick so I wouldn't leave her."

He sucked in a breath. "My God, Ava. What did she do?"

"I don't know. I had prescriptions that quit getting filled. She stopped my education. When I piece together my notes, it seems every time I started sneaking out or seeing boys, she would move us, and then I couldn't remember anything from before."

He shoved back his chair with a squeal and stood up. "I'll have her arrested. She will rot in jail for this."

I held up a palm to make him sit back down. "How would we prove it? Accusations from a girl who can't remember, who has a condition nobody understands?"

He leaned across the table to gather my hand between his, like when we first said hello. When I lifted my gaze to his, I saw what I'd been looking for, the things I'd seen in other fathers and daughters but had never experienced for myself.

Gentleness. Care. It was there.

My father had it.

"I need a dad," I choked out. "I got away from her, but I still need a family."

He rushed around the table. "Ava, I'm here. I'm totally here."

He folded me into his arms. I tried to remember him, tried so hard. I had seen what fathers do with their children, swinging them in the air, pulling them against their chests.

I couldn't picture myself that way. I couldn't see that girl with her headband held in his protective embrace.

But maybe I could feel it.

Dad smelled of expensive clothes and hair products. That didn't connect.

But the curve of his chest. The pull of his arms. The press of his chin on my head.

I felt that. I surged with a sense of calm, of letting go, as if I wasn't in charge anymore. Someone else was at the helm. The impression ran deep, below memory, beneath understanding, and into the marrow of who I was.

I was a daughter.

"Come visit me for a weekend," he said against my hair. "We should all get to know our Ava."

I could only nod against the grip of his arms.

With my seizures, our past had been erased. But Tucker was right. We could make new memories.

CHAPTER 34
Tucker

The VNS worked like a damn miracle.

Within a day of the technician turning it on, my headaches became manageable. And by the time we'd fine-tuned it, I felt like my old self.

I taught Ava to drive while we waited for my license to be reinstated. We trundled around the neighborhood in Gram's Buick, laughing when Ava hit curbs or slammed on the brakes. It took two tries for her to pass her test, and we both got the right to drive within a week of each other.

Ava and I road-tripped to Houston for the holidays to meet Ava's sisters. Amanda was quiet and serious and resembled her mother Tina. Twelve-year-old Jennifer, however, was a mini Ava and followed us around with stars in her eyes, asking Ava's opinions on her hair and clothes. Ava patiently twisted the girl's hair into pinwheels to match hers.

Marcus set up a college fund for Ava. I got my old job at Shelfmart back and started thinking about school again. What did I want to be? The future had broken wide open.

Ava quit her job at Big Harry's to intern for one of the

big-wig portrait photographers in town when she wasn't in class. Some weekends, I would go with her on portrait shoots to carry equipment and watch her work. She was a natural, goofy to get the kids to smile for her, focused on how she wanted to set up the shot. She became more and more like the Ava I knew at the end of our first time together, light-hearted and fun.

Some days we lay on the floor of her apartment, now furnished with old pieces from my life before the accident, staring at the ceiling and reveling in how good we finally had it.

We should have known the easy part couldn't last.

A classmate uploaded an image of Ava from a photoshoot on social media and tagged her real name. The very next day, Ava's mother showed up at the community college, chatting up the professor.

Ava was blindsided by the sight of her mother and took off running. She jumped on a bus to Gram's to wait until I got home.

They sat at the table, drinking tea, but I could tell by the way Ava slumped in her chair she wasn't going to get past this easily.

I sat down opposite them.

"Poor child," Gram said. "Her mother won't leave her alone."

"I'm dropping out," Ava said. "And probably I should get a name change. And maybe I'll move. I could go to Houston. Live with Dad, even."

Gram's eyes met mine over her teacup.

"I could apply to schools in Houston," I said. But I couldn't miss how Gram's throat bobbed when I said it. I'd be leaving her.

"Could you find another big studio in Houston to apprentice for?" Gram asked.

Ava held her head in her hands. "Doubtful. And I'd lose my credits if I left mid-semester. I'd have to start over."

"Let's call your dad," Gram suggested. "He'll know better than any of us what to do."

Ava set her cell phone in the middle of the table and turned on the speaker. Her dad's secretary put us straight through.

Marcus's deep voice telegraphed concern. "Ava, is everything okay?"

"Mom found me."

"Where?"

"At school. Some idiot tagged me in a picture. She must be scouring the internet for any mention of me. She showed up within a day."

"Did you speak to her?"

"No. I ran."

"Where are you?"

"At Gram's with Tucker."

He let out a long exhale, amplified by the phone.

"I don't know what to do," Ava said. "If I drop out, I have to pretty much start over. And Cici just started giving me solo shoots."

"I'll handle it," Marcus said.

Gram leaned forward. "What do you plan to do?"

"Confront her. Threaten legal action. Get a restraining order."

I wrapped my arm around Ava's waist. "Is that what you want?"

"I never want her in my life again," she said. "No

matter how many times my memory restarts, I never trust her. I never feel safe."

"Good enough for me," Marcus said. "Consider it done."

We all stayed at Gram's for a few nights to be safe. When the police didn't find enough to go on for a restraining order, Marcus hired a lawyer to go before a judge with all of her history. It worked, and the paperwork was filed that if Geneva entered any of the places where Ava lived, studied, or worked, she would be arrested.

CHAPTER 35
Ava

Tucker and I thought we were so secure. Tucker's VNS worked so well. My meds kept my seizures away. Once we had the legal protection against my mother in place, our situation felt manageable. We could live like other people.

But at my next doctor visit, everything changed.

Dr. Clark entered the room without his usual smile. He held a tablet in his arms, scrolling and tapping, frowning.

"Everything okay?" I asked.

He sat on the stool and looked at me with dark eyes filled with concern. "Ava, you're a patient I think about a lot. Epilepsy is one thing. Memory loss is another."

I wasn't sure what he was getting at. "My medication has been working for over a year. Things have been good."

"Remember when we talked about the blood test at your last visit? Why you had to do them?"

Unease curled in my belly the way a flower petal shrivels and dies. "I did the blood test."

"And I have the results. We were looking for signs of liver damage. It doesn't happen often, but it's also not really rare. And it's happening to you."

Tucker stood up from his chair. "She has to switch medicines?"

Dr. Clark nodded solemnly. "She has to switch."

It took a few seconds for my throat to loosen enough to speak. "Will the new one work?"

"It should. It uses a similar method of stopping seizures." He patted my shoulder. "We're going to be very conservative. We'll have you on a full working dose before we wean you off the old one. Your liver isn't going to be harmed immediately. We have time to move from one to the other."

Tucker watched as we moved through the usual checks, finger touching, eye following, but we were both distracted.

The moment we headed out of the office, he said, "We need to plan for a reset. Just in case."

I agreed.

"We need to make videos. You talking. The two of us talking. Film your apartment and what everything means. Pictures of people. Your history. Everything."

I took his hand. "We'll get it done. We'll be sure to be ready."

But I understood his fear. When I started over, I knew nothing. Not even him.

We prepared as best we could. Videos. Notes. We typed up our entire story, alternating points of view to make it like a real book of our lives. We created what we called "the sequence"—an organized set of videos, notes, and photographs that would tell me who I am and who mattered. And also, who to avoid.

I would never be more vulnerable than right after losing my memory.

Tucker didn't officially move in with me, but we stayed

together for all of our home hours. For the first few weeks of the transition, everything seemed all right. The new med caused some dry mouth. A few rounds of dizziness. All normal side effects that faded as I got used to the drug.

But then I noticed small things. Frequently, my head would go fuzzy for long seconds. I'd catch myself being asleep, but not asleep, like I'd zoned out.

Dr. Clark was concerned, but felt sure I would settle in. Once the old med was totally out of my system, he inched the dose of the new med higher and higher to stop the small breakthrough seizures.

On an evening a couple of months after the switch, I spread my newest class assignment across the dining room table to be packaged and turned in. The photos were of a baby with a toothless smile, gold bokeh behind her, bits of light I'd captured perfectly out of focus.

"Come look at these," I said to Tucker, who was washing the dishes. "I really love doing this. I'm thinking about getting a bachelor's degree instead of just an associate's."

He shut off the water. "That's great! Still here in Austin?"

"Sure. UT has a great program. I could do any kind of work I wanted. Portrait. Editorial. Advertising. I could be on a billboard!"

"I love it. Dream big, Ava." Tucker kissed my hair and turned back to the sink.

My head went fuzzy again, and I sighed in annoyance. Another partial seizure. I would sit for a few seconds and wait it out. We'd have to increase my dose yet again.

I was about to tell Tucker I would call Dr. Clark in the morning when I realized my mouth wasn't working. I couldn't get a word out at all.

My hand holding the portrait went slack, dropping to my side. That was bad. I hadn't gotten this far before.

My body tilted, more muscles going. My head sizzled. The last thing I saw as I began to fall was the world turning sideways.

CHAPTER 36
Tucker

I didn't know anything had happened until I heard a crash.

Ava had fallen over, her head bumping the table leg as she crumpled.

I dropped to the floor. Her eyes met mine, so she was still conscious.

"It'll be quick," I said. "It will be fine. Just like the carnival. And hopefully this will be the wake-up call to Dr. Clark to try a different drug."

But she didn't respond, her eyes clocking to the right, center, right, center.

Her entire body stiffened. The seizure had generalized.

I counted to sixty while her muscles pulsed. Her leg banged against a chair, and I pulled her body onto mine to cushion her. Ninety seconds was still normal. We had to wait it out. Gram had never had to call an ambulance on me, and the records told us Ava had never been to the hospital for a seizure other than the one she had when we met. This would end soon.

But it didn't. Two minutes passed. Ava turned blue, like in the disco room. I called for an ambulance. They said they were on their way, but it felt like forever before they arrived.

I had to leave her on the floor to go open the door. The paramedics rushed into the kitchen. One of them asked why we didn't have emergency seizure meds. No one had ever told us we should.

I thought for certain she would die.

Ava was out for six long minutes. Her face was ashen, her fingernails purple. She didn't relax, rigid even when the pulsing seemed to stop.

Longest six minutes of my life.

The first breath Ava took was a miracle. She gasped for air, choking on saliva, but they sucked it out.

She was breathing.

We rode in the ambulance while Ava slept. I had no idea if she was really okay. I'd never been with her for a seizure of this magnitude, not all the way through.

They rolled her to a curtained room, and a nurse took her vitals while I filled out forms. I didn't have her medicine bottle with me and had to guess at the dose, since it had changed so often. I banged the clipboard against my knee as I waited for her to wake up.

It was half an hour before her hand lifted to her head.

Her eyes opened, and I could see the pain in her glazed expression. "I'll get them to give you something for the headache." I pulled back the curtain so I could spot a nurse if one passed.

I also wanted to give her some space. Her face contorted with confusion, her gaze shifting back and forth. What Ava was I about to meet? I'd never been with her at the very beginning of a new life for her.

The nurse came around the corner, and I flagged her down.

"Is she awake?" The whip-thin woman in blue scrubs approached the bed.

Ava scooted away from her, drawing her knees close to her body.

"I'm Nurse Helene," she said. "How are you feeling?"

Ava didn't answer, looking from the woman to me and back again. My stomach lurched. I was afraid that she didn't know me, that she didn't recognize her surroundings or what they meant.

"She has a headache," I said. "She usually does after a seizure."

Helene inflated the cuff on Ava's arm. As the pressure increased, Ava's eyes grew wide with panic. She tried to pull it off, but Helene expertly pushed her hand away until it beeped. "Calm down, now. We're making sure you're okay."

But I knew then. Ava didn't recognize a blood pressure cuff. It was all gone.

I moved beside the bed. "She's confused. She gets amnesia. She won't know who she is or why she's here."

The woman's eyebrows lifted. "Is that so?"

My whole body flashed hot. She didn't believe me. "Can you get something for her headache, please?"

But Helene had had enough of me. "Sweetheart, does your head hurt?"

Ava had pushed herself as far into the pillows as she could, creating distance between herself and the woman. She nodded, moving her hand to her head again.

"Are you allergic to anything?" Helene asked.

"No," I said. "Ibuprofen will work fine."

Helene's lips pressed sharply together, but she stepped

back. "I'll get them for you. Now that she's awake, I'll let the doctor on call know he can see her." She held out her hand for the clipboard.

"Her neurologist is Dr. Clark. Can we call him?"

She glanced at the clock. "You can try. But it's late. Tomorrow morning during his regular hours will probably be better."

"But—"

And she was gone.

I sat on the edge of the bed.

Ava held her knees tightly, eyes wide.

"Do you remember anything?" I asked her. I had no idea what she could do. Was it possible she didn't even know how to talk?

Her eyes met mine. I wanted to do something, anything to let her know I was on her side.

"You had a seizure," I said. "In your apartment. You and I had just had dinner. I'm your boyfriend. We've been together for several years. You're twenty years old, same as me. Your birthday was only a few weeks ago."

Her eyes watched me with fear and suspicion.

"Your name is Ava. It's tattooed on your hip in case you lose your memory. There's also a tattoo on your wrist."

Her gaze immediately dropped to her arm, and my anxiety eased that she understood me.

She pushed up her sleeve. Her eyes widened at the words. *Trust only this handwriting. Find the book. Remember your life.*

So she could read. We could do this.

"I'm Tucker," I said. "I love you. I'm here to help you through this."

We were interrupted by the arrival of a tall man in a white coat, a stethoscope slung around his neck.

"Hello there," he said, lines crinkling around his eyes as he smiled. "I'm Dr. Jensen. I heard your new anti-seizure med might not be quite right."

I took in the deepest breath since this ordeal began. This man seemed reasonable.

"What's your name?" he asked Ava.

Her eyes darted from me to the doctor. "Ava," she said.

"Good, good." He pulled a metal object from his pocket. "Can you look at me, Ava?"

He shined a light in her eyes. At first, she shied from the brightness, but he moved it aside and grinned. "Just seeing how pretty your blue eyes are."

She let him look.

"Very good. How old are you, Ava?"

She glanced at me. "Twenty."

"Very good. Can you touch your nose?"

He ran her through all the neurology checks we'd both done a thousand times. Touching fingers. Sticking out your tongue.

"You look good, Ava," he said. "You seem recovered. How often do you have seizures?"

Ava glanced at me. In our short time, she seemed to understand I had the answers.

"Every few years," I said, but before I could explain the additional problem, he interrupted.

"Then I will release you to the care of your usual neurologist, so he can determine what adjustments to make. Call him in the morning."

And before I could say another single thing, he was gone.

The nurse came in right on his heels. "Here's the

ibuprofen," she said. "Looks like you're being released. Let me get some papers, and we'll have you on your way home." She passed the small cup of pills and a bottle of water to Ava. "Dr. Jensen will send a report to Dr. Clark for the follow-up."

"Wait," I said. "She can't go home. She needs testing." I remembered all the things Ava told me about her hospital stay when we met. "Her memory. Her skills. We need to know where she's at so we can help her through this transition."

The nurse's smile became plastic, like it had been carved onto her face. "I'm sure her regular doctor can manage all that. I'll send someone in with your release papers."

Then Ava and I were alone again. Maybe this was the difference between a children's hospital and an adult one. They probably didn't even have an epilepsy center here.

Ava held the cup of pills and the water bottle in her hands as if she wasn't sure what to do with them.

"Do you want me to open that for you?"

She held out the bottle, and my chest loosened. She trusted me at least that much. Maybe she could remember. I had no idea.

I broke open the seal and unscrewed the lid. When I passed it back, she took a sip, still holding the pills in her palm.

"Do you want to take those?" I asked.

Her eyes searched our small space, the privacy curtain, the small table by her side, the white sheets on the narrow bed.

"Ava?"

She set the cup of pills on the bed and held the bottle with both hands. When I shifted to pick up the pills before they were knocked off, she recoiled, holding the bottle close to her.

"What do you know?" I asked.

Her gaze met mine, and I realized my question was too big.

"Do you know the rest of your name? What comes after Ava?"

After a long moment, she shook her head from side to side.

"It's Roberts. Your name is Ava Roberts. You're a photographer."

Her eyebrows drew together at that.

"You take pictures with a camera."

She nodded, understanding registering.

"When you have seizures, you sometimes lose your memory."

Her face crumpled into confusion again.

"You can't remember people or things that happened in your life."

She gazed down at her water bottle.

"Do you still have the headache?"

She nodded.

I held up the cup of pills. "This is medicine to make the headache go away."

She held out her hand.

"Don't chew them. Swallow them like you do the water."

She shook the cup, rattling the pills, then dumped them in her lap. She picked up one and examined it closely. Then she put it in her mouth.

It stuck there, and her eyes widened with alarm.

"Drink the water, and it will push it down," I said quickly.

She took a swig, and her shoulders relaxed as it went down.

"Can you do it again?"

She picked up the second pill, this time managing it better.

A different woman in black pants and a shiny shirt arrived with paperwork. "You guys are good to go," she said. "Follow up as soon as you can with the neurologist. Someone will call you in a week to make sure you've made an appointment."

I took the sheaf of paper from her and she disappeared, leaving the curtain open.

"I guess we have to go," I said. "I can take you home. Will you go with me?"

Ava drew her knees up to her chest.

"I can ask for a social worker. We might be able to get more help."

But something clicked at those words. "Social worker," she said.

"You want one?"

She shook her head. "I want to go home."

Thank God. I helped her down from the bed and pulled up my app to call for a ride. But as soon as her feet were on the floor, she walked ahead of me to the curtain. She peered both ways, not sure what to do, but clearly wanting to do it on her own. I hurriedly requested a car for us.

She looked lost. Of course, she would be. I could barely get around in a place like this myself. "There should be an exit sign."

She spotted it and hurried past other curtained rooms. She stopped abruptly when the doors slid open on their own, then she rushed on through. I jogged to keep up with her as she barreled through the waiting room, then out into the night.

Only when she was assaulted by new sounds and smells with no idea where to go did she turn back to me. "This is terrifying," she said.

I knew exactly what she meant.

CHAPTER 37
Ava

I got out of a car and walked up to a door I'd been told was mine.

Many more doors lined up in a row, all the same shade of brown. The bricks were brown. The earth was brown.

The man who'd been with me since the hospital unlocked the door and passed me the keys before turning the handle. I examined the trinkets fastened together on the keychain. A blue circle read, "Big Harry's Diner."

Then two keys. The man had used one to open the door.

I forgot his name. He told me in the hospital. It started with a T. Tom? Terry?

Tucker. That was it. The name made my stomach settle.

He opened the door. "You can take a look around, or I can show you if you like."

"I'll look around."

The room was large. I could identify most everything in it. Sofa. Table. Television. I spotted a strange black object on the table and picked it up. It had a long protrusion on the end, and many buttons.

"Do you remember how to use it?" Tucker asked.

I set it back down. "I don't even know what it is."

He frowned. I'd said the wrong thing. I'd been doing that constantly. He seemed displeased with me.

We entered a kitchen, and I instantly walked to one cabinet and laid my hands on the door.

"That's where you keep your medicine," Tucker said. "That's a good instinct."

I opened the door. A couple of bottles read Ava Roberts, which Tucker had told me was my name.

"Do I take all these?" I asked.

"No, we keep the old bottles. Anything with a big red X is one you shouldn't take."

"You said this happens every few years?"

"It depends on your medicine. This is the third I've known about."

I passed a table covered in photographs and returned to the first room. Nothing looked familiar, although the smell was soothing. I moved to a hall. There were three doors. I opened the first, a closet full of towels and blankets. The second was a tiny bathroom with a blue shower curtain.

The third was a bedroom with one big bed.

"Is this mine?" I asked Tucker.

He shuffled his feet, eyes downcast. "Sometimes I stay here with you."

So, I slept with this man in this bed.

I drew in another deep breath and let it out slowly. "Will you tonight?"

"No. No. Of course not. But I should stay on the couch. It's almost midnight, a bit late to go back to Gram's."

"Gram's?"

"My grandmother."

I hesitated. "Do I love you?"

"You did," he said. "I completely understand that you don't right now."

Strange. I sat on the bed. "I'd like to be alone for a little while."

He nodded, his face solemn. "Let me know if you want me to help you with memories. We prepared for this. There are videos and notes and photos."

"I don't want to do anything yet. Can I be alone?"

Tucker shoved his hands in his pockets. His hair was tousled. "I'll be in the kitchen if you need me."

When he was gone, I closed the door and turned to my room. I stepped inside the closet and walked among the unfamiliar clothes. I liked jeans and colorful shirts. I had a lot of shoes. Some of the shirts were bigger than the others. I held one out.

This one must be his.

His clothes were here. I'd never get him to leave.

A box tucked in the far back corner of the top shelf caught my attention. It was high and hard to pull out, so I moved on, heading back into the room. The dresser proved full of socks and underwear and T-shirts. The difference in the type of items from one drawer to another told me that some of these were also Tucker's.

There was no escaping him. He belonged here, too.

I moved to the door, listening. He must have been sitting quietly because I couldn't hear him moving around.

I turned back to the room. Should I go out? Ask him questions?

The box in the closet nagged at me. Something about it made my stomach quiver.

I returned to it. If I stood on my highest tippy toes, I could pull it forward. Finally, it landed in my hands.

I took it to the bed and lifted the lid. Inside were stiff circles that read "Big Harry's Diner" like the keychain that opened the door. Big Harry's must be important.

A red plastic badge read "Shelfmart" on the bottom and "Ava" in big black letters. There were photographs and lots of flowers cut from faded colored paper. Were these the things Tucker said I needed to learn who I was?

I pulled out a black and white notebook.

The words on the cover shook me to my core.

Trust only this handwriting.

This is the book.

Remember your life.

I flipped over my wrist. The words were so similar to this tattoo.

Why could I only trust this handwriting?

I flipped swiftly through the book, my eyes glancing off words.

Trust no one.

You were born in the year 2000. Anything else is a lie.

Living in the shelter has taught me one thing—men can't be trusted.

Your journal is taped beneath the middle dresser drawer. Don't let anyone find it.

I dropped the book and ran to the dresser to jerk open the second drawer. I felt underneath it.

There was nothing there!

I returned to the book, flipping quickly for another reference to the journal.

Your journal has been stolen.

My heart pounded so hard my head began to hurt.

Who stole it?

That man out there?

Men can't be trusted.

What should I do?

I turned more pages, pausing when I saw a familiar name.

Big Harry's Diner.

I scanned the page. I worked there. I had friends. It was one of the few places I felt safe.

I turned to the last page. A card was taped there.

Ava Roberts.

Last known address.

It listed numbers and a highway in Wimberley, Texas.

I stared at the closed door. Tucker told me on the ride home that we were in Austin. Not Wimberley.

I didn't belong here.

This man had done something. He'd lied. Stolen my journal.

I fluttered my fingers across my wrist tattoo.

What should I do? Go to the last known address in Wimberley? Or Big Harry's Diner?

Anywhere but here.

I opened the door a crack and peered out. I could see the living room, empty.

A sound in the kitchen meant he was in there.

Men can't be trusted.

I tugged the card with the address out of the book and clutched my keychain. Beneath the words "Big Harry's Diner" was another address on First Street.

How far away was that? Could I find another woman with a car to drive me there like the one we rode here? The car had driven up to the door of the hospital to bring me home.

Would one be waiting outside here to take me to Big Harry's?

I slid against the wall toward the living room.

We'd come in through the brown door. That was how I would have to leave.

I drew in a breath. This was my chance.

And I ran.

CHAPTER 38
Tucker

When a door slammed, I didn't know what it meant at first. The walls of Ava's apartment were paper thin, and it could have been a neighbor.

I left the kitchen where I was planning to make popcorn, a happy smell with good associations that might calm her. It was something Ava and I had brainstormed as we prepared for this day. She'd figured out memories weren't just stored in her head, but in her senses and her muscles, and the ways things made her feel.

The bedroom door was open. I peeked in and saw the box on the bed.

No no no no. We'd purposefully hidden it away. We didn't want Ava starting her journey with fear. That entire scrapbook was full of warnings.

She might run from them.

A quick search of the apartment proved fruitless. I raced for the door, angry I'd waited so long to look. I ran out into the parking lot and called her name.

Nothing.

I raced from one end of the building to the other. She was nowhere.

Where would she go? She didn't know anything yet.

I returned to the apartment and snatched up my phone. I dialed her number.

A buzz sounded in the kitchen.

Her phone was where she'd left it before the seizure, sitting amongst the portraits.

I returned to the notebook for clues. It lay on its front cover, like she'd flipped through the whole thing before closing it. There was no telling what parts she might have read. It ended too soon, before we were a couple again. We'd planned to rely on the videos we recorded and the story we'd written to establish our relationship.

But she hadn't seen any of those yet.

The middle drawer of her dresser was open, so something had made her want to look there. If she found something, I had no idea what it might have been.

I dialed her father, panic making my heart thunder so hard I could barely breathe. It was very late. He'd be asleep.

I got Marcus's voice mail and left a quick message saying Ava had lost her memory from a seizure and had taken off on foot. When I hung up, I wondered, what should I do?

I could drive around. She had to be walking. Most everything was closed this late. I'd take it slow, covering all the terrain.

I'd bring the book. Explain what it all meant. I snatched up the notebook and my keys and raced to my car.

I had to find her.

CHAPTER 39
Ava

Nobody showed up outside my apartment to give me a ride.

The streetlights lit my way as I hurried down the sidewalk. A car approached, but a man was driving.

Men can't be trusted.

I hid behind a tree until it passed.

I came to a street and a green sign on the corner read "Fifth Street."

Fifth!

If I kept walking, I could get to First.

I moved quickly. The next sign read Sixth, so I turned around and headed back the other way. Fifth again. Then Fourth. Then Third.

When I arrived at First Street, I paused. I had no idea whether to turn right or left, or how far down this street Big Harry's would be.

But this was the road we'd driven on from the hospital.

We'd come from the left before turning in. I closed my eyes, trying to picture the route. But I hadn't looked closely enough. I couldn't remember if we'd passed Big Harry's Diner.

This street was wide, with businesses on both sides. A man sat on a covered bench.

I hurried past him. Cars moved in steady lines, their headlights piercing the dark. Two women stood beneath a lamp, talking and laughing.

I scanned the buildings. Auto Service. Pizzeria. Fresh Nails.

No Big Harry's.

I clenched my hands into fists and approached the two women. They wore tall shoes and bright makeup. They paused and looked at me.

"Do you know where Big Harry's Diner is?" I asked.

"That way," one pointed. "About two blocks. Kinda rough part of town, though, for a fresh face like you. Sure you want to be walking alone this time of night?"

My belly quaked. "Thank you," I said. The women shrugged and resumed their conversation.

I stayed close to the buildings and almost jumped when I crossed the street and a car honked at me.

But I saw it. A sign that read *Big Harry's Diner* lit up red on a brick building.

I raced for it and tugged on the door.

The sounds and smells immediately soothed me. I knew this place. Maybe not the sight of it. But something about it felt completely right.

A few people sat at tables in a big room on the right. More lined up on stools along a counter on the back wall. A woman carrying a tray paused beside me. "Ava? That you? Oh my gawd! Harry's gonna be so excited to see you!"

Would he?

She turned toward the bar. "Devon! Look! It's little Ava! Go get Harry!"

A dark-skinned man behind the counter waved his arm and headed to the back corner of the room.

"How are you? How's the pictures? Harry is so proud! He framed that shot of him you took." The woman led me to the big counter and set her tray in front of an empty stool. "Take a load off. Can I get you something? You like Sprite, right?"

This woman knew what I liked to drink. And that Harry had a photo I had taken.

"Yes, thank you."

A giant man with a huge, bushy beard came out of a far door, followed by Devon.

"Ava! My love! You're here!"

He enveloped me in a hearty hug, and I tried not to go stiff. But as he held me, I realized I knew this position, this man, and my head dropped to his shoulder. Tears popped out of my eyes.

When he pulled back, his expression immediately changed. "Li'l Ava, what's wrong?"

I shook my head. I didn't know what to tell him, how to explain.

"I need to get here," I said to him, pulling the address card out of my pocket. "I don't have a way."

He and the woman glanced at each other.

"What happened to Tucker?" he asked.

"I had to leave. I had to get away."

His words came out like a growl. "If that boy hurt a hair on your head…"

I held out the card. "Can you help me get here, please?"

The woman turned the card around. "I can run her out

there if you like. Or we could call for a car. That's a ways. An hour at least to get there."

Harry's eyes narrowed. "I will take her myself. Come on. You can tell Big Harry all about it on the way."

The woman passed me a cold green can and leaned in to kiss my cheek. "You take care, Ava. It'll be all right. Men are pigs."

I nodded. So it was true. Men couldn't be trusted.

But Big Harry was a man. He must be different.

We stopped by his office for his keys, and he led me out a back door into an alley. I followed him to a black truck and climbed in.

When we had been on the road a while, he finally asked, "You want to talk about it?"

I shook my head. Big Harry was helping me get to my last known address. I felt sure that when I got there, things would make sense. Maybe my journal would be there. I could check the dresser.

I wished I had brought the notebook.

"So, what's in Wimberley?" he asked. "Where am I taking you?"

"My last known address," I said.

"Where you lived with your mother?" His heavy eyebrows drew together.

I lived with her last? A mother sounded like a very good thing.

"Yes."

"I thought you hated the sight of that woman."

Did I? "When was that?"

"When you first worked for me. I'm glad you made up with her. Family is family."

I had family. I could ask my mother questions. Figure

out what was happening and why I was with a man when men couldn't be trusted.

I must have fallen asleep to the rumble of the engine because I jolted awake when we turned onto a dirt path in the dark.

"Google says this is it," Big Harry said.

A tiny yellow light by the door pierced the dark.

He pulled up close to the porch. "I'll come with ya, just in case."

I opened the door and jumped down. The front window brightened.

The curtain shifted, then a few seconds later, the front door flew open.

"Ava? Is that you?" A woman hurried out, holding tight to the front of a robe.

"Mother?" I ventured.

"Oh my God, Ava. I can't believe you're home!" She rushed down in bare feet and wrapped her arms around me. "What's happened?"

Big Harry walked around the front of his truck. "She showed up at my diner, asking me to drive her here."

She held my cheeks with both hands, staring into my eyes. "Ava, what do you remember?"

I held her gaze. Something felt wrong. Now that I was here, my stomach flipped.

Big Harry stepped close. "Are you all right, Ava? Is this what you want? To be returned to your mother?"

Did I? It was my last known address. She wasn't a man. Men couldn't be trusted.

I nodded slowly.

"All right then. I've got to get back. The overnight shift is light." Big Harry patted my shoulder. "You come by anytime."

I followed my mother up the steps to the house, feeling less sure by the second. But she led me to the kitchen table and pulled out a chair. "Let me make you your favorite tea. You can get some sleep, and we'll get it all sorted out. Does anyone know you're here other than that man?"

I shook my head.

"No one else?"

I shook it again.

"When did you lose your memory?"

"Today."

"Thank God you made your way home. Thank God." She turned on the kettle and the little noises calmed me. The clink of the metal tea canister on the counter. The scrape of the mugs as she pulled them from the shelf.

I knew this place, deep down. When the water hit the tea, the smell made me want to breathe deeply. And when Mother gave me the cup, the first taste was beautiful, warm and cinnamon and sweet, like everything good.

I had done the right thing.

I was home.

CHAPTER 40
Tucker

I'd been driving the streets surrounding Ava's apartment for twenty minutes when I decided to stop at her place and try Marcus again.

His voice wasn't sleepy at all, despite the hour. "I missed your call. What's happened?"

"The new meds failed. She seized for six minutes. We got to the hospital, but they wouldn't listen about the memory loss. They sent us home, and she ran!"

"When?"

"About half an hour after we got back. She asked me to leave her alone, so I waited in the kitchen to give her some space. She found her old notebook full of warnings to herself, and I think she got spooked. I've been driving around looking for her."

"Have you called the police?"

"I thought I'd spot her. She can't get far on foot."

"Call them now. I'm jumping in my car. Call me back as soon as you've talked to them."

I hung up. I was about to dial 911 when something occurred to me. Where were the keys I'd handed her?

I retraced our steps from when we walked in. The kitchen. The med cabinet. Her room. Nothing on her dresser or on the bed. Nothing in the closet.

She had her keys.

Maybe she saw the keychain and thought of Big Harry.

I raced back to the kitchen and snatched up her phone to plug in her passcode.

Big Harry was in the contacts.

I called him and listened as it rang and rang. When the recorded message kicked in, it gave the hours and location of the diner. It wasn't his personal line.

Damn it.

Now it was time to call the police. With a heavy heart, I dialed the numbers.

The woman's voice was chirpy. "911. What is your emergency?"

"I have a missing person to report. It's urgent."

"I'll connect you to the police."

I paced the living room while I waited. Another woman answered. "Austin Police. What is your emergency?"

"My girlfriend is missing. She has amnesia. She can't be off by herself."

"I understand," the woman said. "Can I have your name?"

The process of giving her the information took forever. Finally, she asked, "And what is the age of the missing person?"

"Twenty."

"And how long has she been missing?"

I glanced at the clock on the wall. "Over an hour!"

"Sir, have you tried calling her on the phone?"

"I have her phone!"

"Have you contacted her friends?"

"She has amnesia. She can't remember who her friends are."

"Sir, I have filed a report for a missing adult on your behalf. We will enter the information into our database."

"That's it? She has amnesia!"

"Do you mean dementia or Alzheimer's? I can note this on the form and the information will be forwarded to that unit for immediate processing."

"No, she doesn't have dementia or Alzheimer's."

"Then we will contact you when it is processed. In the meantime, continue to try to reach her at all known contacts."

"This really is an emergency," I said. "She's defenseless. She doesn't know anything."

"Sir, does she know her name?"

"Well, yes."

"Does she know where she lives?"

"I guess so. She left from here."

"Then we will process this form and let you know when it is in the system. Is there anything else I can help you with?"

I hung up. Nobody understood.

But I could go to Harry's. The diner was open late. Big Harry was almost surely there. I called Marcus as I drove over and updated him on the police issue.

"But it's in the system?" he asked.

"Yes."

"Where should I meet you when I hit town?"

"Ava's apartment. She might go back. I think she has her keys. I'm headed to the diner where she used to work. She can walk there, and it's a path that might be muscle memory to her."

"I'll see you in about three hours, less if I break all the speed limits. Call me with any updates."

I hung up as I stopped the car in front of Harry's. I tried to steady my breath. She would be here. I knew it. Even if she didn't consciously know where she was going, her feet would lead her here.

I tugged on the door. Only a few stragglers sat on bar stools at this hour.

The youngish man behind the counter looked me up and down. "You'll need ID to order a drink."

"I'm looking for Ava Roberts," I said. "Has she been here? Do you know her?"

His eyes widened. "Who's asking?"

"I'm Tucker, her boyfriend."

The man waved at another server, a woman with big hair and a tray. "This guy's here looking for Ava," he said.

Her eyes narrowed. "Are you the reason she ran off?"

My breath caught. "So you've seen her? Tonight?"

"Maybe I did and maybe I didn't. If you want to know anything, you'll have to ask Big Harry." She cocked her hip, clearly none too pleased with me.

"This is important," I said. "Ava was in the hospital today. She's sick and scared. I need to find her."

The woman's body relaxed from its hostile posture. She glanced over at the other bartender. "What kind of sick?"

"She has epilepsy. Seizures."

"She never had none of that when she worked here."

"It's true, though," the bartender said. "I once asked her why she didn't drink. She said she took pills."

"Bloody hell," the woman breathed. "She left with Big Harry. Wanted to go to an address she'd written down."

My heart hammered. "What address?"

The woman bit her lip. "You're welcome to get it out of Big Harry."

"Do you have his cell number?"

"We always call him here. He practically lives here."

Damn. "Can I wait?"

She tilted her head toward the back wall. "Wait in his office."

She led me back, and I sat on a folding chair among the stacks of receipts and paperwork.

I had nothing to do but sit and think. What address would have been in the notebook? It was too old to have Gram's or her father's house.

I snapped my fingers. The old duplex address was in the scrapbook multiple times. She knew to trust Grandma Flowers.

Despite the hour, I had to call her. If Big Harry had taken Ava there, she'd be up, anyway.

The phone rang for several long moments. I was about to give up when a sleepy voice said, "Hello? Tucker? That you?"

"Yes," I said. "Ava's gone missing, and I thought she might have found your address. Have you seen her?"

She cleared her throat. "No, son. But I will keep a lookout. Did she lose her memory?"

"Yes, earlier today. I was in the kitchen and something in her old notebook spooked her and she took off."

"Oh, Lord. I'll keep the light on just in case."

"She might show up with her old boss from the diner."

"I'll keep that in mind."

"Please call me the minute you see her."

"Of course, my boy. I will."

I hung up. I had no idea how long ago they'd left. I was

about to go back into the diner and ask when my phone rang.

Gram. I hadn't talked to her since I sent a message from the hospital while Ava was sleeping. She must have been waiting to hear.

"Tucker? How's Ava?"

I swallowed hard. "She's okay, physically. But she lost her memory and got scared and took off on foot. I'm trying to find her."

"My Lord. Have you called the police?"

"Yes. And her father. But she came to Big Harry's. She's with him."

"Oh, thank goodness. Will he bring her back?"

"I don't know. They won't tell me where he took her."

"Maybe to his house?"

"No. He lives behind the diner. She had some address where she wanted to go."

"Well, I'll stay here in case it's this one," she said.

"That's a good plan. I'll keep you posted."

"Please do."

I hung up, and somewhere out by the bar, drunken friends roared with laughter. Their lives went on normally, while mine was at a standstill.

Where would she ask Big Harry to take her? The list of places was short. But maybe the shelter? The old Shelfmart where she used to work?

I called the shelter but the woman who answered wouldn't tell me if Ava was there or not, per their policy. I asked for Sheila, and thankfully she came to the phone. She confirmed that Ava hadn't shown up there and promised she'd keep an eye out for her.

The diner shut down, but I refused to leave. The big-haired waitress got testy. "We want to go home."

"Then call the cops on me, because I'm not leaving until Big Harry gets here."

She tilted her head at the bartender. They were the only employees left. "Let's drink. We usually hang out anyway."

I could do nothing but wait. Since I knew Ava wasn't going back to her apartment, I texted Marcus to meet me. He arrived at the diner a few hours later.

He looked like hell, eyes red, his wrinkled shirt unbuttoned at the throat. "We might as well wait together."

"It sure is taking a long time," I said. "Either the place he went is far, or he's sitting with her somewhere."

"No telling."

Marcus perched on the corner of the desk.

"What's Harry's number?" he asked. "Maybe he'll talk to me."

Before I could explain about the cell, Big Harry himself strode into the office.

We both stood.

"I figured I'd be seeing you," he said to me. "She'll contact you if she wants."

"Is she safe?" I asked.

"I reckon so. She seemed to be in good hands."

"Whose hands?" Marcus asked.

Harry crossed his arms over his protruding belly. "And who might you be?"

Marcus seemed to remember himself and stood straighter. "Marcus Roberts. I am Ava's father."

"Huh. She never mentioned you in all the time she worked here."

"I live in Houston."

Harry circled his desk and plopped down in his chair. "I take it you and the girl's mother are divorced."

At the word *mother*, we both lunged forward. "Did you take her to her mother?" I asked.

Harry held out his hands. "Now, I know Ava wasn't too fond of the woman. She said as much when she first worked here. But they had a right fine reunion. She's safe from the likes of this one." He pointed at Tucker.

"What have you DONE!" Marcus shouted. "We have a restraining order against her!"

Harry shot up. "I saw their happy hugging with my own eyes!"

I reached out to Marcus. "We know where she is. Let's go."

We whirled around and raced out of the diner.

"My car," Marcus said, clicking the remote to a sleek Mercedes.

I jumped in. "What do we do when we get there?"

"Pray that they are still there. Didn't she always move Ava when she had a memory reset?"

My chest tightened. "At least twice. It's only been a few hours. You think she could get it done that fast?"

"I don't know," Marcus said, banging his hand on the wheel. "How did this happen?"

"Obviously she didn't read about her mother or spot the tattoo about her. Or else she didn't understand."

Marcus squealed out of the parking spot. "She has a tattoo about Geneva?"

I hoped Ava didn't mind me telling him. "She has three tattoos. The one on her wrist you've probably seen, about only trusting her own handwriting."

"Right."

"She also has less visible ones. One is her name and birthdate. The other says, 'Mother is bad.'"

"So the first time she sees that, she's going to realize she's done the wrong thing."

"Yes. And probably run again." Ava was already in full panic mode.

Marcus blew out a long gust of air. "Let's assume that hasn't happened yet. What would she be using for information?"

"She must have found the section in the notebook about her time at the shelter. There was a police report in there with her mother's address, in case she wanted to go back home."

"And you didn't think to get rid of it?"

He was right. We should have. "I will now. The section of her book on the shelter was when she was the most scared. She had notes about the things the women taught her. Not to trust men." My stomach lurched.

Marcus slammed on the accelerator to blast through a yellow light. "So, she reads not to trust men, realizes you're a man, grabs the address and heads to the diner."

"And Harry takes her out there and of course Geneva is happy to see her."

Marcus's eyebrows gathered in a scowl. "Damn it. Damn it. Damn it. She'll move her. Get away from the restraining order."

"It doesn't count if Ava goes to her, does it?"

"They won't enforce it." He drew in a long breath and let it out. "Surely she won't bolt in the middle of the night. Ava would know something is up."

"And all that is only until Ava sees the tattoo about her mother."

The Mercedes barrels through the night, out of Austin and onto the dark highway. We had to get to them before any of these disasters struck.

CHAPTER 41

Ava

I didn't sleep well at my mother's house. I kept hearing noises in the night. Rustling. Drawers opening and closing.

But when I tiptoed to the door and peered out, all was dark and quiet.

Mother was still fully dressed, putting papers in a box.

When she saw me, she said, "Can't sleep?" She held out another mug of tea. It shook, the surface trembling.

"Is everything okay?" I asked.

"Right as rain," she said. "It's almost dawn. Why don't you go water your roses by the porch? They've missed you."

"Okay." I sipped the tea and followed her down the hall.

"The hose is at the corner of the house!" she called, heading toward the back door.

Why was she pushing me out the front?

The sun was just peeking over the hills. When I saw the flowers, a breath of happiness unfurled in my belly. I set my mug on the porch and hurried to the water hose to tend to them.

The parched earth soaked up the moisture. My hands reached for the dead blooms, expertly plucking them off. My body knew the flowers. My heart opened.

Mother came out on the porch again. "Let's go for a drive." Her hands shook.

"What's wrong?"

"Nothing, my darling. I thought you might like to see the places you used to love."

"But it's so early."

Her expression shifted for only a moment, but my throat tightened. Something was wrong.

"We can pick up some breakfast. There's a pastry shop you loved a lot."

I took a step back. "I'd like to stay here a bit longer, if that's okay."

Her smile looked painted on. "We really must go."

"Why?"

"It's—" Her voice faltered. "It's not safe for you."

My heart thundered. "It's the men?"

She nodded. "They're coming for you. You can't trust them."

I hurried onto the porch. "Do they know I'm here?"

"I don't know. We can't risk it. My car is out back. I already packed some things. See? I will keep you safe."

We crossed through the house and Mother led me out the back door to a rusting car. The back seat was loaded with suitcases and boxes. She had been packing in the night.

"Hop in, darling. Let's make a trip of it."

I glanced back at the house. Something flashed in my mind—the squish of soggy cool grass. But it must have been from some other time. Today the grass was dry and crunched when I walked. Fear crept through me. The back door was bad. Everything was bad.

I stumbled away from the car. "No. Something's wrong."

Mother grabbed my arm and led me to the passenger door. "Get in before it's too late!"

I had no idea what to do. My heart beat so hard that it hurt. But what scared me? The men coming for me? This place?

I opened the door and sat on the cracked seat.

"There you go, darling. We'll have a lovely time. We'll get reacquainted and all will be well."

She started the car, which chugged and groaned for a moment, but eventually fired up.

Mother let out a long sigh. "Everything will be as it was."

She drove across the dry earth, bumping and lurching as we rounded the house.

But when we arrived at the driveway, a sleek, shiny car blocked our way. Mother slammed to a stop in the dirt.

"No!" she called. "No!"

I opened my door, panicked. "Should I run?"

She turned to me, tears on her face. "No, my darling. There is no need to run."

But my fear blasted through me, hot and terrible. I lurched from my seat and stood by the open door, the wind blowing dust into my hair.

Tucker was in the other car. I swiveled to sprint away.

He jumped out. "Stop!"

I hesitated. What was happening here? Mother turned off the engine and sat with her back straight, tears dripping onto her pale green dress.

Another man emerged from the car. Something about him calmed my breathing. I knew him.

"Who is that?" I asked.

"Marcus Roberts," Mother said. "Your father."

Tucker approached. "Please, Ava, stay right there. Your dad's here."

"Come with us, Ava," the other man said. "Get in our car."

I shook my head and backed away. I almost fell on the rough terrain, broken clods of dirt and spurts of weeds tangling my feet.

"Let's go in the house," Mother said, sighing. "It's long been due for us to talk like civilized people."

"Yeah right! You were about to steal her away again," Tucker shouted.

My father held out his hand. "She's right. We'll talk. Let's sort this out to avoid future problems. Ava's medicine isn't settled yet. We need to all be on the same page until her condition stabilizes."

"Restraining orders are the page you like," Mother said.

Restraining orders?

I retreated to the porch, away from the door, watching them all walk up. Tucker was stiff and angry. Father clenched his fists, but walked calmly. Mother seemed to slump in on herself, tugging her skirt when it snagged on a cactus.

When they were all on the porch, I moved to the farthest corner. Mother opened the door. "Come, Ava. We didn't make it."

What did that mean?

"You knew better," Father said. "You would have been violating the order."

Mother's laugh echoed on the weathered slats as she entered the house. "How? By being happy to see her when she showed up at my door?"

They all followed her inside, but I hesitated. Should I run away from all of them? They seemed so angry, so upset. I wanted to get away from the heat of their misery.

Tucker waited by the door. "Please come in, Ava. We all want to help you. I won't let anything bad happen to you."

I didn't believe him, but what could I do? I needed to know what was going on. I scooted past him into the room.

Father stood firm by the door to the kitchen, arms crossed. "I've gathered enough evidence to bury you. Prescriptions you stopped filling. And this place." He gestured at the house. "I sent more money than this. You should have been able to live better. And the way Ava described your shopping trips. What happened to the money? I bet a financial audit could figure it out."

Mother sat on a chair and arranged her dusty green skirt. "You don't know anything. Nothing at all."

Tucker settled on the sofa. I shifted to the opposite wall, as far from all of them as I could get.

Mother pulled a worn shoebox from the shelf beside her. "These are all Ava's prescription bottles." She passed them to Father. "You'll see everything is in order."

"Then why wasn't the last one refilled?" he asked.

"It quit working," she said. "Unfortunately, the meds the doctor gave her next had terrible side effects. Nightmares. Dizzy spells."

Father sorted through the box. "So, what? You decided not to give her anything else?"

Mother smoothed her skirt over her knees. "I took a chance on an alternative route of medicine. It's been working for quite a lot of epilepsy cases." She glanced over at me. "I did my research. Unfortunately, the regimen is illegal here in Texas, so I had to allocate most of the money I got each month to procuring it."

Dad set down the box. "And what was that?"

Mother folded her hands together. "Marijuana."

"You had her smoke joints?" Tucker asked.

She shook her head. "This was medical grade. There are several compassionate growers who refine it. But it's expensive. I had one who was providing it for free for a while, and Ava bloomed with it. Just remarkable. Took to her studies so quickly." She turned to me. "You were so lovely and kind. We got along so well."

"Sure, if she was high all the time," Tucker said.

"I had every reason to believe I was seeing a miracle. Reports of it were even making the news. Kids with fifty seizures a day, cured. But the man giving it to me was arrested, and I had to find another source as fast as I could, before I ran out." Her hands knotted together, thumbs flicking against each other. "I was terribly afraid of getting caught. I could go to jail. I didn't want Ava to know anyone, meet anyone, talk about it accidentally. She was so guileless, so sweet."

"Is that why you didn't want her to go anywhere?" Father asked.

She nodded. "She took it twice a day. No one could know."

I glanced over at Father. He'd relaxed into a chair, his mouth a deep frown. "And you were going to hold her here—indefinitely? Lie to her about her age?"

Mother's eyes cast to the floor. "I just wanted to buy myself some time. Her seizures weren't that common. I needed to know if we were stopping them. If she thought she was sixteen, I had two years, plenty of time to know if they were truly gone."

Tucker leaned forward on the sofa. "You kept her prisoner," he said. "She had no friends. No contact with the outside world. You had me arrested."

Mother nodded. "I did. She was so impressionable. She'd tried to run away before, with a group of no-good hooligans. Keeping her safe during those tumultuous years was hard enough without outside influences." She met my eyes. "You seduced her."

Tucker frowned. "It wasn't like that."

Dad set the shoebox on the floor. "We are working on drugs for Ava. She has plenty of people who love her. You, however, have a history of stealing her from everyone. That is no way for her to live."

I was beginning to understand the situation. "She forced me into her car."

Mother gasped. "I'm the one who has kept you safe all your life!"

I shook my head. "It sounds like prison."

"Your condition is your prison!" she shot back. "I gave up my whole life to help you with it. Your father walked away!"

Father stood his ground. "Ava and I have worked through that."

We had?

Tucker turned to me. "Ava, you read your old notebook from when you were lost and scared. If you let us show you all the things we planned to help you get your life back, I think you'll understand."

I flattened my back against the wall. This was too intense. To ease the pressure, I pushed my fingers against my temples.

"What will help you, Ava?" Father asked. "We will do this any way you like."

I gulped in air, trying to think. My head felt empty, like the sky. I had so little to hold onto. I sorted through my memories, settling on that hug in the diner. "Can Big Harry be with me?" I asked.

"Of course," Tucker said. "I'm glad you believed in him. He's the best."

Mother clasped her hands in her lap. "Do I get to see Ava at all?"

"That remains to be seen," Marcus said. "Clearly you can't be trusted."

"Maybe if I had a role in her life, no one would need to worry about anything," she said.

"You have to earn it," Father shot back. "Just like I did."

I moved to the window, the white heat of the morning bleaching the landscape. The purity of it was easier to look at than the expressions of all the people behind me. "Mother, do you have a phone?"

"Yes."

"Give Father your number. You can ask him when you want to know something about me."

"And that's it, after all these years?" Her voice wobbled.

"That's about the best I can do." I headed for the door. "I'd like to go back to my apartment. I'd like Big Harry to come over, if he's willing." I turned to Tucker. "And I'll watch the videos now."

His shoulders dropped in relief. "You'll go with us?"

I nodded. "I'll go with you."

When I was outside, the open sky in front of me, wind blowing dust across my skin, I felt calm again. The others were taking their time inside the house, so I plucked one of the biggest blooms from the rose bushes. Something told me this bright red flower wasn't going to last much longer, and it would like to go with me.

Maybe I would come here every once in a while, with Tucker or Father or Big Harry, and care for the spindly bushes, help them grow strong. Something from this part of my life should be salvaged.

Epilogue: Tucker

I switch my cell phone to selfie mode and start recording.

"It's a big day." I turn it to show Ava sitting on the floor of our house. She sticks out her tongue. I love it. Twenty-two going on thirteen.

I turn the camera back to me. "It's day three of Ava's latest reset and we're about to engage the new sequence. We're not sure we'll always be able to do all these steps, so we're recording this one for posterity."

I sit next to her. "And here she is."

Ava fakes a smile. "Hey, Ava. I'm you. Just another you. I've started a new medicine. We're hoping this is the one. We're on what—number five?"

"We are," I say. "We're hoping this drug is the one."

"I'm feeling okay," Ava says. "The side effects aren't too bad. I'm thirsty all the time." She holds up her big green water bottle. "Easily solved."

I turn the screen back to me. "We're heading out in a minute to make our rounds of 'This Is Ava's Life.' And hopefully this sequence will be the last for a good long while."

Ava nods. "Not loving this journey for me."

I let out a chuckle. Ava watched an entire season of *Schitt's Creek* last night, and she definitely loved Alexis. She's quoting her constantly.

I shut off the camera so we can move on. "You ready?"

She nods. "Just you and me?"

"If that's okay."

"Sure."

We lock up the house and get in my car. I've taken the week off from my job, like I always do when she resets. It takes a while for her to be alone safely, as she still easily jumps to conclusions based on what she finds and reads first.

We don't tempt fate, ever. We're fastidious about movies we see and places we go. Strobe lights are stupidly ubiquitous in entertainment. Amusement parks, haunted houses, and even roller rinks and indoor mini golf can be treacherous.

But things are good. Ava's classes are going well despite the wild ride of medicine roulette. Her professors are informed, and Marcus got a specialized plan put into place ensuring they couldn't fail her because of her disability. But it's been fine. So far, people are more curious than anything.

Today, it's time to remind her of who she is outside of our house.

"So first we see the lady I lived next door to for a few years," Ava says, consulting the book of photographs we've put together. She doesn't yet know she took them all herself.

"Right. You bonded with her over the flowers on her balcony. Her name is Maya. Grandma Flowers in your notebook." We switched to using Maya's real name after the last reset because Ava insisted on seeing photo IDs that time.

We park in front of the duplex and stomp up the steps. Maya rises from her porch chair to envelop Ava in a big hug. Ava is gracious, even though she often bristles when new people act too familiar.

Maya also believes that the heart remembers. When we first created the memory reorientation sequence, I suggested she be less touchy-feely at first. But Maya insisted that her hug would bring back more connection with Ava than any conversation or photograph. As usual, she's right, and Ava melts into her.

Maya shows Ava the shared back porch and talks about the flowers Ava loved the most. I point out the window I crawled through the fateful night of my arrest.

Several college boys live next door these days, and Maya clucks her tongue at the beer cans strewn around the yard, saying, "This too shall pass."

We drink lemonade and eat cookies while I video their interactions. Eventually, I recognize the glow in Ava's face that lets me know some piece of herself has returned, not in memory, but in the emotional connection. So, I tell her it's time to move on.

Maya leans close to me and quietly whispers, "Good luck, sweet boy." I know she means getting Ava to return to me, which is always the hardest relationship to reestablish.

Next, we visit Big Harry's Diner. As we park in front of the dive, Ava turns to me and asks, "Where the heck are you taking me?"

"You used to work here."

Ava peers out of the car window with trepidation. "Was it safe?"

"You were epic. You could handle the most belligerent customer with a practiced hand. Besides, if anyone gave you an ounce of trouble, Big Harry would have thrown them out."

Despite Ava's insistence that she isn't familiar with the place, she knows exactly how to tug on the cranky door to make it open.

"He should fix that," Ava says.

"You say that every time."

Our gazes clash. "Does this get old for you?" she asks.

"Nope." And I mean it. I will take her through this sequence a thousand times if, at the end, she comes back to me.

Inside, a smattering of people sit at tables. Two couples play beer pong on the bar side, and a cluster of college kids throw darts on the back wall.

"Okay, the smell of this place is making me want to eat fried food," Ava says.

"Your clothes always smelled like it."

"I can almost taste it."

Big Harry emerges from the back office. "Ava! You're darkening my door again!"

I start the camera as he walks straight up to her and envelopes her in an oversized embrace. He wouldn't give up his Ava hugs either.

Ava peeps out over the tattoos of his meaty arm with a look of *who the heck is this?*

"This is your old boss, Harry," I say.

"You're still no bigger than a mite," he says. "Can I fix you your regular?"

Ava looks up at his grizzled face, mostly hidden by a scraggly beard. "What is my regular?"

"The concoction you drank to pretend you were

boozing it up like the rest of them," he says with a laugh. "As if we didn't know."

He walks behind the counter and expertly flips a glass from one hand to the other. "Let's see, I believe it was Sprite, a splash of Grenadine for color, and a wedge of lemon?"

Ava shrugs. "Maybe?"

Big Harry drags a shovel through a trough of ice. "You worked here during a pretty good run. Everyone got along, and we would talk in the wee hours when the crowd was light."

"Ava was a force to be reckoned with," I say.

"Oh, she was." Big Harry passes the glass to Ava and pours himself a beer in a big pewter stein. "She was like a whirlwind. Nobody messed with her. If they didn't catch on quick enough, I made sure they didn't mess with her."

He leans over and stares me in the eye. "I seem to recall tossing you out on your can the first time you showed up here."

Ava laughs. "I've heard this story!"

"He earned it," Big Harry says. "And I woulda kept doing it, but he was smart enough to sit on the bench outside."

Big Harry sets his stein on the bar with a thump. "I never saw a boy more determined to woo a girl than this fella right here. He sat out there on that bench, sometimes for hours, just to get a glimpse of you. It coulda softened an old codger like me, if I still had a heart."

"Now that's a lie," Ava says. "I've only known you for five minutes, but I can already tell that your heart is bigger than your beer mug."

He holds his mug aloft. "Don't you tell a soul, or I'll have to feed you to the sharks." He laughs again. "Well, from what I understand, you two have a big day ahead." He claps my shoulder. "Good luck, young man."

He rounds the counter to envelop Ava in another hug that almost makes her disappear.

"Give him a listen, girl," he says. "This boy only has your best interest at heart." He turns to me. "But I still don't regret throwing you out on your can."

I shake his hand, and Ava kisses his cheek. We head out of the diner to my car.

"Since you've been drinking so heavily," I say. "I guess I should drive."

Ava laughs. "It's hilarious to know I would lie about my drink to fit in. That was fun. Where are we going next?"

"It's an unusual stop," I say. "I had to make special arrangements. But I got it done."

She buckles her seat belt. "Now you have me curious."

"You'll know it when you see it, even if it's not from your memory."

"You think so?"

We exit the freeway, and Ava says, "I think I've been this way before."

We drive up a boulevard that ends at our destination. My nerves jangle to the point that I can almost hear ringing in my ears as we approach the complex.

"What's that tall tower ahead?" Ava asks.

"I think it's supposed to be a beacon of hope or something," I say. "No one has ever fully explained it to me."

We pass a hospital sign, and Ava sucks in a breath. "This is the children's hospital."

"It is."

Ava peers out the window. "This is where we met."

I pull into the parking lot.

Ava is rapt, staring at the entrance. "Do they still have the disco room like in our story?"

"They do."

"Well, this is exciting."

I park and lead her to the front entrance. A security guard in a blue uniform opens the door.

"We're headed to the epilepsy monitoring unit," I tell him.

"Are you visiting someone?"

"We were here a few years ago. It's how we met."

He chuckles. "Well, that's a new one. I don't know of any couples who met here at the hospital."

"We were seventeen."

"I don't think they let just anyone up, even if you met there," he says.

"I made an arrangement with a nurse. Marsha Stephenson. She said you could call up and verify it."

"Let me contact the unit." He picks up the information desk phone.

The hospital is quiet. Stuffed animals fill the window of a gift shop. Ava examines the art installation near the information desk, where a series of balls travel through a complicated maze of pulleys, tunnels, and obstacles.

The security guard sets down the phone. "You guys are cleared. Do you know the way?"

"I think I can find it again," I say.

I take Ava's hand, and my heart soars when she lets me. So far, so good.

We wander the halls of the hospital. It was built around a courtyard, so the wards branch off a central square. We climb a set of stairs and follow the signs until we arrive at the circular layout that makes up the epilepsy unit.

"This feels strangely familiar," Ava says. "I don't recognize anything, but the way the rooms make a circle seems right. I feel like I know my way around."

"Your way *around*?"

She elbows me.

I lead her to the second pod. "That was my room," I say, pointing to 210. "And this was yours. 205. We used to stand in our doorways at the top of every hour and wave at each other."

A nurse in pale yellow scrubs approaches. "You must be Tucker and Ava."

"Marsha?" I ask.

"Yes. We all thought your story was super cute. We've never had this happen on the unit. Do you remember where the disco room is?"

"Maybe," I say. I feel a little turned around.

"This way," she says.

"Can I take a peek into an empty room first?" Ava asks. "If you have one. This place is leaving a strong impression on me, even though I can't remember it."

"Sure," Marsha says. "Do you know what room you were in back then?"

I point to 205. "That one. It looks unoccupied."

We peer inside. It's almost completely unchanged. The high television. The sofa that converts into a bed. Only the signs on the wall are different.

Ava walks in. "I feel a lot of emotions here. Anxiety. Anger."

I take her hand again.

She looks down. "You doing that calms me immediately."

"We did a lot of this in the hospital," I say. "You called me out as your boyfriend straight away."

"And here we are."

I know it's wise to slow things down. Let her process the parts of her memory that are activating. Sounds. Smells. The emotional history that her brain still connects to this place, even if she can't pull forward an actual image of it in her mind.

Ava lets go of me and moves through the room, trailing her hand along the bare mattress and the metal frame. She picks up the wired remote that calls the nurse and works the television. I subtly record her walk with my phone.

She seems most interested in looking from the bed to the door. "Did I watch you from here?" she asks.

"You couldn't see me from the bed," I tell her. "But maybe you were as anxious as I was for the clock to move so we could see each other again."

"I'm trying to imagine myself jumping up and racing to the door before my mother could stop me," Ava says.

"That's probably about how it went down."

Ava heads for the door. "So, where is this disco room?"

Marsha leads the way out of the circular ward and down a hall.

"Here we are." She steps aside so we can enter. "It's all yours."

My fingers slide around Ava's, squeezing lightly. The disco ball sits dark and still in the center of the ceiling. The room is brighter than the first time we were here. A different style of speaker sits in the corner, and the gray floor shines with wax. It doesn't look like any more people come in here now than when we did.

I pull my phone from my pocket and unlock it. I'm about to head over to the speaker when a familiar voice says, "I can get that."

I turn. It's Nurse DeShawn! He's dressed in jeans and a T-shirt, so he must have come especially for us.

"You're here!" I say. "How did you know?"

"Marsha wanted to surprise you. I'm one of the few people who have been here that long." He tilts his head at Ava. "She doesn't remember, does she?"

I shake my head.

"I've never seen another case like Ava's. She's one in a million."

"She is."

DeShawn pats my back. "You stay the course, my friend." He takes my phone. "The one that's queued up?"

"Yeah. Thanks."

DeShawn crosses over to the speaker while Ava and I wander the room. After a moment, the music begins, and a slow, easy melody breaks the silence.

"Is this 'Highway to Hell'?" Ava asks.

I have to laugh at that. "No, that one's heavy metal. A head-banging song."

"Oh. That doesn't seem like a very solid beginning."

"It gave me a pick-up line," I say. "A terrible one, but one just the same."

She laughs. "You know, you could have left it out of the story, and I never would have known."

"I wouldn't change a word of our love story." It's true. From that first time I saw her, each step of this journey has felt right to me.

And every time I have to convince her that we belong together, I get to watch the magic envelop us both all over again. I no longer doubt that it will happen. I don't need faith when I have years' worth of proof.

We finish the slow walk around the room as DeShawn moves to the switches on the wall by the door.

"We haven't danced yet this time around." I pull Ava

by the hand until we face each other, and put my arm around her waist.

"We danced that first time?"

"No, I mean, since you started your new memories."

"I don't know how to dance."

"I never have known," I say. "And, luckily, you've forgotten how terrible I am."

She smiles. "Show me what to do."

I pull her close. We don't actually take steps, more rocking from side to side as we shift our weight. But it's the best part of dancing. Bodies close. Oneness with the music.

She lays her head on my shoulder, and we get to simply *be* for a while. The overhead dims and the disco ball begins its gentle turn, sprinkling color through the room like confetti. I glance over at DeShawn. He gives me a thumbs-up and slips out of the room. We're alone.

The rest of the world ceases to exist. Bits of light cross our bodies, as if they are the memories Ava could catch and hold onto if she simply held out her hand.

Sorrow washes over me that she's forgotten our story. We have so many bright moments that can no longer be played in her mind. One day, she might forget this one, too.

But isn't that what time does to everyone? Robs us of our history, leaving only fleeting glimpses of emotion when we hear a certain song or encounter a particular scent?

"I love you, Ava," I whisper close to her ear.

Her arm around my shoulder squeezes. "I believe you."

I hold us still for a moment and pull back to look into those blue eyes I know so well. I'm aware my face isn't as familiar to her, but hopefully since her last reset she's begun to understand who we are together.

"Ava, I want to be the keeper of your memories. No matter how many times you lose them, I want to be there to remind you of who we are."

Ava watches my face. I wait, suspended between anxiety and what is next. She's run from me before, feared me, gotten angry, and I've had to fight to get her back.

But I will not walk away. Not today. Not ever. Not as long as there is a chance of getting her to return to the love that binds us once she finds it again.

"You're not going to give up on me, are you?" she asks.

"You're all I want."

"We should record this, then," she says.

"My phone is busy at the moment playing the music."

She pulls hers from her pocket. "We'll use mine."

She flips it to show our faces and presses record.

"I'm Ava Roberts, and I'm here with Tucker Giddings in the disco room of the children's hospital. Apparently, this is where we met."

"We've chosen better music this time," I say. "But as long as we're together, it doesn't matter where we go or what we hear. The heart remembers."

"I like that," she says. "The heart remembers. Maybe I'll get that tattooed on me to go with the others. Right over my heart."

"I'll get one, too."

"It's a plan." She tucks the phone back into her pocket. "So, are you going to kiss me or what?"

"You ready for that?"

"Does a girl always have to ask for her first kiss?"

"It's not exactly your first kiss."

"Okay, so not my *first* first kiss. Or my second." Her face scrunches up as she thinks.

"It's our fifth," I tell her. "Our fifth first kiss."

A smile breaks across her face. "All right then, Tucker Giddings. What does a girl have to do to get her *fifth* first kiss?"

I draw her close. The colored light washes over us, the music humming from the speaker. Taylor Swift, of course. In every iteration, Ava is a Swiftie. We resume a gentle sway, and I swear the world goes completely still as my lips meet hers. She's back to me. I can feel it in the tingle that passes between us.

We're back. Another new beginning.

I'm the luckiest man on earth.

With this kiss, we get to fall in love all over again.

Thank you so much for reading *This Kiss*. In the Aftwerword, I talk about how epilepsy has affected our family.

For my other emotional reads, I recommend my *USA Today* bestselling book Forever Innocent about how baby loss affects a young couple. Or Forbidden Dance for how a secret adoption is impacted when a birth mother is unexpectedly famous after falling in love with a celebrity.

I find peace in the ups and downs of my life by creating dynamic new situations involving the issues from my own home. They help me cope. I hope they help you, too. *XO, Deanna*

The heart remembers.

Afterword

Three things made me write this book.

The first was all the times I went unconscious as a teen. People always laughed that I "fainted" so easily, as I was heat sensitive and walking from an air-conditioned room into a Texas summer day often caused me to hit the ground.

I collapsed in bathrooms, in doctor's offices, at the optometrist, and once, while riding my bike. Mostly I just went limp, but starting in my twenties, these events began to include "tonic posturing" where your arms and legs go stiff. This is the hallmark of a seizure. But because I didn't know about epilepsy back then, and was always fine afterward, I more or less let it go.

All this was merely a footnote in my medical record until I seized in front of my adult family practice doctor. They took it very seriously, and I got wired up for an EEG.

In the end, I was not diagnosed with epilepsy, but vasovagal syncope, two things that can look very similar. But those years I struggled with syncope were definitely

AFTERWORD

on my mind when my daughter Elizabeth had her first seizure at age six.

Which leads to the second thing.

I learned about the disco room at Dell Children's Hospital in Austin, Texas, during a seven-day stay with Elizabeth when she was fifteen. She'd been battling epilepsy for nine long years and we were desperate for answers and help, as her anti-seizure medications kept failing, much like Tucker's.

I loved the entire concept of the disco room—letting teens meet other teens while also tiring them out with a dance party and ultimately helping bring on a seizure to collect the necessary data. The disco room was intended, at least back then, to help with the hard cases.

The conversations with staff, the layout, and the events on the epilepsy unit in this book were lifted directly from our experience. Also like Tucker, Elizabeth never had a seizure on the ward even with sleep deprivation, antihistamines, and riding a bike in the middle of the night. And just like her nuclear medicine technician said might happen, a seizure occurred that very night when she got home.

AFTERWORD

Then, about a year later, when Elizabeth had a seizure at a movie theater on a class trip, I raced to the mall to find two fire trucks and a half-dozen tricked-out firefighters walking out.

They'd been there for her. She was going to have a story to tell me about them!

But she didn't. She had no memory of the firefighters, of feeling bad, or roughly half an hour leading up to the seizure. It took a good hour for her to orient herself with a chunk of her life missing.

I started researching memory loss with seizures.

This led to the third thing that brought about this book —a news story about a young woman who lost her entire life's memory after a seizure. It turned out that this was a well-documented phenomenon, and several memoirs exist about it.

Looking at the medical reasons for the loss of memory due to seizures, I realized—this could happen. And if this was the type of seizure that was normal for someone, it could happen over and over again.

And so my thoughts churned. What if it did? How would you love anyone? How could anybody stay in love with you?

So I created Ava and Tucker to find out.

The heart remembers.

Special Acknowledgments

My agent, Jess Regel, who championed this book so hard.

Janet Wilson, MSN, CPNP-PC at Dell Children's Hospital, who has been with us from the very beginning and always remembers that Elizabeth loves cats (even in her 20s, Elizabeth still makes sure she wears cat things for you!)

The staff of Dell Children's Hospital in Austin, Texas, who kept Elizabeth safe, even if they never convinced her to go to the disco room.

The members of the Parents of Children with Epilepsy Facebook group, who were an amazing support network in the hardest years.

Elizabeth's father John, who was a great partner and co-parent through all the ups and downs we never could have foreseen.

Kurt, my husband. You got a step-dad medal of honor for all the seizures you helped with, including racing through New York on our wedding day trying to find meds for your very-soon-to-be step-daughter.

SPECIAL ACKNOWLEDGMENTS

Emily, my eldest, who has been part of Elizabeth's safety net all her life, and still is, and will continue to be. We are grateful for you.

Deanna Roy is the six-time *USA Today* bestselling author of new adult romance and women's fiction.

She writes passionately from her own life experiences, spinning them into stories. Her books follow the complexity of baby loss (*Baby Dust, Forever Innocent*), adoption and foster care (*Forbidden Dance, Conversations with Little Dude*), and living with epilepsy (*This Kiss, Elektra Chaos*.) She lives in Austin, Texas, with her family.

Learn more about the author at
www.deannaroy.com

Join her email or text list for new release notices at
deannaroy.com/news

- facebook.com/deannaroyauthor
- instagram.com/deannaroyauthor
- goodreads.com/Goodreads
- bookbub.com/authors/deanna-roy
- tiktok.com/@deannaroy.author

Also by Deanna Roy

THE FOREVER SERIES

A young couple reunites in college, four years after the death of their newborn.

Book one Forever Innocent *is FREE on all venues.*

- Forever Innocent (Corabelle & Gavin)
- Forever Loved (Corabelle & Gavin)
- Forever Sheltered (Tina & Darion)
- Forever Bound (Jenny & Chance)
- Forever Family (Corabelle, Tina, Jenny)
- Forever Christmas (Corabelle & Gavin)

- Boxed Set: First Three Books
- Boxed Set: Final Three Books

- Stella and Dane (Standalone)

THIS LOVE SERIES

A woman with a form of epilepsy that causes repeated amnesia resists falling for the man who has pledged to always love her.

- This Kiss
- This Love

- This Life

THE LOVERS DANCE SERIES

A sheltered ballerina is lured into the life of a brash TV reality show star.

- Forbidden Dance
- Wounded Dance
- Wicked Dance
- Tender Dance
- Final Dance

- Lovers Dance Boxed Set

- Billionaire's Dance (a standalone prequel)

OTHER BOOKS

- Conversations with Little Dude (Nonfiction stories with her son who was adopted from foster care)
- In the Company of Angels (A fill-in-the-pages baby record book for babies lost to miscarriage or stillbirth)
- The Magic Mayhem trilogy of action/adventure books for children ages 9-12.

IF YOU PREFER YOUR ROMANCES WITH NO GRAPHIC LOVE SCENES OR COARSE LANGUAGE

You will love Deanna's pen name Abby Tyler. As Abby, Deanna writes funny, feel-good small-town romances with a recurring cast of feisty senior citizens and the couples they push together, by hook or by crook.

Made in United States
Orlando, FL
11 November 2023